april showers

janay harden

I will never have this version on me again. Let me slow down and be with her.

april showers

by Janay Harden

one

. . .

P eace Lily.

The slender woman carried it with two hands wrapped like it was gold. It was drooping something terrible and looked like it hadn't been loved on properly in a while. She towered taller than most women I'd ever seen.

Peace lilies were funny like that though. One minute they were tall and strong, and minutes later they could be dramatic and fall limp. My makeshift greenhouse on the rooftop of our building housed at least three of them, and they reminded me of a bad little kid—always up to something.

The last day of school in the middle of June lasted just a few hours, and I dreamt of a steamy New York City afternoon in which my brownstone neighbors and I popped open the fire hydrant and cooled off while someone bumped Will Smith's *"Summertime"* from their car's speaker. Instead, I scrunched my face up at the sky, examined the clouds, and peered at this vertically elongated woman hauling droopy house plants and boxes marked *'living room'* and *'bathroom'* into our building. It rained like cats and dogs and instead

1

of the giddiness I thought I would feel on the final day, I couldn't name two things I was excited about.

I watched from the stoop; covered by a small awning protecting me from the rain. The asphalt smelled just like the city—rubber, a stench of piss, and something savory. We were in uptown Harlem where everything was an emergency but done with love. We lived in Harlem all my life, and now and then me and my parents visited the surrounding boroughs but always came back home to where the streets were paved with music notes to Langston Hughes and syrupy words to Zora Neale Hurston. Hairdressers, poets, wanna-be ball players, nurses, a few doctors, and a solid middle class called our neighborhood, home. The city that never slept was always up, always on, and always ready. You had to *stay* ready. We devoured Harlem and all its delicacies like a big breakfast—easy on a Sunday morning. If the rest of Manhattan was the bacon and sausage, Harlem was a thick slab of sweet, French toast and every morsel had me more addicted.

Harlem was home.

I rubbed my legs together. They were smooth; not a hair in sight —just like I liked them.

"Shane, honey. Take this for me. It's killing my arms." The woman complained.

A lanky, brown boy with dimples in both cheeks and a hat flipped to the back slammed the trunk door down and rushed to the woman's side. He eyeballed me up and down as he helped his mom. "Here, Mom. I got them."

"Well, how are we supposed to move in woman, and all you want to do is carry plants?" A man with a round stomach and a frown emerged from the front of their Tahoe truck with a Connecticut license plate. His patchy beard was peppered with gray hairs, and laugh lines squeezed the corner of his eyes. The three of them laughed together and hustled toward the building as the rain picked up. I eyed the sky again and shook my head at their luck.

Another younger boy spilled from the car with his head buried into a tablet with the volume sky high. He left the car door wide open and walked towards the building without a care in the world.

"Marcel! Get back there and grab something, boy! Always with your head in that computer."

"It's not a computer, Mom, really?" Marcel sighed and walked as slowly as he could back to the truck.

"Nice to meet you, little lady. Do you live in this building?" The older man stopped in front of me.

I spied Shane behind his dad and my words caught in my throat, refusing to come to the surface and speak up for herself. All I could do was nod.

Marcel grabbed a set of pillows from the truck and scowled next to Shane behind their dad. With all three men standing in front of me with similar copper skin and lanky statures, they were the same make and model and looked like off brand versions of each other.

"Yes. She lives here, and so do you now! What's y'all's last names again?" Mr. Fred held the front door open as Shane and his mom breezed through right past me.

I crinkled my face at the scent of our landlord—Mr. Fred assaulted my nose. He always smelled of something strong from his lair of an apartment that could probably put hair on your chest. As the owner of the building, Mr. Fred lived here too, but however he got the property was a mystery. One day, he was nice and then if Harlem blew through a cold gust of wind on any given Sunday, his mood could be just as chilly. With a permanent frown and Grinch-like tendencies, he was our feared leader, and we tried to stay out of his way.

"We are the Walkers. That was my wife, Yolanda, who just went inside with our son, Shane. He's sixteen. Our youngest is Marcel, and he's over there with the pillows." Mr. Walker motioned. "He's ten. We've been driving for a few hours and just arrived. Are you Mr. Fred?"

"Well, how about that? You found me." Mr. Fred smiled and flashed his many missing teeth. His fat tongue rolled around in his mouth as he peeked his head around at Mrs. Walker. For someone representing the building, he made a show of being anything but welcoming.

My stomach churned.

"Yes, I am your brownstone landlord and owner." Mr. Fred flapped his gums. On the stoop next to me, he banged his cane. He covered it in stickers from all the different countries and places he'd been and carefully wrapped it in some special cloth he said he got on a religious trip to Peru back in the day when he was in the service. He strutted with that thing like he was Beyonce waltzing down the Coachella stage and he wasted no time showing off each sticker. With his fedora cocked to the side, he plastered on his fakest smile for the Walkers. "I thought I recognized you folks from the application you sent over. Your apartment is ready. It's on the third floor. Now I regret to inform you that the elevator is broken. There is a ticket in to have it fixed soon, but we have an old-fashioned dumbwaiter that some of these little kids like to use. Right, April?" Mr. Fred nudged me with his cane.

I was sixteen years old, and he called me a *kid*. Shifting my eyes between him and the Walkers, I wondered if this alleged ticket was really in for the elevator. No one had been to the building in months to fix anything, let alone the prized elevator. I cleared my throat as my back stung a little from the nudge of his cane. "Yeah, sure thing."

"And what floor are you on, dear?" Mrs. Walker peered down at me as she and the men breezed in and out carrying boxes.

I caught Shane's eyes again and I became aware that I was sitting on a stoop in the rain on the last day of school with eight sets of curious eyes staring down at me. Rising to my feet, I stood and cleared the way for the Walkers to bring in more of their stuff. "I'm on the second floor with my parents." I smiled.

The front door chimed, and I heard Jorge, my next door neighbor's voice. "I'm not eating no beef patties, Ms. Gloria; I told you I'm a vegan." He chuckled. Jorge escorted Ms. Gloria by the arm as she gripped her umbrella like a weapon against the rain. Why were old women always ready for the rain? Ms. Gloria limped, and her lower leg and ankles looked painfully swollen.

I excused myself from Mrs. Walker and sprinted to her side. "How you feeling, Ms. Gloria?" I put my hand on her head and squeezed her arm.

"Don't be feeling me up now. I'm okay. My diabetes just got me a little swollen, is all. I already took my water pill, and it should go down in a few days." She swatted me away and tilted her head so she could get a better look at all the unfamiliar faces she stumbled upon in the lobby of our building. Perfect timing for her.

"I told her to leave that orange juice alone! One sip and you got the sugar." Jorge rolled his eyes and his heavy Spanish accent shined through and dotted yellow love notes and seas of spicy red on this dreary day. His bright, blue silk blouse and tightly fitted pants looked nice against his tinted sunglasses. Even though there was no sun right now—Jorge was always photo fresh and did not waste a moment to show off when he was out of his drabby hospital work uniform.

"Oh, we didn't mean to interrupt." Ms. Gloria checked everyone out as she hobbled to the front door, pushing past Mr. Fred. He jumped out of the way and his cane got caught in the door, twisted, and yanked from his hands.

Giggling to myself, I stood off to the side. Ms. Gloria was quite vocal about her dislike for Mr. Fred. These two had been living in the building together for over thirty years. He as the owner-landlord, and she as the tenant. We were in apartment 2B, Mr. Fred in 2D, Ms. Gloria in 2A and Jorge in 2C. We ruled the second floor and got along well. Rumor had it they dated back in the day, but whenever I asked Ms. Gloria about it, she changed the subject.

I sized up Shane's pecs through the window of the front door littered with raindrops. My temples throbbed too. What a sucky day to move in, but I was glad I was here to scope out the action.

"April, baby. Come here." Ms. Gloria called to me from the bottom of the stoop.

Jumping out of my stupor and rushing to her aid, I held her arm and guided her to the front where she stood with her walker, waiting for the senior citizen's bus.

"Yes, Ms. Gloria?" I breathed, not taking my gaze off him. Shane whizzed by me, heading to the truck to grab more boxes. I caught another glance of him and smelled his scent as he walked by. I wanted to close my eyes and melt in it for a while. He was kind of funny looking; his eyes were a little farther apart. I stared at him anyway.

"Don't you have plants to tend to? A brother to check on? Honey, go in the house, and stop staring at that boy before your dad comes out here and knocks some sense into ya!"

two

. . .

Parlour palm. Flamingo lily. Even my dracaena was happy. The rainbow signified the end of the storm, and it calmed down enough for me to take the steps two at a time, racing to the brownstone rooftop to check on my plant babies.

I didn't choose the plant life. The plant life chose me.

My best friend was Ianesha, but we called her Ivy. That was how we met. I went to a farmer's market over in West Harlem with my mom, gathering ingredients for our biweekly platter sale. She said they had the best Caribbean spices, straight from the islands, and we made the trek to pick up scents that made my eyes water and nose tickle. One day, there she was. Waving to my brother, Gage, and palming a leggy bamboo tree at a plant sale. I think we both fell in love with her; me and Gage. She looked bored to tears and was following her mom around like a lapdog when she and Gage started making googly eyes at each other. I couldn't help but wrap my pointer finger around a vine on the plant in her cart. We struck up a conversation, and I ended up bringing both Ivy and the plant home. In my head, I pronounced us best friends.

I checked out the sky and cursed the rain. Too much could cause over-saturated soil and pesky gnats. Too little welcomed crispy dirt that was fried, died, and laid to the side. The brownstone was positioned just right overlooking East Harlem and received full sunlight. In the summer, it was always a fine line of watching the plants for burning, and bringing inside the ones who didn't like so much sun. *What kind of summer will this year be?*

I looked around. I went online and ordered a special tarp to help with the winds and sun, but it wasn't being delivered for a few days. We lined the brownstone rooftop with all different plants and green turf. The entire perimeter squeezed plant after plant next to each other. I carefully palmed some of them and gently gave the leaves a good press to assess if they needed more water. With Tems on my mind, I hummed a song to my plant babies, so they knew I was here. Throaty words escaped my mouth without a stitch of musical talent, but I didn't care. I sang to each of them I grew from little buds. None of them were purchased fully grown, they grew as I grew.

When Gage moved out, I placed a few plants in his room that couldn't be outside and before long, plants were lining the floor and snaking down the walls of his old room. Empty fish tanks Dad picked up from a thrift store were filled with terrariums and special grow lamps. Mom had to beg Mr. Fred to give me a small corner of the rooftop when all the foliage became too much for Gage's room and our balcony terrace next to our three-bedroom apartment. After Mr. Fred saw Gage's room bursting at the seams, he said, "ain't nobody giving y'all no extra square footage so that girl can play in dirt." He stomped his cane into the ground. It was another moment I wanted to rip it from his arms and bang Mr. Fred's entire stumpy, five-foot frame into the next day.

Fortunately for me, Mom smiled sweetly, bestowed her famous pound cake that took her hours to make from scratch and presented it to him. She added some bass to her voice—and asked again. Mr. Fred offered me a corner on the roof and Dad didn't even have to get involved. When she told him the story, she said Mr. Fred offered it and she winked at me out of the corner of her eye. That was how a lot of things went in our house. It was like magic sometimes. Mom would get people to change their minds with food.

Mom was on me something serious to find a job, but I didn't blame her. She was funding all of my planting needs and whenever I brought her a new item I needed for my makeshift greenhouse; she took care of it. Gage was upset that I had more space, even though my "space" was nothing more than a bird-poop filled slab of concrete covered in shrubbery. I was grateful when he moved out and got his own place with his girlfriend. He officially made me an aunt, and made our parents,' grandparents, with a chubby-cheeked little girl named Milani. Our place wasn't but a New York minute big, but when she came over, her eyes told stories of a maze filled home with her family around every corner.

I opened the small storage bin where all my supplies lay and I pulled out my gloves, fresh soil, and scissor shears. Pulling the gloves over my hands, a muffled yelp ricocheted off the brick building. I leaned over the side of the roof and squinted to see what the commotion was. Shane's dad dropped a small box onto his foot and was hopping around howling in pain.

"Dad, pretty soon I'm going to have to put you in a home." Shane held his dad's arm and steadied him from falling over.

"Get off me, boy." Mr. Walker chuckled and pushed his son's arm away. They shared a smile and when Shane cocked his head up at his dad, he caught me staring at him from the rooftop. He frowned and stared back.

"Shit!" I fell to my knees and hid behind the wall. My chest rose, and I banged my head on the wall in peeping embarrassment for having been caught.

"You're supposed to be up here starting a rainforest, and she's up here cussing Mrs. Mays." Ivy tee-heed to my mom as she burst through the heavy storm door from downstairs. Ivy didn't really have a filter and said the first thing that came to her mind. Fortunately, my mom found her funny when others would find her crass for a teenager.

Caren with a C and not with a K—as she liked to tell people—always smelled like melon and pound cake. Smooth mahogany skin up against her heavy-set stance proved the perfect combination. Mom kept her hair done even though most days she didn't go anywhere since she stayed home to take care of the house and our bellies. For years, she sold platters every other week to the brownstone tenants. No one officially gave her the okay to open up shop, but it had been standard for so long that no one batted an eye and they looked forward to her meals. A steaming platter of something always seemed to calm even mean old Mr. Fred. She charged a standard twenty dollars per plate, and the menu changed. No one asked what she was making. They just *knew* it would be worth the surprise. Whatever she cooked, she searched out every farmer's market she could find for the perfect ingredients. The key ingredient, though was love. She sang prayers and affirmations over every pot of food she stirred, the same way I sang to my plants. Dimples in both cheeks and a Sensattionel wig about ten years old—Mom was hood fabulous and the best cook this side of Harlem.

"Don't be lying on my baby!" Mom shouted at Ivy and pulled the door closed behind her.

"And why are you on that dirty floor, anyway?" Mom eyed me suspiciously.

"Ugh, nothing," I stammered and hopped to my feet. I moved around cleaning up some of my mess, but my nerves were bad, and I hoped she didn't see me looking at Shane.

You okay? Ivy mouthed. She peered over the ledge and saw Shane and his dad. She raised an eyebrow without a word.

She knew, and she always knew.

I guess that was the perks of being best friends with someone since grade school. By the time 10th grade rolled around, she knew me damn near better than I knew myself. Even so, nothing was wrong with looking.

"I was just watering the plants, Mom. You heading to the mailroom?"

"Yes, when I saw Ms. Ivy Lane heading right past my house without stopping to say hello, I thought I would come up here too." Mom waved her hands like, how dare Ivy not stop and speak to her.

I collected my thoughts and put Mr. Shane what's-his-name out of my mind. "I'm just about done here." I closed the lid to my plants' supplies and pulled off my gloves. I wiped my damp forehead with the back of my hand, pulled my wet t-shirt from my chest, and peered up at the sun now shining and sitting high when minutes ago it was overcast. Just like that. A New York minute.

The brownstone mail room, or, Town House like I called it, was popping with people, food, and body odor. It was always noisy, and people anxiously waited for the mailman to come with news. Now what kind of news depended on the day and who you spoke to. One thing was for sure, we all waited for checks from *somewhere*. You could expect anyone or anything to happen.

With the elevator constantly out, delivery people couldn't get to and from each apartment, so we had a central location for mail. The more tenants congregated in the Town House to get their mail and chat; my mom sent me downstairs with bite-sized food samples to taste her cooking. Mr. Fred began keeping complementary bottles of water in the fridge, and for years now, it became the late afternoon hang-out spot to wait for the mail. That was the only nice thing I could think of Mr. Fred doing. Ivy loved to tag along some days, and with her leading the way, I was thrilled.

Mom, me, and Ivy made our way downstairs and ran smack dab into Shane and his mom.

Just my luck.

"Well, hello Mrs. . . Mrs . . . What is your name?" Mom extended a hand.

"Hello, I'm Mrs. Walker. My family and I just moved from Connecticut."

"The third floor, right?" Mom questioned. She leaned in like she needed to share a deep secret that only she and Mrs. Walker understood.

Mrs. Walker nodded. "We're just getting settled. It's been hard without an elevator, and I'm sure we already saw a rat the size of Donatella."

Mrs. Walker and Mom shared a laugh and touched each other's forearms.

"So, what made you guys move from Connecticut?" Ivy cut in.

I wanted to pinch Ivy's butt for chiming in, but Mrs. Walker smiled and said, "my husband is a recruiter for the NBA. They reassigned him to the New York division, and he's from Harlem, so it worked out."

Shane and I stood behind our parents while they made small talk. People buzzed in and out of the busy room, retrieving their mail and checking out the various flyers on the walls. I eyed Mrs. Walker's plant that she brought in earlier sitting lonely on one table. It was still a pitiful sight, and I didn't know why she left it there. Taking gigantic steps across the room, I fingered the brown edges of the leaves and examined the soil. They needed some love.

"Can-can you help?" Shane shrugged and fumbled over his words.

My words were missing in action again. Why did this happen with him? I wondered if he would think I was deaf if I didn't respond.

"My girl can help you do anything!" Ivy burst into the conversation—if you could call it a conversation. She was in a heated debate with Marcel about if Cheez-Its and Cheese Curls were actually cheese. Her small pudge poked out the top of her jeans and her oversized t-shirt held breasts way too big for any teenager to manage.

"Yes, she's the plant whisperer," my mom chimed in behind me.

"I put some basil and collards in her hands as a child, and she grew them from seeds. She can do anything." Mom's eyes sparkled.

I was a regular girl. Even though Mom taught me as a child how to grow vegetables and fruit, it was the plants that made my heart sing. Greenery grew all around me and we found a home and a friendship in each other.

"I'm really not." I waved them away. Plopping down at the table seemed like the right thing to do to put some distance between me and their far-fetched ideas.

"I bet she can help you with yours, Mrs. Walker. That thing looks sad." Ivy snorted and pursed her lips at Mrs. Walker's droopy, depressed plant.

I kept my hair pulled back in a tight bun at my neck and I was on the thicker side. Missing meals was something I didn't do, and big, flannel sweaters hid my chubby waist. But the summer meant skin was out—and I scoped mine like a crazy person searching for unruly, overgrowing hair. If I sucked in my breath and thrust my breasts high, I looked slimmer and trimmer. But the last time I tried that I almost passed out. Ivy and I were coming off a rough 10th grade year, littered with confusion. She had my back through every fist fight, argument, and secret.

"You think her plant is sad?" Marcel emerged from under the table and giggled. He was quiet like a cat and climbed out of nowhere. His front tooth was missing, and his lips were red from sucking on something sweet. He looked like the neighborhood troublemaker already

"What are you doing, little boy?" Mr. Dawson, fourth floor tenant, spewed. Marcel gasped at Mr. Dawson's disheveled clothes, bugged eyes, spit flying from his mouth—and skedaddled behind his mom.

"Calm down, boy. It's okay." Mrs. Walker held Marcel. He stared at Mr. Dawson with a wide eye that said he would probably be afraid of him for a while.

Mr. Dawson *had* that effect.

Most days, his lips were wrapped around a bottle too, just like Mr. Fred's. But Mr. Dawson seemed to always be in pain, and he was angry about it. It was either his back, or recurrent headaches, or stomach pains. People avoided him because of his ailments and disgruntled mood, and he seemed okay with it. *"Just steer clear of him,"* my dad always said. Yeah right. It was always me who ran into him at Town House and not my mom or dad. Mr. Dawson had the tendency to go off on long tangents that left him with bloodshot red eyes and full of anger directed at everyone and no one. His apartment was scattered, and Mom offered more than once to go in and help him clean, but he was a man. And a man could clean his own house and his own self according to Mr. Dawson. In the meantime, the rest of the building had to put up with his cross-mood.

Mr. Dawson slammed his mailbox shut and backed out of the Town House. When he left, Mom and Mrs. Walker eyed each other. "He's harmless—really." Mom tried to reassure Mrs. Walker. "Say, how about my April help you with your plants? She really is a whiz." Mom winked in my direction.

Man was she *good*.

Out of habit, I pulled out my phone and began scrolling. I was comparing the best hair removal systems for girls. I hated hair and it hated me. Hairs trapped odors and I didn't like odors. Maybe if I looked busy enough, Mom would stop volunteering me for stuff.

"What you think, Miss April? Can you come by and save my *sad* houseplants?" Mrs. Walker smiled and winked at Ivy. I noticed the laugh lines on her face and her olive-brown skin. She was a beauty—and she had made a funny-looking, equally beautiful son. Ivy was playing on her phone beside me and not paying much attention. Her leg bounced up and down as she hearted a picture of Coco Jones on Instagram. But I noticed Shane. I noticed him noticing me.

I wondered if Shane was like Chase. Or Chase was like Shane.

three

. . .

Before rapping on Shanice's door, I smoothed my gelled hair. Shanice lived on the fifth floor and when I delivered platters, I always started on the fifth floor and worked my way down since the elevator was out. I loaded up the steaming food containers and traipsed up and down the brownstone — dropping off food, collecting money, and containers from the weeks prior. That was Mom's only request. She wanted all her containers cleaned and returned, so she didn't have to buy new ones every month.

"Coming!" Shanice shouted from behind the door. She unbolted the locks and pulled the heavy door open. It sounded exhausted, like someone had precisely opened it that way thousands of times before.

"Hi, April!" Deja waved from behind her mom and giggled.

"Come on in." Shanice made some space for me walk in with tired eyes. She looked how the door sounded.

The spicy scent wafting from Shanice's apartment made my nose tingle. She was from Jamaica— born and raised, and besides Mom, could also cook her behind off too. She always bought a platter from my mom.

"It smells so good. What are you making?" I leaned against the door frame.

"Fish and cabbage." You wan' take your mom a plate?" Before I could answer, Shanice breezed by me into the kitchen and was dishing out food into a to-go container.

"So, what are your plans this summer?" Shanice quizzed. There were loud bangs and shrieks coming from the room behind us and I knew Deja and her brother, Corey, were probably back there knocking each other's heads off like only siblings could do. Gage and I had a few wrestling matches that could rival the pros.

Shanice never batted an eye. I guess when you worked all day at a lawyer's office bored to tears, your tolerance level was a little higher and shrieks didn't faze you. Shanice's daily routine consisted of working and cooking it seemed. She and Mom talked a lot; and juicy, grownup conversation was a fruit I loved to taste. Shanice hoped the kids knew she loved them, but was just too exhausted to show it. She hoped that around 9 p.m. the kids would drop, and she had about an hour or two to herself before falling asleep to do it all over again the next day.

Sometimes Mom agreed with her.

I raised my voice so she could hear me over the noise that was her kids. "Nothing, really. I'm too old for camp, if that's what you're thinking." This was the question of the summer. What was I doing for the next three months? Mom wanted me to stay home where I was safe and could help around the house, but when I was in the way, she wanted me employed and out of the house. I did want to get a job, but the more I thought about an interview, the more I wanted to lay down and forget about it all. The movies made it look easy, and that's how I wanted it to be. Waltzing into a pizza shop after seeing a *Help Wanted* sign outside, I'd point to it and say, *'hiring?'* and they would say, *'Sure thing. Can you count?'* I would nod, and they would say, *'great, you start right now.'* And together we would tackle a lunch rush and become fast friends. Could it be simple like that?

"Well, if you wanna work, I need someone to help with Corey and Deja. Deja is a little older. You know she's ten. But Corey just turned six, and I think I actually saw his head spin off like the girl in that *Exorcist* movie."

Stifling back a giggle, my hand shot to my mouth. "Let me think about that. I have to do something." Leaning back, the wall behind me supported my weight and worry. Ever since my fateful 10th grade school year ended, my head was in the clouds. Taking any steps not completely planned and perfectly laid out drained me. Flashbacks of Chase, Ivy, and dozens of staring eyes had me in a mental chokehold, and most days, the only thing that brought me joy was found on the rooftop or the terrace. What I *could* control. What I *wanted* to control.

I checked Shanice out as she closed the lids and milled around the house. Her body was out of this world. Shaped like the number eight with not a stop sign in sight. When we ran into her at Town House, the men stopped and stared at a taste of the island's forbidden fruit. Some of them even knew what time she usually came down, and they waited for her—just to catch a glimpse. Shanice chomped her gum and never looked their way. Even though she was single, I never saw a man in her apartment. She donned short black hair with tight ringlets of curls. No matter what fake smile her face held, the truth laid behind those tired rings around her eyes. She always looked put together; not purposely, though. Like one of those girls who didn't know how beautiful they were because life hadn't afforded them the luxury of slowing down to see.

Biting my lip and stealing glances in her directions, I wondered. What was it like to be drop dead beautiful and have everyone want a part of you, but you are oblivious to it all? Last year I thought I was that person—that girl. A stupid boy named Chase made me believe otherwise. Watching Shanice move around the kitchen made me feel heavy. I mean, I'm no spring chicken, and every time Mom took me to the doctors, they said I could stand to lose about ten to fifteen pounds. But today I felt heavy. On the inside.

"Here you go. Now give this to your mama and tell her let me know what she thinks. I've been toying with a new sauce, and I think I'm on to something good." Shanice winked. The wall behind us banged again, and I jumped in place. "Corey! Cut all that playing around!" Shanice yelled over her shoulder only to be met with a fit of giggles.

I bustled through the rest of my deliveries and counted the money. Everything was there—plus some extra in tips. Good. A new electric razor caught my eye on our last Target run, but I didn't want to ask Mom to buy it for me. With summertime meaning *skin* time, I had to be ready. Now I could get it myself. If people continued tipping like this, maybe I didn't have to get a job after all.

"Hey, Ma." I burst back into our apartment. She had Prince blaring from the speakers. When she cooked, she needed music to get her in the mood. Prince was her absolute favorite. When I was younger, she found these purple toilet bowl tablets and every time we flushed and checked between our legs, the water was raining purple. And when the music was *extra* loud, she cooked something *extra* delicious. "Here's all the money. And this is food from Ms. Shanice. She said to tell her what you think." Sitting everything on the kitchen counter, I plopped down, banging my elbow onto the table and yawned.

"I have one more order I need you to take upstairs."

"Ma! I'm tired. I didn't forget anything this time! All the orders were delivered, and nothing was left over, I swear!" I whined. My bed was calling my name, and I knew it fluently. I wanted to wrap up and not think about Chase or Shane.

"Girl, go on and do what ya' mama said, now." Dad strolled into the kitchen.

"Dad! I thought you weren't home until Sunday?" It was one o'clock on a Friday and he was never home this early. Dad drove trucks for a food company and when he was gone, it was for a few days. When he returned, he had heaps of new foods and desserts for us to try. Those days were the best. Between Mom cooking her way into the history books with the bacon, and Dad bringing the bacon home; it made sense why the doctor said I could stand to lose a few pounds.

"I took a few days off. I missed my woman. Me and your mama going on a date." Dad grinned.

"Ohh can I come?" I squealed.

"Uh, no. It's a date. Hence, I'm taking my lady out for lunch, and she's even allowed to get cheese on it." Dad palmed the small of Mom's back.

"Oh hush, Kyle!" Mom giggled.

A knock at the door gave Dad a second to plant a wet kiss on Mom's cheek.

"Are you guys ever *not* feeling each other up?" Gage shook his head. The vein in his arm bulged from carrying Milani's car seat.

"Hush your mouth, Gage, and bring my grandbaby here." Mom leaned into Dad and tugged at his beard. She gave him that, '*straighten up in front of the children,*' look.

Mom and I crowded around Milani, ready to give her as much love as she gave us. She was resting and snoring lightly. Mom and I just stared at her sleeping, unable to make a move away from her. She was sweet as caramel.

Dad shot questions at Gage. "Did you call the doctor back? Is that girlfriend of yours back to work? What did my man uptown say about that job interview for you?"

These two were like oil and water.

A few months ago, he decided he needed a new job because he was tired of collecting tolls at the Brooklyn Bridge. When Dad landed him an interview at the food trucking company he worked for, Gage returned with no job offers, but he had locc'd up his hair instead of his usual buzz cut he left with that morning. "Do you like it? This feels more like me," he said to Dad, moving his head from side to side.

I watched a few veins pop out of Dad's head. Everything happened fast after that. Dad said he was too immature to be a father, and he had to learn the hard way. So, he kicked him out and my new plant room was born. He never invited us over to his new place and we only met LaToya a few times. I prayed that he and Milani were okay.

Gage scratched his head and sighed. His bubble jacket inched up toward his waist. I could see his sagged pants around his hips. I winced for Gage, knowing Dad already spotted his pants around his waist. The next few words he spat at his oldest son were icy. Why did he have a bubble coat on in June, anyway?

Like he read my mind, Dad stood and folded his hands. "Why do you have that coat on, son? And pull up your pants."

"I had to go downtown to the courthouse. It be mad cold in there." Gage peeled it from his body and slung it across the back of the couch.

"Was your ass cold too? You couldn't pull up your pants?" Dad folded his arms across his chest and poked it out. Minutes ago, he was smiling and preparing for a day date, and now his eyes darted between Milani and wanting to kiss her face, to being a stern father to his ornery son. The lines in his forehead deepened the way they only seemed to do for his oldest child.

Gage squared off his shoulders and stood up straight in front of Dad. Too straight. He wore Milani's baby-bag slung across his chest, but I could tell by the way the straps were frayed and twisted, it wasn't made to be a sling bag. Coupled with his puffy bubble coat, he looked hot and stuffed. He tugged his pants up and rolled his eyes.

"Can we not today, Dad? I'm not in the mood. I just came because Mom said she hadn't seen Milani in a few days."

"Days? It's felt like weeks! Bring my pretty grandbaby here." Mom leaned down and unbuckled Milani from her car seat.

"What was at the courthouse?" Dad pressed.

Mom snipped and snapped at the contraptions holding back Milani, and she was cooing in her face within seconds. She blew her kisses and gently placed her in Dad's arms.

Dad's jaw softened, and I saw a glisten in his eye. Dad stared at Milani, and his breathing changed. He asked Gage again, but this time softer with the tone of a grandfather.

"What was at the courthouse?" he whispered. His eyes never left Milani, his only grandchild and the new love of his life.

"LaToya had an interview. She going to be some sort of court clerk. We were waiting for Mommy, right Milani?" Gage smiled at Milani. She made a girdling noise and shot large, wondrous eyes at her family. "And I have some interviews set up. I'll find a job myself. And yes, I called the doctor, Dad. They said it was just a little cold and Milani will adjust."

We stood around Dad and admired Milani's beauty. Our beauty.

"Good." Dad smiled down at Milani. She giggled, and Dad's face beamed like he had just won the lottery.

"Gage. April still has to finish delivering some platters. How about you go with her? Let me and your mama watch the baby for a second." Dad said it like it was a suggestion, but he walked into the living room, plopped into his favorite chair, and rocked back and forth before Gage could say anything.

"I thought y'all were going on a date?" My neck whipped around in confusion.

"We can go another day. Toss me a bottle, Gage. And April, you get back to work." Mom and Dad grinned into Milani's face, showing all their teeth.

"That is fine by me. Give Daddy a break." Gage patted his stomach and stretched into a goofy yawn.

"There are no breaks, son. None." Dad rocked back and forth in his chair as Milani squirmed in his arms.

"Where am I taking the last platter, Mom?"

"It's the Walker's apartment. That new family that moved in?"

Cayenne pepper coughs filled my throat.

"Cat got your tongue, April?" Gage snickered.

I couldn't go up there. My day wasn't complete without a shower *and* shave. My braids were frizzy and were ready to come out. I looked a mess, and she wanted me to go upstairs to Shane's house when just the sight of the boy sent me into mental hysterics. I wondered what he was doing right now... But why?

Parents just didn't understand.

"Ma!" I shouted again. "I can't—"

"Girl, hush up and take this food upstairs! And I told Mrs. Walker that you would see about her plants, so please go see about them."

I stomped my foot and sighed. "Why you gotta cook for all these people all the time, anyway!" I sucked my teeth.

"Don't be sucking those teeth unless you want a knuckle sandwich," Dad warned.

"Now gon' and do what your mama said. We'll probably be gone already when you get back. We gon' take the baby to Chuckie Cheese."

"Chuckie Cheese? Dad, she's four months!" Gage raised his voice but cowered under Dad's glare. Where Dad had a dad pudge, Gage was stocky and muscular. He worked odd job after job that required him to lift and be on his feet. Me and my big brother were the exact same color. Chocolate as midnight. Skin went on for miles. Mine with more soft valleys and his with chiseled peaks. He towered over Dad but never disrespected him, even though they both could be iceboxes.

"We'll take good care of her, son." Mom grabbed Gage's jacket off the couch. She pulled a blanket from the foyer closet and placed it on the floor. She and Dad got down on their knees with Milani and began playing with her.

Gage sighed.

I pulled my sneakers back on and looked at myself in the bathroom mirror. A new pimple popped up overnight on my face and my eyebrows were bushy and long. The extra weight hid behind my favorite pair of tights, pulled all the way up so everything was tucked and in its place. My ankles were covered with long socks so no skin or hair would show.

Taking stairs to the third floor two at a time with Gage hot on my heels, I wanted to get it over with and hopefully, Shane wouldn't be there and see me. Why did I care, anyway? Chase was the last boy I dated. Love wasn't for me. Relationships weren't for me. They were icky, and confusing, and if this is how I had to feel—they could keep it. Boys reminded me of some of my plants. They thrived in low light because they were sneaky. They took little water, but when they went too long without it — they were dramatic. At least that's how I looked at them. Maybe Shane wasn't like that, and he would be like my favorite plants and wanted to stand in the sun.

I wanted to stand in the sun.

I forced out a trapped breath and knocked on the door.

Shane, I gulped.

"Hey. Come on in. My mom is waiting for you in the kitchen." He smiled.

"Thanks," I muttered and followed him into the foyer.

"Hey, my man." Gage dapped with Shane. "I'm April's brother, Gage."

"Giants or Jets?" Shane questioned. He shot it out so abruptly that I turned and stared at him.

Gage didn't skip a beat. "Giants, of course," he countered.

So he liked football. I could do football. He licked his lips and smiled in a way that told me he was comfortable around me and my brother, and I wasn't sure if I liked that. He made me squeeze my legs together so my coochie didn't bulge. He was grinning away. Apparently, I didn't have the same effect on him he had on me.

While they talked football, I checked out the Walker's apartment.

They filled it with a bit of everything. There were boxes piled so high they covered the windows. Bikes, exercise equipment, and loose sneakers littered the hallway. *Where the heck would they put all this stuff?* The building was laid out over five floors with six families per floor. Delivering platters every two weeks for Mom allowed me to check out each of them intimately, and this one was intimate. Family photos, vacations, professional baby pictures, and shots of Shane in a boxing ring leaning against the walls, ready to be displayed. Mr. Walker had a few photos with NBA players, and they framed those in shiny, gold trim. He wanted those seen—first.

Each apartment had their own smell. Not good or bad smells, just their own unique scent. Even though they were far from moved in, the Walker's home smelled like roses. I inhaled and explored the scent of flowers. Feminine. Beautiful. Lovely.

"So — April, is it?" Shane asked.

"It is." I leaned against the wall to steady myself and prayed stage fright didn't invite me to drop dead.

Shane smiled and cocked his head to the side. "So . . . so what's good with you?" he stammered. "I see your plants. That's pretty cool."

My eyes widened. For a second, I became real life weak in the knees for the boy with the funny shaped head. Was he trying to be funny? Did he think my plants were immature?

"No one thinks my plants are cool," I muttered. Crossing my arms at my chest, I looked away. Mom would have to make this delivery in the future herself. Coming back to his house was not on my list of favorite things to do. My body responded to his words and his scent like it used to do with Chase, and I couldn't have that. Didn't want that.

"You determine what's cool." Shane shrugged.

Gage shared a glance between the two of us. He could jump into the conversation any moment, but I think he reveled in seeing me sweat.

"And plants are indeed—cool." Mrs. Walker sauntered into the room. "Is this your mom's food? It smells delicious!" Mrs. Walker slapped her hand against the kitchen counter and grunted as she taste-tested the gravy.

Clearing my throat, I turned to Mrs. Walker. "This is my brother, Gage. He's helping today. I can check out your plants. You know, make sure they are happy." I bit the inside of my cheek. My underarms were already shaved, and silently, I was thankful because I was sweating like a big dog.

Mrs. Walker cackled. "Hello, Gage. Nice to meet you." She nodded to him. "Honey, they are for sure—not happy. You go out on the terrace and look. Shane, show her." She pointed to the terrace.

"I'll take you," Shane said, leading the way through the apartment. Walking behind him, I wanted to place my hand on his back like Dad did to Mom. His t-shirt clung to his broad shoulders, and he walked like he was good on any MLK Boulevard. My bulging stomach became the focus of my attention, and I wondered if Shane liked skinny girls. I made a mental note to Google how to lose weight in a few days and I hoped the answer wouldn't be crack or something. Maybe I could talk to Mom about adding some salads to the platter menu.

"Here they are." Shane pushed the balcony door open. The sounds of the city assaulted and tickled my ears. New York City was loud, demanding, and in your face. Summertime in the city was delectable. With something to do on every block, there was no reason for me to feel so alone. But I did. The beauty of living in Harlem was finding out which kind of day it was going to be and how to tell the difference. There was artistry in the neighborhoods, each block having their own distinct aura and colors in the wind. Some blocks were modern and fresh. Stucco and matte black decorated the buildings. Others were full of flavor and gusto, bursting at the seams with zest and essence of history and culture. Feet slapping against the pavement. The air hung heavy with desperation and dreams deferred.

The stench of immediacy, permeated with a little rudeness, but a whole lot of heart infiltrated the air. I didn't care. It was fucking home.

I sucked in a gulp of Harlem air and closed my eyes.

"You smell it too." Shane grinned.

"You're a newbie around these parts. What do *you* smell?" I poked out my chest, ready to defend my city.

Shane held his stomach, fake wincing in pain. "Ouch! Newbie?" Shane inhaled. "I smell . . . chocolate."

Thinking about chocolate dripping from his lips made me squeeze my legs together again.

I bent down next to Mrs. Walker's plants and stuck my finger into the soil. The dryness crumbled between my palms. Using my plant shears tucked away in my bag, I cut some of the dead ends and stems drying out. I turned on the hose and clicked the head three times before a small spraying stream emptied from the spigot. The rain cascaded over the thirsty plants and drank all they could take.

"That should do it." I stood to my feet. My knees cracked loudly.

"Wow, that was beautiful." He sat dumbfounded.

I squinted at him. Was this guy for real? He thought this was cool?

Couldn't be.

This was the part I hated about boys. You never knew if they were serious or if they meant what they said. It was easier to not want them. Not believe them. Not believe *in* them. Last year in school, Chase walked up to me, and he said, *"would you like to go to the movies with me this Friday?"*

I closed my locker and looked around. For sure, he wasn't talking to me. We ran in two different crowds and while his crew wasn't better or worse than mine, it still made me pause to make sure I was who he was referring to. When I saw that no one was behind me. I pointed to myself. *"Me?"*

"Yes, you." He snorted, and I felt silly that I thought it wasn't me. Why couldn't it be me?

"Sure. Thanks for asking," I managed out, trying to sound nonchalant. The late bell rang, and although I was late for gym class and would probably have to stay after school for detention, I didn't care. I held onto my locker for support. My fuzzy sweater had my armpits a wet mess underneath the light-hearted gaze of Chase. His eyes dreamt of sunsets and chocolate cake.

"Come on. I'll walk you to class." He smiled. His varsity jacket clung snug to his body like they made it just for him. He was old-school, still rocking four cornrowed braids to the back. I wondered whose legs he plopped down between every week to keep them looking so fresh. Probably skinny legs. Not these golden-brown drumsticks I had. Two football championships from freshman and sophomore years, creased brown dimples on both cheeks, and a gift for the gab, made Chase a *catch*. All the girls wanted him. Me and Ivy pointed and laughed at girls falling all over themselves to get his attention. A few fistfights were standard in the name of who thought they belonged to him and who disagreed. They always claimed they were dating, but I wasn't sure he was dating *them*. Or if they even knew. Yet, he wanted to take me to the movies? I brushed those thoughts from my head. Just because I was heavy-set didn't mean shit. Mom always said the prettiest girls had some meat on their bones. Besides, I was draggin' a wagon.

"You know what—" I rolled my eyes and focused my attention back to Shane.

"Wait— do you hear that?" Shane shushed. He placed his finger to my lips and my stomach ached in delight and brushed my thoughts about Chase away. I wanted to know Shane. Hear what he heard. The thought left me deliciously scared and terrifyingly nervous all at the same time.

Focusing my ears, sure enough someone was screaming. "What is that?"

Gage stood and held a hand up so he could listen. *Was Mom okay?* I headed toward the door.

"We have to go, y'all."

Gage was already stomping across the living room, his eyes focused on the front door.

"Wa-wait — we'll go with you." Shane motioned to his mom.

Mrs. Walker licked the spoon and rushed out the door beside us.

The same way I walked up to the Walker's apartment, two stairs at a time, I lumbered down the stairs with Shane and his mom in tow. I hustled toward Town House, where Mr. Fred and a small circle formed. Ms. Gloria was scowling in a chair, both hands resting on her walker. Shanice was yelling at her kids to behave, and Jorge was dressed in his factory uniform fresh from work. He looked like a totally different person on his days off.

"Who did it?! Who did it?" Mr. Fred spewed. He hopped around the room and dragged his foot. Something looked different about him. His eyes were bugged out of his head, and he was red in the face. That was probably because of the bottle he hid horribly in a breast pocket in his jacket. The bottle was jostling around in his shirt, threatening to fall.

"Who did what, Mr. Fred?" Deja asked sweetly. She had one hand behind her back and was swinging side to side, looking much younger and sneakier than her ten years.

"Somebody took my walking cane! Somebody stole it. I can say I won't get mad, but I'm pissed off. I ain't never did nothing to nobody and don't even want to be here! My cane got all my special stickers and tickets from where I been. Y'all ain't never been nowhere! And it better turn up in the morning or I'm calling the police, god dammit."

"All this is over your cane, Mr. Fred? Are you serious?" Jorge scoffed. He scratched at his neck and tugged at his pressed collar until it left a red mark.

"I want my shit! I better have it tomorrow or there will be hell to pay. Wait, you see!"

"Well, when did you last see it, Fred?" Ms. Gloria huffed, clearly annoyed.

Mr. Fred paused and recalled something that within seconds made his eyes land on Shane. "You. You came to Town House and asked me to help your mom with unlatching the terrace door. I went on up and left my cane here. Only you were here." He wagged his finger at Shane.

"Ridiculous!" Mrs. Walker stood in front of Shane and shoved him behind her. "My boy don't know nothing about no cane. We just moved in."

"It-it-it wasn't me." Shane's chest rose as he fumbled over his words as the accusations lingered in the air. "Really, it wasn't. I just grabbed a bottle of water and then . . . I went outside for a second."

"And what were you doing outside? It was raining, remember? Making off with my cane. That's what you were doing. The boy stole my shit!" Mr. Fred grabbed a nearby chair and tossed it to the ground. He pulled his foot across the floor and almost tripped over the chair he threw. He shuffled upright and sneered back at us. Without his cane, he was slower, meaner, and held on to the wall for support. He stalked out of the room, leaving a trail of four-letter words behind him.

"Okay. Who did it? Marcel? Corey? New boy? What's your name?" Shanice questioned Shane. The bangles around her wrist screamed in frustration with every movement of her body.

Mrs. Walker cleared her throat and her back stiffened. "My boy don't know nothing about no cane. Like I said, we just moved here."

"Then why was he outside in the rain?" Shanice questioned with a hand on her hip.

Mrs. Walker frowned and took a step closer to Shanice. "I didn't know it was a crime to go outside in the rain."

Shanice cleared her throat. She backed down and turned to me.

"Then April? Come on, it *has* to be one of the kids. Just give the crazy man his stuff." Shanice tapped her foot against the table leg and stared at each of us. She stopped to check the time on her phone every few seconds.

"Alright now. Us old folk don't like when people mess with our stuff. I know you gotta let the good Lord use you as *He* sees fit. But I don't think this is the way to do it, y'all. Does anyone have it?" Ms. Gloria rocked back and forth in her seat. I could see her ankles screaming for relief in her compression socks and an inflamed red ring dented her skin. She rested her hands over her round stomach, and blinked at each of us, while *we* blinked at each of us.

Silence.

four

. . .

"I s your mama going to the Town House meeting tonight?" Ms. Gloria furrowed her eyebrows.

"We all are. Even Gage."

"Gage going too? He misses his neck of the woods, huh?" Ms. Gloria chuckled. She sat back in her favorite chair. It was worn out and should've been replaced a long time ago. She parked it in the room's corner, surrounded by her small houseplants that I grew from little buds on the roof.

"Ms. Gloria, do you really think someone stole his cane? I mean, a cane — really?" I sulked. The sun finally peeked through the clouds and today was a hot one. Someone rode by blaring Bhad Bunny from their stereo attached to a bike. I almost slid off Ms. Gloria's plastic covered couch from the heat and my sweat. She said the air conditioning was too cold, and she couldn't hear her stories over the loud humming noise.

"You just sit still and be quiet. It ain't even that hot once you focus," she said. I made sure I was never without something cold to drink while here.

"First of all, where was he at when it went missing? Fred says he left it in Town House, but yet, Shane says he was outside? I mean, it's pretty suspicious. It *was* raining off and all day. But his mama was right— going out in the rain ain't no crime."

"And they were moving in! Of course, he would be in and out. His parents, Marcel, and Shane all were." I added, ready to defend my man who wasn't my man.

"You right. You right, girl. I just don't know who would do such a thing. That's like somebody stealing my walker, and these chicken legs ain't nothing without my walker. But God don't be making no mistakes. I don't think he should've called the police, though. But I don't know, you young folks is different, think everything is funny and then go and put it on that Snap Talk."

"Snap Talk?" My eyes flung open from her couch as I tried to focus. I couldn't hold back a giggle. "Do you mean Snap Chat?"

"Whatever y'all call it!" she mused. "I'm just saying. I'm in too much pain all the time to fight. My knees are bad, and I have arthritis. Shit, I guess if it came down to my walker, I probably would've called the cops too. We gotta pray to Saint Anthony!"

I sat up on the squeaky couch and agreed. "I can't believe he called the cops!" The situation became dicey when the police arrived, and they threatened to ticket him for misuse of calling 9-1-1.

Ms. Gloria scratched at her left knee and flinched in pain.

"Ms. Gloria, when is your daughter taking you back to the doctor? Your sugar has been kind of high?" I recalled the meter when she showed it to me that morning.

"Oh girl, don't you mind me. Ms. Gloria will be just fine. Let's talk about you and this boy?"

"What boy?" I said in a shaky voice.

"*What boy?*" Ms. Gloria mocked.

I fell back onto Ms. Gloria's couch and slid downward onto the floor from sweat. We cracked up when I hit the carpet and my knee banged into her coffee table filled with cigarette butts and Ensure bottles. Once we stopped laughing, I cleared my throat and whispered. "I don't know, Ms. Gloria. He seems nice, but I don't really have anyone to compare him to." I never told Ms. Gloria about Chase. My mom knew that we dated, but that was the extent I was ready to share. What would I say anyway? I thought he liked me and turned out he didn't. But it was the words for me. The words he chose to describe me. The way he saw me. I looked at Chase and saw someone who made me want to put my phone down.

He didn't *see* me at all.

"Well, you is old enough. And you pretty enough. You gotta come up for air sometime and talk to the boy. You can't keep staring at him like that."

"I don't stare!"

"And my name is Halle Berry! Tell a lie, shame the devil!" Ms. Gloria shouted and tapped her chair.

My head fell back onto the couch, and we giggled again. These were the days I loved. Laughing with Ms. Gloria about nothing. I came by to water her plants, and she watered me with laughs. Having a job was great, but this was great too, in its own way.

There was a knock at the door, interrupting our amateur comedy hour.

"Go'on and see who that is, baby," Ms. Gloria directed.

I slid off the carpet and flip-flopped my way to her front door. My stomach hit the floor when Shane himself was staring back at me through the peephole.

"It's him!" I whipped around and whispered.

"Who?"

"Him! Shane!" I hissed.

Ms. Gloria's pudgy stomach rumbled in her chair, and she gurgled out a rippling laugh.

"It's not funny!" I slumped my shoulders. Did he hear us talking about him behind the door? Maybe he held his ear close and heard us say his name?

Before I lost my nerve, I ran a hand through my hair, still pulled back tightly in a braided bun at the nape of my neck. I smoothed down my jean skirt and felt my upper thighs. No hair. I checked my toes. Not a chip in sight.

"Hey." I cracked the door and wrung my hands.

"Oh, uh—hey. I saw your, uh—mom downstairs grabbing the mail. She said you were with Ms. Gloria. I, uh—was going to walk to the bodega and get some ice cream. Want to walk?"

My shoulders dropped from around my chin, and I relaxed. He wanted to walk to the bodega. With me. He swiped right. On me. My mind and heart were flowing in two different directions, wanting different things. My mind wanted to keep me safe and recalled of rushed and confusing encounters with Chase. My heart . . . my heart didn't speak in words. It spoke in glances, moments, and aromas of chocolate. Both sides were me, and so that was what I wanted? Right?

With curiosity leading the way, I grabbed my purse. "Sure." I breathed. "Ms. Gloria, I'll come back tonight, and we'll check your sugar again." I turned around as Shane waited for me in the hallway.

Ms. Gloria leaned back in her chair and grinned. "Go'on, baby, I will be fine. Y'all have fun now, you hear?"

Shane and I took the stairs down to the ground floor, and our arms touched along the way. He was almost a whole foot taller than me, and when we faced each other, I had to look up into his eyes. His eyes were soft. My mom always said, you could tell good people by the look in their eyes. I thought Chase had beautiful eyes, but clearly missing the mark was an understatement with him. Maybe I didn't have that gene. That knowing gene, that seeing gene, like Mom did. What was his angle here? And did he have one? When he held the door open and smiled at me like he knew me from a long time ago; I decided I had that gene. He was so good so good so good.

Shane saw me wincing from the brightness of a midday Harlem summer. "Do you want my sunglasses?" He dug into his pockets. He pulled out a pair of sunglasses and my eyes widened at the stocky gold frames.

"Where did you get these from, the Jeffrey Dahmer collection?"

Shane's bottomless laugh was deep and full of life. I wanted to make him laugh a thousand times again to see his dazzling smile.

Walking down the street as slow as I could, I pulled the glasses onto my face, and together, I pointed out our new neighborhood. "And that is where the middle school kids go to vape. They have a little hideout behind that alley over there. Sometimes I walk by and play a police siren on my phone, and they scatter. It's so funny." I jumped over a large puddle, but Shane didn't see it and traipsed right through it.

The puddle splashed Shane's white Air Force Ones, and he sucked his teeth and splashed off the excess water. "And what's that over there?" He pointed to a beautiful brownstone on the corner. It was painted matte black, and the owners had new hardwood and windows installed. It was easily the nicest home on the block, but it rarely looked lived in.

"I really don't know. My mom loves that house. She says the kitchen is probably out of this world. But it always looks dark and cold to me."

Shane hovered in front of the stoop and looked the building up and down. "Doesn't look like there's love there."

"You can see love?" I chuckled.

He searched my face and paused before responding. "Yes."

Casting a magnetic spell with his gaze, I wanted to know what he was thinking, and if those thoughts consisted of me. He was growing leaps and bounds, infecting every empty space in my heart I froze when Chase left. But Shane burst through my energy fields with a flashlight, shining a light into places I longed to keep hidden.

We grabbed ice cream, sunflower seeds, and Slim Jims from the bodega then retreated home. Not wanting to miss a moment, my pace was even slower. There were still a few hours before the sunset, and the owners of the after-hours lounge were washing the windows and preparing for a night of Bachata and line dancing. I talked faster, giving him a condensed tour of his new residence and the neighborhood.

"So, your dad works for the NBA? That's cool." I licked my cone. Kids were whizzing by on their bikes and I wiggled my waist to make sure they didn't run me down. This was how I remembered summer break. No rules, no adults—just fun.

"Yeah, it's been fun. We get a lot of tickets to games."

"Did you want to move here? I couldn't dream of growing up in Connecticut! What's there?"

Shane grinned. "Before you say it, yes, there are Black people there. That's the only thing about the NBA. They can re-assign you anywhere they need recruits, and you kind of just have to go. This is our first move, so we haven't had it too bad. Besides, my dad grew up in Harlem. This is his home." Shane held the door for an older woman coming out of the welfare office. When he turned back toward me, I noticed a thick, brown scar above his right eyelid.

Without thinking, I placed my hand on his face. "What happened here?"

He pulled away from my hand with enough force that made me want to apologize and look the other way. "Oh, that's nothing." His pace increased on our stroll home. My stomach lurched. He clearly didn't want to be touched and here I went, putting my hands on him.

"I'm a boxer. I took a couple of hits in and out of the ring," he stammered.

"By the looks of that scar, did you give any out?" I laughed.

"I did. A lot, actually; thank you very much. But part of the game is about being able to take them too." He shrugged.

He. Was. So. Different. Than. Chase.

Chase Rickles, the boy that had ruined all the boys for me.

My sophomore year jinx.

The scar over not my right eye—but my heart. So many girls in school were having a grand ol' time having sex, wearing the boys' varsity jackets, and making TikTok videos together. The one time I liked a boy and actually did something about it, I became the laughingstock of the school.

"Have you even thought about it?" Chase asked one night on the phone. I was under my blankets and the rain raged outside. The sandman called me to sleep hours ago, but Chase phoned me and dared me to stay up and talk to him. His parents were never home, and he could always talk at any hour of the day. It was exciting. Knowing my parents were in another part of the house sleeping, and I was on the phone talking to a boy who I liked and liked me too. My phone conversations were reserved for Ivy as we talked about other people and planned our futures.

"I've thought about it, of course. I just don't know if I'm ready. Like, what do we do afterwards? Pretend it never happened? Do it again?"

"We do whatever you want to do. Listen. I want you to be comfortable. It's not a big deal to me."

Chase and I went to the movies, just like he requested. The new Marvel movie looked pretty cool, but we hardly watched it. He wanted to explore the back of my throat with his tongue instead. I'd kissed boys before, and they tasted like a penny and fumbled their way through dry, unsure lips. Chase kissed like he *kissed, kissed*. Like he knew what he was doing and practiced many times before. It was pretty intimidating, trying to watch the movie and kiss at the same time. I said nothing, though; I didn't want him to think I wasn't interested, so we swapped spit, popcorn kernels, and stole glances at the screen.

I snapped out of my thoughts and wondered if Shane tasted like a penny or something sweeter. My body buzzed with slippery feelings I wanted to go away, but I also wanted to know what he tasted like.

"How did you get into that? I saw your boxing pictures in your house." I pressed with a raised voice. We were getting closer to our brownstone and people were driving by blasting music through their speakers and laughing.

Shane's lip twitched downward. "You know, just life, I guess."

"Have you found a gym out here? You know Harlem is famous for turning Cassius Clay into Muhammed Ali."

We made it to the crosswalk in front of our building, and he grabbed my hand and led me across the street. "I don't plan to be Muhammed Ali. Just Shane Walker." He flexed a muscle and gave a silly smile.

Electric jolts shot through my body as I squeezed his hand back. I was glad I was wearing his sunglasses. I didn't want him to see the sparkles forming in my eyes and the way he was tip-tapping at my heart.

"When's your birthday?" I asked.

"July 27th. You?"

My eyes lit up. "Seriously?! Mine is July 24th!"

"Wow, small world. July birthdays are the best." Shane clapped his hands together.

When we punched in the keycode and headed back inside, we were hit with a blast of cold from the central air, and even more icy tones in the Town House.

"That's not fair!" I heard my dad's voice.

When we rounded the corner, both of our parents were standing in a straight line against Mr. Fred. The air between them was thick with tension, and I wasn't sure who was upset the most.

Mr. Fred did not look good. The bit of hair that was left on his head was sticking up, and I could smell the liquor permeating through his pores. "It's not about fair. I'm doing what's right and what should've been done a long time ago."

"What's going on?" Shane frowned.

"Mr. Fred here has decided that April's greenhouse on the roof is a fire hazard, and she has to move it." Mom's nostrils flared.

"What?" I cried. "You said we couldn't keep it on the balcony terrace, and we had to move it to the roof!" I banged my hands on the wall. This couldn't be happening. He told us it was okay to move it there! We didn't even know the rooftop was accessible until he showed it to us.

"Well, things have changed, young girl. And until they return my cane, there are new rules around here! I gave y'all an inch, and you been skating ever since."

"Now, Mr. Fred." My dad waved his hands in defeat. "This is not right. I don't know nothing about your cane, and I will even help you find it. But don't take this out on April, she ain't did nothing." My dad backed away from Mr. Fred and gave him some space. "Now, where was the last place you saw it? Maybe you misplaced it?" Dad crossed his arms at Mr. Fred like he was a parent wheeling and dealing with an unreasonable child.

Mr. Fred stomped in place just like one too. "I left it in Town House and that Shane boy was there, just like I said before. When I came back in from helping the Walkers, it was gone. And did y'all hear what I said? Maybe I'm speaking that Spanish y'all love so much. I said move it by next week or until someone turns over me cane. And that's final!"

Rage surged through my body and my head was ready to pop like a balloon. "It's not right!" I screamed.

"Mr. Fred. Me and April were talking, and we decided that we're going to find your cane. You don't have to do this." Shane swept his arms. He was trying to keep the peace, and I wanted to cry.

"Now that's the most sensible thing I heard all day. Finally, and it took a Connecticut boy to figure it out. Maybe it wasn't you." Mr. Fred smiled. His mouth was blank and hollow from missing teeth.

"Watch it." Mr. Walker pinched his lips.

Glancing at Shane, I wondered when we came up with this plan to find the cane. I didn't want to find anything. I wanted to walk to the bodega with him, help Ms. Gloria check her sugar, and drop off platters for my mom—not a summer homework assignment.

five

. . .

"I don't care, Ivy!" I shouted into the phone. She was working her summer job at Chick-fil-A and she was outside flailing her arms directing traffic while Facetiming me.

She sat her hand on her hip. "Really April? He could've made you completely move it. I know it's not ideal, but bringing your plants back to the terrace could be worse."

"The terrace is filled with Mom's overflowing cooking pots and Gage's room is already overflowing with plants," I whined.

"Then you'll have to move them, April!" Ivy shouted into the phone as a car honked at her in the drive-thru.

"You know what, Ivy. I will talk to you later." My eyes narrowed.

"But—" and before she could get another word, she met the red end button.

Pulling the terrace door open, a blast of heat slapped my face. Friday night in Harlem meant music, laughter, and spades. The Old G's in the neighborhood were setting up their card tables and the women were in the houses with the windows wide open, frying chicken and tossing large barrels of rice. Getting ready for a night in the city was where memories were made. I dug into the cool soil in the container beneath me and let it turn my fingertips brown. The hairs on the back of my neck stood up, and I slapped my skin, expecting a mosquito to be feasting on my melanin. When I looked up and squinted at the setting sun, Shane was peering down at me from his third-floor terrace.

"Why do you do it like that?"

"Do what?" I cut my eyes and returned my gaze to the soil. What the hell did he want? I was mad at everyone today.

"Roll your fingers between the dirt?"

"It's not dirt, It's soil. It's nourishing. To them, at least," I said without looking back up.

"I'm going to come down and see."

"Don't you come down here!" I shouted and whipped my head up so fast that my neck shot out a pain.

Shane chuckled. "See you in a minute!" He ducked off the terrace.

"Ouch!" I cried, scrambling to my feet and stubbing my toe on the sliding door. "Mom. Shane said he was coming down."

"That boy who likes you?" She wiped her hands on her apron and had specks of flour sitting in her hair.

"He doesn't like me," I grumbled. "He just feels bad for me because I have to move my plants."

"Well, why wouldn't he like you? You know, ever since you dated that one boy, Chase, you have been closed off. I don't get it. Did anything happen with you and him?" She let her words trail off, along with my nerves. Mom's jaw hardened, and she stopped breathing for a second. I wanted to comfort her and say, *hell no, nothing happened.* But that wasn't true. The truth laid somewhere between dirty motel sheets and a few blocks over where I left my virginity, and the last time I felt something other than ice.

"Did something happen with who?" Gage said, paddling his way down the hallway and lightly patting Milani on the back. He usually lumbered into the room, taking up space with laughs and jokes, but fled when the energy turned sour. Dad was usually the sour energy for him, but for me and Mom—he was so sweet.

"Nothing happened." My temples throbbed.

"Gage, where is that child's mama? You been here every day this week with her. Her mama don't watch her?" Mom questioned. As if on cue, a chess board crashed outside below the terrace where the men were seated playing cards and highlighted Mom's lingering question.

Gage cleared his throat and gently laid Milani down in her playpen in the living room.

"You say I don't come over and you want to see Milani more. When I come over, my room is overrun with plants and has turned into a rainforest, so there's nowhere for her to really rest and get comfortable. No offense, sis." Gage shot me a sympathetic smile. "So here we are, and now and you say we *'been here every day this week.'*"

Gage rocked his head back and forth and did his best impression of Mom. His brows furrowed just like Dad's did when he was frustrated. Milani cooed in her playpen in the dining room and I ached to hold her and tell her everything would be okay, and her silly daddy and Pop-Pop would make up. I would tell her they weren't always like this—and they used to be fun and each other's favorite person. I wanted her to know that I was worried they wouldn't forgive each other or let go of whatever had them at each other's necks these past few years. It seemed like the older Gage got, the more he walked, talked, and acted like Dad. And Dad went harder on him and expected more. Expected him to be something he wasn't and didn't know himself to be yet. But I said nothing to Milani.

I stared at her and hoped and wished from the armchair next to the terrace. The room was now quiet, just us Mays family.

"Well, are you working, son? We just want to make sure you are okay."

"You care, but does Dad?" Gage's voice rose, and it made me

jump in my seat. I wasn't afraid of my big brother, but I was shocked at his flared speech. He skipped the skim milk and opted for the full fat on his tone and words today. He brought himself back down almost immediately, but he seemed to shrink in the chair because he knew what I knew too. I held my breath and turned to Mom, waiting for the theatrics.

Mom's eyes bugged out of her head and one look told me that Gage even thinking about raising his voice was disrespect. Mom's wig cupped her chin and the first few pieces of hair on her forehead were plastered to her skin because of her sweating, cooking, and now fussing.

"Excuse me!" Mom rolled her neck. "You won't be hollering at me in my house and will *not* disrespect me in tone and pitch! This is my house!" Mom rose from her brief reprieve from cooking and huffed around in the kitchen. Pans banged together and Milani jumped in her sleep from the noise.

"Got my grandbaby woken up! All because my oldest child is screaming at me in *my* house!" Mom shouted to no one from the kitchen.

Me and Gage stared at each other, trying not to break until our eyes were full from holding back funny tears. The lady could perform when she wanted to. Sometimes she was the voice of reason between Dad and Gage, and other times I wasn't sure how she felt. Maybe that's what being a parent was about. Deciding solely based on how something felt in the moment.

Tap Tap!

Someone rapped on the door. *Shit!* Shane was here. I broke Gage's gaze and shuffled to the door, taking a few deep breaths and running my tongue over my dry teeth.

Minutes ago, I wanted to see no one. Minutes ago, he demanded to see me. And now—I wanted to see him. And be seen. Kick every Chase memory, chasing me through the scaffolds, darting between white sheets to the curb.

"Hey, Shane." The door held my weight and courage.

"Hey, yourself." He grinned, leaning against the door frame.

"Heyy." I took a step closer until my chest rubbed against his. It was bold of me, and not particularly *ever* feeling like a bold girl, I surprised myself.

"Heyyy," Shane breathed. His eyes locked on mine, and we stared at each other and spun a silent poem only we understood.

"*Heyyyy . . .*" Gage giggled from the living room. Even Milani let out a small grunt-chuckle.

"And y'all can stay in the living room and on the terrace. April— ain't nobody going in your room. Your dad will be home soon." Mom had a way of giving direct threats—indirectly.

"Come on." I motioned and grabbed his hand, leading him to my therapy. I felt the makings of a headache coming on. Why did boys make you feel like you were having a heart attack? You sweat. Your chest gets tight. You feel itchy all over, your nerves were bad, and your mind raced a mile a minute. Was it all some colossal joke to make you think you might absolutely, positively die right before . . . love?

We returned to the terrace, and I tended to my smallest plants. Shane sat in a corner and watched the city come alive around us with weekend vibes. Someone had a spotlight waving back and forth from the westside, and in the distance a few planes were landing from different directions. He slung his shoulders over the terrace and watched the rowdy chess game below. He closed his eyes and took a deep breath.

"This is nice."

"It's perfect for when you want to get away. That's why Mr. Fred can't take it away. First it's the rooftop, and next it'll be this." As I kneaded the soil between my fingers; I stopped breathing once I felt him watching me. What did he see when he looked at me? What was he looking at? Were my legs hairy? Did he like what he saw? Most days I liked what I saw, and other days I needed to be reminded by someone who insisted.

"What do you want to get away from?"

Dirt blackened my fingers and when I looked around, there was nothing to wipe my hands with.

"Here—wipe it on this." Shane leaned in and pulled his white shirt toward me.

"Are you serious?"

He shrugged. "We wash clothes. Haven't done it yet since we moved in, but that was only days ago. Maybe tonight will be the first night." His brown eyes locked hold of mine and for all the tea in China, I tried not to blink, so I didn't miss a thing.

"Okay . . ." I scooted closer. We sat cross-legged in front of each other. We were so close our knees touched. My filthy hands painted ballads across his broad shoulders. Sweeping my fingertips across his shirt, lullabies sauntered laps around his heart, and molded Gold Coast hymns baked in future memories around his belly. Melodic, warm palms lit up like a piano, prickling his chin and pulling his face closer.

His white shirt was filthy. And my hands were clean.

Please God, let me be his only lyric.

A smile crept to my face, and I exhaled.

"How do you do it all? All this?" His eyes flickered around and touched the side of my face.

Clearing my throat and scooting backward, I knelt down on all fours. "I give them fertilizer first. It's a delicate dance between sunlight, water, fertilizer, and checking the soil. You should also wipe the leaves clean once per week and at least mist them on days they're not being fully watered. But really, you just have to listen to them. They usually tell you what they need."

"Do you listen to anyone?"

My poor neck. I whipped it up and stared at him. "What do you mean?"

Shane leaned in toward me. "I know I jumped the gun with Mr. Fred. I shouldn't have said we were going to find his cane. But maybe we should be! Let's work together and figure this out." He emphasized.

"Work together and figure this out? This isn't CLUE." I shook my head. Mr. Fred was going to do what he wanted regardless. He was a mean old man, and now he had the space and opportunity to be even meaner. "I think we should just leave it to the adults to figure out. It has to turn up." Water from the hose splashed around inside my water pail and onto Shane's new kicks when I pressed the nozzle. He didn't flinch when the water hit his Jordan Retros, but I knew he wanted to.

"Well, I could use your help. You're not the one he's accusing." He uncrossed his legs so his shoes weren't right in the line of fire. "You know the lay of the land better than I do. It's been a few days, and no one has come forward yet. He's making you move your greenhouse. What else will he do? I just thought before the next Town House meeting we could figure something out. At least look like we're taking him seriously."

Turning my back to Shane, thirsty plants stared back at me for water and answers. The reprieve from his eyes was welcomed, even for just a few seconds. In those seconds, my mind wasn't scrambled like eggs with American cheese, and I didn't get lost in the already painted future memories of us in my mind. In theory, he was asking to spend more time with me . . . right? And Mr. Fred already did make me move my greenhouse. Shane was right. What else was he capable of now that his cane was missing?

I had to help Shane. This was on me too.

As if reading my thoughts, Shane said, "I mean, I had to stalk you from the third floor waiting for you to come to the terrace just so I could spark conversation." He slapped his knees and pretended to faint.

I put my fist to my mouth and stifled back a giggle. "You could've just gone to Town House. Every day, I check the mail at the same time." I was a predictable girl and not buying this, he was 'waiting' for me jazz. Chase had me down that road of tall tales from the hood before.

Thoughts of Chase stuck to me like a wad of annoying gum.

"Why didn't you show up yesterday?" Chase asked. I shut my locker door, and he was standing on the other side. It was second period, and I was rushing to grab my gym clothes and get changed. His deep, questioning eyes pierced my soul like they always did, and blanketed my waning confidence like a cloak of darkness. A wizard, he was. With each late-night phone call, I touched myself under the blanket to his voice.

"Hey, Chase." I steadied myself against the locker as the bell rang. "When I got there, you were already gone."

"Bullshit, April. I waited and called you three times. Is everything okay?" He leaned in and cupped my face.

We made plans to meet at a motel a few blocks from our school. It wasn't anything nice, at least from the outside looking in. We planned it for at least two weeks, and I rode past there with my bike to make sure when the big day came—I knew how to get to and from with no issues, and no adult needed. "You don't need to be going to no motel," Ivy scolded. She was angry at him for even suggesting it and even angrier at me for considering it. "You can do so much better for your first time. This guy is not it."

"He cares about me. We're not officially together, but we're working towards it. He loves me," I told her. The weight of my denial was heavy. I wanted to convince her not to worry, and we had things handled. I was mature. Inside, I racked my brain searching for one good reason; I agreed to go. It was what he wanted, and I didn't want to disappoint him. For me that was answer enough.

When school ended that day, I ran home, showered, and zoomed back to the motel. My heart was racing and praying and praying and racing. Please God, let no one who knew Mom and Dad see me riding closer and closer to a motel. Sweat clung to my clammy skin and my eyes burned deep. The city noises around me seemed so much louder than ever before and I snapped my hands to my chest. I thought a heart attack was coming on.

"Honey? Are you okay?" An older woman grabbed my shoulder. As soon as she touched me, my bike released from my grip and my body crumpled into her arms. "Are you hurt? Sit down. Let me get you some water." She wore scrubs and had the brightest red hair I had ever seen. Flashes of images ran through my mind. Chase. Ivy. Mom. People at school. Was everyone having sex? Me and Ivy weren't. Were we the last ones?

"I'm, I'm okay." I gulped the water bottle she gently sat in my hand.

"Count with me. Breathe in for five seconds. Hold it for five seconds. Release for five seconds. Hold again for five seconds, release for five seconds, and repeat." She placed her hands on my shoulders and counted with me.

I followed her lead and concentrated on counting to five in my head and calming my body. After a few minutes, my mind slowed down, and I wasn't sweating anymore.

"Good. Very good," she commanded. A small crowd formed around us as people scoped out the distressed teenager, wondering if she was on drugs. Could I be high off love? Did love do this to you?

"How do you feel?" Red Hair asked.

The answers caught in my throat. "Better. Much better. Thank you." Heavy words croaked from a place in me on display for everyone to see.

"I think you had an anxiety attack there," she explained. "Have you had one before?"

I shook my head.

"First one is always the hardest. Your body is overstimulated. But just because your brain thinks it doesn't make it true." She tapped her

temple and then tapped mine. "You are stronger than your brain. If it happens again, breathe your way through it."

"Breathe my way through it," I repeated with a deep belly sigh.

Once I settled, the crowd dispersed. She handed me her card and said, "My name is Trista. I'm a psychiatric nurse at a counseling wellness center. Check us out sometime." She winked in my direction and walked away, red head bouncing in the wind.

Turning my attention back to the motel looming in front of me, I felt a magnetic pull to finish what I started and enter a new chapter in my life. The magnet that was Chase was propelling me forward, but after my fake heart-attack I felt . . . dirty. My skin now ashen and itchy from sweat. Red Hair said I was overstimulated. Funny, that's what Chase was supposed to do. Frozen between one last look at the motel beckoning me to enter its fortress of secrets and home tugging at my heart. My knuckles gripped the handlebars.

I turned around and rode back to the brownstone.

How did I explain to Chase that I had an anxiety attack at the thought of having sex? How did I tell him I wasn't ready for what I told him I thought I was ready for? I wanted to get to know him better, but did that have to include sex?

"I just backed out, I guess," was my answer for Chase at the locker.

He was quiet for a moment just as the late bell rang. "April, we don't have to do

anything you don't want to do. It's okay" He took a step back and gave me space.

"But I do. I'm just, like, not ready."

"I have to get to class. Come on, I'll walk you to the gym." He grabbed my elbow.

Then he didn't talk to me for three days.

Didn't respond to any text messages and when he saw me waiting for him at his locker, he turned and walked the other way. He blocked me on social media. When the burning sensation of unanswered questions *seared through my body and waves of anxiety attacks washed me up to sea, intrusive thoughts of who he was talking to ravaged my veins like drugs. Each second, each moment that passed, I convinced myself he was falling less and less out of love with me. There could only be one answer. The cure was also my drug. When I finally texted him and said,*

I thought about it, and I think I'm ready.

He was at my locker the next morning with donuts.

I snapped out of my Chase thoughts and snapped back to Shane. *God, let me stay in the moment,* I prayed. "It's actually about time to get the mail, anyway. Do you want to head down? We can head to the bodega for some ice cream?" I suggested. Jabs at the soil, and stupid thoughts of Chase interrupted me tending to plants. I stopped harassing the dirt and plopped down in the lawn chair across from him. A cool shower called to me even though I took one the night before *and* this morning. I needed to shave. Again.

Shane didn't hesitate. "Ice cream, huh? Is that a yes? Are you waving the white flag? You'll help me with Mr. Fred then?"

I sighed. "That is a yes."

"You will help? Yes!" He jumped up from the chair and pulled the sliding door open. *The Golden Girls* was blaring from the tv as my mom cooked and snickered from the kitchen.

"Y'all heading out?" Mom stirred the pot. "I found something for you, April, hold on." Mom took her apron off from around her waist and ran into the living room. Rummaging through her purse, she grunted and cursed under her breath until she found it. "Here it is," she breathed.

"What is it?" I frowned.

"It's a Home Planters for Teens Contest. I saw it in the *NY Times*. I thought maybe you could apply." Her voice dropped like she was nervous to say what was on her mind.

Me? Apply for . . . What exactly? I read the small press release and sure enough; they were looking for photos of your best home-grown houseplants; teen edition.

I had tons of those.

"Thanks, Mom." I tucked the clipping into my pocket and kissed her cheek. Standing beside me. That's where I could always find her.

"Don't you just love, love?" Shane grinned and made an Eddie Murphy voice.

"Bye, Shane!" I rolled my eyes. "I'm going to take a quick shower. Can you wait a few minutes?"

Shane leaned in and sniffed. "You smell fine to me. Let's roll." He walked across the living room and opened the front door, holding out a hand for me to follow.

Mom cackled from the kitchen. "That boy is something else." She shook her head.

He sure was. He sure was.

We trekked down the steps and my flip-flops made slapping noises. The noise was so loud, I tried walking quieter. It must've been too loud for critters because when I got to the first-floor landing, a mouse scurried in front of my feet and ran into a hole.

"Ahhhh!" I yelped and fell into Shane's arms.

"Whoa, it's okay. It- it- it's okay," he stuttered. His heart was beating just as fast as mine. I could feel it through his shirt.

"He's so worried about this damn cane when we have rats as big as your head running around!" I huffed.

"Now what did I do? Why does my head have to be put in it?" Shane cuffed the back of his neck and leaned against the wall.

"Don't y'all have somewhere to be?" Mr. Dawson's words were laced with disgust and made us jump from the intrusion.

"Hi, Mr. Dawson." Shane waved. "We're getting the mail—just like you." Shane towered over him, and Mr. Dawson had to look up at him to even see his face.

"I ain't got nothing to say to you or your family." Mr. Dawson shooed Shane away from him.

"Uhhh. Did I do something wrong?" Shane tripped over his words and squeezed his eyebrows together.

Mr. Dawson's face was turned up and contorted like he smelled something stinky. He looked up at Shane. "All I know is everything was fine before you and your people showed up. Now we got things missing. Rats coming out in the middle of the day. It just ain't right. I don't know what's going on here. But I'm watching you and the rest of your city-slicking NBA family. Y'all steal too."

I cringed, watching one Black man size up another.

"Mr. Dawson. That's not right. We don't know who it was. Shane and I are going to find out, though." I locked my fingers around Shane's and he shot me a surprised glance. He squeezed my fingers.

"Humph. Don't you get yourself all wrapped up in things you don't know nothing about. After all, they are from Connecticut." Mr. Dawson limped away, shaking his head.

six

. . .

S hanice crossed her arms and pulled her sweater around her waist. It did nothing to cover the round mound that was her behind.

Mr. Dawson stared at her through stolen glances and well-concealed scowls. It was not with the same contempt that he had for Shane when he cornered us.

Our biweekly brownstone meeting couldn't have come at a worse time. We were fed up with Mr. Fred. One week. That's how long it had been since his cane was stolen and yet, no one came forward to turn it in since our last impromptu meeting about it.

Everyone was a suspect these days, and poor Shane was at the center of it. He was the new kid on the block and given his dark skin, and cuts to his face; he was an easy target to accuse. It angered me that Mr. Dawson accused him, and even worse—he was flapping his gums to anyone who would listen. Other people were giving Shane curious looks and judgmental eyes. According to Mr. Fred, he was upstairs helping Mrs. Walker when his cane disappeared and Shane was the only one in Town House. Not to mention, we never had any burglaries in the building and the drama began when his family moved in.

I stared at him, hoping he wasn't pulling a Chase on me. Was he who he said he was? Did he take the cane? And if so, why? Was I just a terrible judge of character?

"Like I said, until they return my cane, life around here is about to get real hard." Mr. Fred stood in the center of the room, hunched over, and chin pointed in the air. He tried so hard to stand up straight, but without his trusty cane by his side, he gritted his teeth through the pain and hurled it back at us.

"But, Mr. Fred, you ain't even done nothing about the rats." Ms. Gloria banged her walker on the floor. She sat in the center of the room with Shanice to her left and Jorge to her right. Everyone formed a semi-circle around her. The longest-standing brownstone tenant that everyone loved. She was the glue. Mr. Fred sometimes bowed down to Ms. Gloria, but today his jaw tightened and his voice clipped for even her.

"Ms. Gloria," he started. "I tried to do something about the rats. I told you that before; but this *is* New York City." He swept his arms around the room. "I set out traps, and I called them animal control peoples and ain't nobody did nothing."

"Well, you also shouldn't be accusing people either." Mr. Walker stood. His voice boomed over Mr. Fred's and a hush settled across the room. He faced Mr. Fred and towered over him. Marcel sat next to his dad, head buried in his iPad, and not paying attention to the fussing grown-ups.

A shifty gaze had my head whipping back and forth between Mr. Fred and Mr. Walker. This was not good and getting worse by the minute. I squeezed my toes on my sandals. My feet were sweaty and cold from nervousness.

Mr. Fred didn't flinch as he stared Mr. Walker in his face. He said, "And Jorge, make sure all that Bachata music is turned down by at least six. I don't want to hear it no more at 9 p.m."

"Six!" Jorge stammered and jumped from his seat. "I don't even get home from work sometimes until seven, so it ain't always just me. Now I know you lying!"

"Well then, whoever that man is that you keep up in your apartment that you think I don't know about—tell him to turn the music down."

Shanice took in a sharp breath at Mr. Fred's last sentence. Even Deja and Corey were sitting still and not bopping around. The energy was thick with truths even their young ears tuned in like a radio.

"There's-there's no man!" Jorge's face reddened.

This was a sad sight, and it was bringing out the worst in everyone. Jorge stood out of the crowd, whether or not he tried. With his white and black pinstripe pants and matching tucked shirt, he clinched it together with a flea market Gucci belt. He slicked his hair to the side with a part in the middle and gold rings adorned his fingers. He worked in a hospital and hated it; the uniform did nothing to bring out his personality. When he was off from work, he came alive, and so did his clothes. He did as he pleased, and that included having a man in his apartment—but *that* he didn't talk about. I saw him a few times when I was dropping off platters, but Jorge never fully disclosed who or *what* he preferred.

"Okay, everyone, just calm down," my dad said. "This can't go on all because of a cane. Now listen, we all know how important it is to Mr. Fred, so someone just return it so we can get back to our regular lives. Summer is usually a fun time for all of us here. Let's not ruin that by some stolen cane."

"Have you ever thought that maybe you accidentally left it somewhere, or you threw it away?" Shanice suggested.

Mr. Fred's eyes bugged out of his head, and he glared at her. "No, I did not lose it. I keep all of my important stickers on there, all the places that I've been, and things I've seen. Stuck right on there. I told you; I sat it down in Town House and ain't seen it since. It's mine and I want it back! I don't do nothing to you people! I try to help as much as I can, and this is the thanks I get." Mr. Fred slapped his hand against the table. "I have nothing left to say to you people, meeting is adjourned."

"But we didn't even talk about the Fourth of July bash!" Ms. Gloria countered.

"You think I'm okaying a BBQ for you mental midgets? There ain't going to be no Fourth of July bash until I get my shit!" Mr. Fred scolded and stalked out the room. He would have the last word one way or another.

The crowd murmured amongst themselves in disbelief. I stared around the room at my neighbors. We saw each other. We learned each other. Waves of happiness, sadness, and pain visited everyone in this building in different ways, but we all made it out and empathized with one another. It felt like a war sometimes living in New York City. You had to be tough and ready to pivot at any moment. But our little alcove in Harlem was where white flags always waved. Everyone's reason for feeling how they felt was personal to them, but today everyone's pain was the same.

Mr. Fred.

Which of our neighbors would even do something like this, and wasn't telling the truth? Everything really *had* started when Shane's family moved in, but I refused to believe he had something to do with it. My heart lurched when Ms. Gloria wiped a tear from her eye. Before we got to the meeting, Shane and I planned to talk to each of the residents and get a sense of if they were good for this crime. *Crime.* A damn cane.

Ms. Gloria was on my list even though I already knew physically she couldn't take his cane. The way her ankles were set up, she would collapse like Bambi trying to do anything too strenuous. Nonetheless, everyone had to be ruled out. I would do just that tomorrow when I went to check her sugar levels.

Back in Shane's apartment, we sat in the living room discussing the meeting. "I already talked to everyone on the third floor," Shane said with a pen and highlighter. He had a piece of paper with boxes drawn on it with everyone's apartment number and name listed.

The boy was thorough.

"And what did you learn?"

Shane shook his head and frowned. "Well. . ." He took a breath. "Some didn't want to talk to me since they think it's me. But the ones I did talk to, I just don't think any of them are good for it. They all have alibis."

The scar above his right eye seemed to shine today, and I wondered if he was a little sunburned. Instinctively, I reached my hand up and touched his thick eyebrow.

"Ohhh, I'm going to tell Mommy that April is kissing your face," Marcel teased in the corner, his iPad now screaming fight sounds.

"Marcel, what are you doing?" Shane's eyes shot around the wall to where Marcel was peeking.

"I'm watching you and April kiss." Marcel made kissy sounds with his lips.

I felt red inside with embarrassment. Marcel was always somewhere doing something. He giggled and ran down the hallway, slamming his bedroom door shut. I heard his PlayStation game power on seconds later.

"Sorry about that. Damn kids." Shane gave a nervous smile. He took my hand and placed it back on his face. His entire body calmed under my touch, and he closed his eyes.

"Some days it looks darker than others." I rubbed the scar where it was a little mushy in the center. "I just can't see you boxing." I chuckled.

Shane nodded. "I hear a lot of people say that, but I gets the job done. I actually found a gym in the neighborhood. I'm going to start training again next week."

"That's great. Am I allowed to come see you get your Creed on?" I lightly jabbed him in the shoulder and giggled.

He grabbed my fist and squeezed. "Of course. I want you in the ring with me. I see you're good with your hands the way you make love to your plants. Let's see what else you can do." His eyes roamed my face. His fingertips brushed against my cheeks and softly pressed into my dimples. It was like he had to touch me. Couldn't help himself and I didn't want him to. It was the same way my hands relished him. And for once, I knew a boy I liked, liked me back.

"By the way," I breathed. "Give me the names of the third-floor tenants who wouldn't talk to you. I'll follow up with them."

He smiled, and I knew. We were in the same book, in the same chapter, and on the same page.

Shane's mom and dad were in their bedroom, talking in hushed voices. Probably about the way Mr. Dawson was treating Shane. He seemed to have it out for him and believed him good for the crime. *Believed him good for the crime.* My God, they had me talking like this was Unsolved Mysteries.

When they emerged from the room, Shane pulled his hand down from my face, and cut his eyes at his mom. I hope she didn't see us touching, even though my hand was literally pulsating from needing to feel his warmth again.

"Did Shane tell you he's a boxer, April?" His mom began cooking.

"Yes, he did, Mrs. Walker. He said he just found a gym. I hope to see him in action one day." I smiled. Maybe he would beat the shit out of Chase.

"It's such a barbaric thing." Mrs. Walker shook her head. "I hated it when his dad suggested it and I kind of still do. But I get it—you know it's a man thing."

"Once the kids started messing with Shane, I knew something had to be done."

"Messing with Shane?" I sat straight up and question marks peppered my face as I shot an interrogating look at Shane and his mom.

"Don't you have somewhere to be, Mom?" Shane peered over the couch where we had highlighters and hand-drawn maps of the building spread out. His intense gaze laser penetrated on his mom and whatever it was she was about to say that he didn't want her to say.

"Anyway, I guess that is my cue to stop talking. Thanks again for my plants, April, they are looking better than ever." Mrs. Walker shrugged and winked at me like she was in trouble.

My heart swelled. Hearing someone's plants were doing well with my help made me feel good. My own babies were struggling but doing okay since their great migration from the rooftop, at Mr. Fred's insistence. I split some on the terrace and the rest crammed into Gage's room. Even though their environment, light, and rain intake changed, they thrived.

So much had changed since Shane moved in. When a flower was cold, it closed up to protect itself. After learning that I was nothing to Chase and the laughingstock of the school, I closed up, too. My hair, clothes, face. Everything became something for me to worry about. Something to change or make better. I focused on over-fertilizing myself.

"Did you pick out the plants you're going to send in for your competition?" Shane changed the subject.

Fortunately for him, I loved talking about my plant babies. "I'm still deciding. I have a few days before I mail the entry form back. You want to go to the terrace and help me?"

"On two conditions. One, please understand that I don't have a green thumb. My thumbs are strong in other ways. But I will do my best." He placed a hand on his chest and swore to God.

"Okay?" I snorted.

"And two. I am sparring at the gym next week. First time in the state of New York! Will you come?"

My mind ran through all the scenarios in my head. He *wanted* me to come. He *wanted* me to be there. If it was next week, I had more than enough time to make sure I was shaved and looking presentable. "Of course! I told you I would. Are you guys, like, going to beat the shit out of each other?" Not that it made a difference. I would be there with bells on and even carry the number card inside the ring like those skinny girls did.

"Oh, man." Shane covered his face and laughed. "No, nothing like that. It's kinda like practice. Nothing gruesome."

"Okay, deal. I wouldn't miss it." My hand rested on his knee like there was nowhere else for it to go.

"Now let's get upstairs and pick out which plants you're gonna use. We'll take some slamming pictures. You're going to win this competition. Yours have love."

Shane stood up and held out a hand for me to rise to my feet. "That they do." I beamed. By the end of the week, I would email pictures and the entry form for the Teen Home Planter's competition. The form said they would announce the winners in one week. In the meantime, Shane and I would walk to the bodega and build. We would cross people off our suspect list. For a lazy, hazy summer that I had planned—this was turning into an adventure.

I wanted to be the type of woman who would bloom whether I was watered or not. But could I bloom with him?

seven

. . .

"It's normal, Ms. Gloria." I ripped the pressure cuff off her arm. I tossed the cuff onto her pile of medications and medical gadgets.

"Really? Chile, I thought with this headache, it would've been higher. How about that?" She shrugged. "You know what? I was thinking about Fred. Do you think he is playing us? Maybe he just lost his cane or he hiding it. I mean, really. Who would do such a thing?" She leaned over and pulled a small notebook from beside the lamp.

I tipped my chin. "What's that?" I asked.

"You and Shane ain't the only ones taking notes. I gotta help y'all figure this out. This is a crime of passion!"

"A crime of passion?" My throat cinched back with a giggle.

"We ain't never had nothing like this happen here. This stupid cane got Mr. Fred all in a tizzy and canceling tradition. Our Fourth of July bash is the event of the season. Tradition! And here he go, crying. I tried to have sympathy for him because, as an old woman, I understands. But no rice and chicken? No hot dogs? No pernil? No ice cream? You can drop dead, Fred. Respectfully."

The laugh hiding in the far corner of my throat burst through, and I cracked up until my belly hurt. There wasn't a bone in my body that suspected Ms. Gloria to be the person who stole the cane. Every year, the brownstone tenants put money together and threw a large Fourth of July block party. Ms. Gloria said it started with our block and every year, another block joined the party until years later, you could walk for what seemed like miles down the street and everyone was partying, laughing, and beating the heat. For as far as your eye could see, you didn't know where the party started or ended. Mom looked forward to the big shindig too, and her sample sized lemon cakes were a hit every year. She made a lot of money, and I made tips when I helped her. It was a good time had by all when the neighborhood came out and came together. This year was going to look a lot different and couldn't end just because of a damn cane.

Ms. Gloria rambled on about how she used to get into fights when she was younger, and that's how she knew she could take on Mr. Fred if she had to. When the doorbell rang, I paddled to the peephole to check it out.

"Who is it?" I peeked.

"Keri! I'm here to do Ms. Gloria's hair." She chomped down on her gum through the tiny looking glass peephole.

I whipped around and glared at Ms. Gloria. "You didn't tell me Keri was coming over today to do your hair. You know I hate her!"

"Oh, girl, please. She ain't did nothing to you and you too scary to do anything to her. Both of y'all need to toughen up. But be on that Snap Talk with all the confidence. Have it in real life. Now open that door. I need my hair done," Ms. Gloria commanded from her wheelchair. She brushed a long piece of hair out of her face and shooed me away with the wave of a hand.

If I didn't love Ms. Gloria so much, I would've cursed. Keri went to my high school for half of the day. The other half she went to the cosmetology vo-tech school. She wasn't a newbie, though; the girl could *do* some hair. It was a win-win for Ms. Gloria. Keri got her clinical hours she needed toward her licensure and Ms. Gloria got a student discount on her hair and she never had to leave her home.

Keri was friends with Chase. And I didn't want to be around anyone who cared anything about Chase.

I took a deep breath and pulled Ms. Gloria's door open.

"Finally." Keri breezed through with an eye roll. "My bag is so heavy. I'm going to have to get one of those rolling carts or something."

"You need one? I got like three. One for my groceries. One for my clothes and one for all this booty I'm tooting," Ms. Gloria grunted and laughed.

"Ms. Gloria, you never gave me a cart as many times as you've seen me hauling Mama's platters," I scoffed. I was half-joking— half-serious.

"Don't worry, you'll get yours when I'm long gone." Ms. Gloria flipped the channels on her tv.

"Do you want a regular press and curl?" Keri interrupted. She set all her materials on Ms. Gloria's massive kitchen counter. She even brought a wax kit that she plugged up to wax Ms. Gloria's bushy eyebrows and mustache.

"Sure thing, baby girl. You know what I like." Ms. Gloria coifed her curls in her hand and giggled like a schoolgirl.

"So, April, have you talked to Chase." Keri popped her gum and smirked. She wore a headband holding back her long hair and her gold earrings glittered against her vile words.

My stomach knotted so bad; I was sure I would shit my pants.

"Who is Chase?" Ms. Gloria squinted.

"No. Why would I?" I coughed, skating right over Ms. Gloria's question.

Keri turned on the kitchen sink sprayer and dabbed at the water with her fingers until it was warm enough to wash Ms. Gloria's hair. "You guys ended kind of . . . fast. . . I just thought. I don't know. All that stuff he was saying. . . . It's none of my business. I guess."

My cheeks reddened. I wrapped my hands around my elbows and held myself upright.

God, not in front of Ms. Gloria.

"What did he say? April? Keri? What did he say?" Ms. Gloria tried to lift her neck from the kitchen sink and ended up in a fit of coughs.

"Nothing, Ms. Gloria. Nothing." The words fumbled from my head and heart. Keri scratched at Ms. Gloria's scalp and soon she closed her eyes and dissolved into a fit of ohhs and ahhs. Keri's phone rang, and she wiped her hands and slipped on her AirPods while washing her hair. Before long, she was giggling on her phone and not thinking about the shit storm she literally and figuratively almost started.

Frozen by the past. Pushy memories were hell bent on coming back and making their presence known. Was this what people did? Bring up someone's greatest shame and then continue with another conversation like nothing happened?

Well, it happened.

I thought Chase liked me. And when he asked me to the Valentine's Day dance after the first non-motel incident, I counted down every day, and every calorie until the dance. With the help of Mom's Spandex and a lot of self-courage, I slipped into a tight little black dress that made me sparkle when I twirled. I looked beautiful. I felt beautiful.

Chase introduced me to his friends, including Keri, and cupped my hand. He didn't call me his girlfriend. He said, "this is April, I think you guys have the same lunch." But he said April like he meant it. Like he wanted to grab me and claim me as his and didn't care who knew it. Or maybe that's what I wanted. Maybe that's what I wanted to sense in his words that were never really there.

After the dance, I let Chase take me back to an all too familiar place. Parts of me wanted to be there. Other parts wanted me to grab my bike and pedal home as fast as I could, just like last time. I felt the same magnetic pull to go home, but today we drove in Chase's friend's car. Them in one room, us in another. Nowhere to turn and run.

And then the night wasn't so beautiful.

Ms. Gloria's front window had the worst view of the complex and pointed directly to a brick wall and an alley. I stared out anyway, willing myself to forget about Chase. When I looked down, Marcel was out there bouncing a basketball. When he looked up and saw me looking at him, he fanned a wave and continued playing alone.

My phone buzzed in my pocket, and when I reached for it, I saw Shane's name in a text message and smiled.

> Shane: Me. You Bodega. 10 minutes after Town House?

> Me: See you soon 😊

Shane told me he would go to my school starting in September. I bit down on my lip, worried about the different scenarios that could play out. Maybe he would see that I wasn't cool. Not like Keri. Not like the other girls. I didn't wear my lashes long and pile my head high with hair. Some of my best friends were plants. Maybe he would meet Chase. And Chase would befriend him and tap him on the shoulder and say, *"man, you can't date, April. Let me tell you a story. . ."* And Shane would run off laughing. I had reason after reason he wouldn't like me. None of which—or all of which—could be true.

I looked down at Marcel, playing by himself. He was alone, but he never seemed lonely.

I didn't want to be lonely—no matter how safe that was.

I wanted to walk to the bodega with Shane.

eight

. . .

Milani's clothes were still warm from the dryer. I lifted them to my nose and sniffed. They smelled baby fresh against my skin. With the new plants from the terrace mixed in with the old ones, Milani invaded my indoor greenhouse/Gage's old bedroom. His sad lump of a twin sized bed was stuffed in a corner and the blankets were crumpled. He never made his bed. It looked like he woke up and knew he would be back soon enough, so there was no point in wasting time tucking sheets. A Pack 'n Play took up one corner and her bassinet was on the other side. Clothes and clean diapers littered the floors around my lush, green habitat I created in his absence. A speckle of sun peeked from the blackout curtains, and I flung them back, letting the light take photos and synthesize my babies. Before Gage moved out with LaToya, his room wasn't exactly clean, but it wasn't exactly dirty either. It was just enough to throw Mom into a tailspin. For someone who didn't live here anymore, his old room was sure enough looking like his old room.

"Are you the cleaning lady? Thanks, lil sis." Gage wore Dad's blue robe from out of the shower. His hair was wet and cheeks flushed.

"Do I look like your cleaning lady, asshole? Move." I playfully shoved my brother.

"And you better get out of Dad's robe before he sees you and his head blows clean off," I warned.

Gage did a little Diddy dance in his robe and slid across his room, twisting his hips. He didn't get far and tripped over a rattle toy. "Ohhh asshole, am I? Don't let Dad hear you talking like that—not his perfect April." Gage grinned and continued dancing.

"Where is Milani?" I changed the subject and sat down carefully on his bed. It was missing a box spring, and the floor met me with a heavy thud.

"She's with her mom. I'm on my way to pick her up now."

"Did she kick you out? I get it, though. I throw up when I see you in the morning too." I looked around the room. "Looks like old times around here."

Gage shoved me and grinned at my sisterly love-hate joke. He milled around on his dresser, and when he found his cologne, he sprayed himself at least five times.

"You know how me and Dad are." He shook his head. "I don't think we'd make it under the same roof again, anyway."

I held back a choke from the heavy musk scent making its way through the room.

"Well, I want you here. And Milani," I confessed.

Gage and I spent long summers in Harlem together. Ripping and running up and down the streets, taking the train too far and wondering how we would get back before the streetlights came on. Water fights, BBQs, street festivals, tent revivals. Gage and I experienced the city together. Things felt a little more normal with him here and all of us together under the same roof.

Gage stopped spraying himself with cologne and stared back at me from the reflection in his dresser mirror. If he cut off his locs, softened his face, and smiled, he would be the spitting image of our dad.

"We want to be here too, April. Trust. But that's not up to me. We'll talk more later. I have an interview."

"Another one?" I fell back onto his bed and squeezed my eyes shut, pretending to faint.

Gage chuckled. "Shut up! I have to take care of Milani." He grabbed some twisting cream and began twisting his hair.

"Where is the interview?"

"It's at a club; they need a promoter. This was the same interview from before, they called me back for a second interview." Gage gave me a sheepish look in the mirror. His voice trailed off, and he looked embarrassed to say the words. Too many arguments with Dad about the direction of his life and getting a "good" job weighed heavy in the Mays' household. Gage was the oldest and felt the brunt of that.

"Good for you. You should do something that you want to do." I beamed at my brother. Gage needed a win, and I hoped this club thing worked out for him.

"I just can't do those stuffy regular jobs. I barely made it out of high school. You have all these things you're good at, I just had me. I don't know what I'm supposed to do, but I have to figure something out now that I have Milani to worry about. It's bigger than me."

I leaned back on my elbows and stared at my brother. The man who looked so much like his harshest critic. How did he see himself? How did he see me? Gage was my big brother and to me—he was good at everything. Why did he think that he wasn't? Maybe it was the same reason I clung to my plants. It was the one thing I knew I was good at.

I already filled out the application form for the Teen Planter's competition. I picked up my PinStripe plant and turned the ceramic jar in my hands. It was in the calathea family and could withstand serious heat and humidity. Sticking my finger in the soil, it was moist inside and retained water well. Its leaves were thick and shiny with pink lines running through its veins.

This was the *one*. When Shane helped me narrow them down the other day, this one was his favorite too. My other plants were still struggling since the move from their cushiony home on the rooftop, but not this one. The terrace welcomed me and my thoughts as I stabbed at the semi-dry soil and rubbed it between my fingers. When I examined all the leaves, some were varying shades of yellow and brown.

It was all Mr. Fred's fault. I jabbed the dirt some more. "Dammit!" I fussed as I spilled a half-opened bag of soil. The dirt landed on my legs, staining the bottom of my khaki shorts.

The hair on my legs picked up speckles of dirt, which made my blood boil.

I shoved the bag closed and kicked it underneath the lounge chairs on the balcony terrace. Hopping in the shower, I scrubbed and scrubbed until every fleck of dirt was removed from my body and not trapped in hairs. I pulled out my shaver. It was an expensive one I read about in one of those girly magazines. It said it was the next best thing behind laser hair removal—which was next on my list to check out.

"Your skin is so soft," Chase said to me one day when we snuggled close in his mom's car.

"Thanks," I breathed back. And I was thankful. Thankful that he chose me. When I studied the curve of his nose and turned my head, it was a perfect fit for our lips to touch. Was this technically my first love?

"I think you would just know if it was love. You wouldn't have to

question it," Ivy answered when I asked her thoughts on the matter later that week. She still was not team Chase. I knew once the three of us spent time together she would like him—just like I did.

"What do you think is up there?" I pointed to the sky. We parked in a movie theater's lot. The sun was setting, and the sky was a brilliant shade of orange and red. The New York skyline was behind us and so were my thoughts of anything outside of what me and Chase could be. He could play basketball like he wanted. I could be his number one fan and go to all of his games. He would want me close to him and would wrap his arms around my waist, so people knew I belonged to him, and I wasn't just some girl that he spent time with outside of school. That's what I saw ahead for us.

Chase shook his head. "I don't know. Never really thought about it. I try not to think too far ahead or in the clouds. One day at a time and keeping things to myself works for me. Besides, when you tell people your thoughts, they have a way of ruining them and making you think you're wrong for even having them. I try not to tell anyone my thoughts." He leaned over, kissed my cheek, and smiled. He slid his fingers over my thigh, and I jumped at his warm hand. Somewhere, I felt deflated. Like I was a balloon and there was a slow leak of air, but I didn't know where. I talked to get to know him better, but he always had a ready-made answer with something that didn't require a follow-up statement.

"Have you told your friends about me?" I held my breath and waited for his response. The air slowly leaked from somewhere.

"I don't think there's anything to tell just yet. We're hanging out, right?" He turned his head and looked out the window. When he faced me, his perfect teeth gleamed, and I knew the slow leak was coming from my heart. I wanted it to be filled with truth, acknowledgment, and consistency, but he skated out of those questions and left my mind more confused than when I started.

"Have you told your friends?" He searched my face for answers.

I wanted to tell him that my only real friend was Ivy, and she already hated his guts. I wanted to tell him that if he listened closely, he would know I only talked about Ivy, and there were no other friends to speak of. If he listened. Instead, I tucked those thoughts away and snuggled closer to him while we watched the sun go down. I focused on keeping my head out of the clouds. Besides—maybe he was right. People have a way of ruining things.

A tap at the front door interrupted my thoughts. Mom and Dad were both at the market uptown buying groceries for the next platter sale and they normally damn near banged down the door when they wanted help carrying in the groceries.

Maybe it was Mr. Fred. If it was, he was ripe for the picking because I was ready to give him a piece of my mind. When I peeked through the peephole, Shane stood before me.

"Dammit!" I crouched behind the door and kicked myself for not putting on any lotion.

I took a deep breath and cracked the front door. "Hey. What's up?"

"Heyyy," Shane sang. "It's beautiful outside. Do you want to walk with me before Town House?"

I wanted to walk. But I wanted to run downstairs and cuss out Mr. Fred too because of my plants.

"I can't." I wrapped the towel tighter around my waist and became keenly aware that I was standing in a doorway wrapped in a towel with a smart, handsome boy who thought the city smelled like chocolate. Did teens say handsome? He was. It was the only word to describe him when I looked him up and down, standing before me in my doorway.

"Why?" He frowned. He shifted his weight and put his hand to the door.

Racking my brain for a reason to say no, instead unintelligible noises came out of my mouth and heat washed across my forehead.

Hot tears sprang to my eyes. "My plants. They are. Not happy." I gulped and cried and cried and gulped.

Shane slid his arm down past me in the hallway and maneuvered me back into the apartment. He softly shut the door behind me. I paddled to the couch and sat in my dad's favorite chair and sobbed in my towel. Shane knelt down in front of me and rubbed my knee through my towel.

"We're gonna find out who stole the cane. We're going to get your greenhouse back."

Shane's eyes were filled with concern, and I hated to be the one he was concerned about. We were days away from the big Fourth of July bash, and Shane would surely meet more friends and more girls. They wouldn't be a blubbering, crying mess over plants.

I searched Shane's face for confirmation that it wasn't true. Making things up in my head was a gift and a curse. But. . . did Shane's stomach do the same flips mine did when he saw me? Or was I to be a summer fling, one that would be long forgotten by the time school came back around? We would both be starting our junior year of high school and once Chase and Keri got a hold of him, who knew how that would change things and the way he saw me.

"Let me get some clothes on." I wiped my face and stood. I needed to put some distance between us. What I was feeling made no sense, and all these electric jolts of energy oozed inside of me with no outlet to catch them. Between Mr. Fred and his antics, and Shane tip-tapping on my heart, who and what was I to believe in?

"April." Shane grabbed my hand and stayed sitting on the couch. He palmed the back of my hand and kissed it. "We'll figure this out. Together." He rose to his feet and looked like he had more to say. We searched each other's eyes for what seemed like forever before I pulled my hand away and returned it to my towel. My body was super-hot.

Shane made my body hot.

"Besides the bodega, I'm really here for something else." A smirk sat on his face. "My mom sent me down to ask your mom if she cooks pig's feet?" Shane's shoulders jumped up and down as he giggled.

"Pig's feet? Are you serious?" I coughed out a laugh.

"Swear fo' God!" Shane put a hand to his heart.

"Grown-ups are disgusting." I shook my head.

"Truly." He nodded.

"Let me get some clothes on and I'll meet you at Town House. Then, an ice cream run. My treat."

Shane beamed and rubbed his head. "See you downstairs. Oh, and—April. I love your pig's feet." Shane pointed down to my toes.

I laughed out loud and pushed him out of the front door.

Gage peeked his head out of his bedroom door and didn't say a word, just grinned at me and blew kissy faces.

A short while later, we walked to the bodega after Town House. Three blocks, two lefts, and one right, and we were there. I eyed the different plants native to the city, and I named them all for Shane as we walked and talked.

"You don't care that Mr. Fred and Mr. Dawson are telling everyone that it's you?" I questioned and licked my ice cream cone.

Shane's jaw tightened. "I-I-I, I don't know," he stuttered. "When we lived in Connecticut, I was bullied a lot. It's the reason my dad made me take up boxing, and part of the reason we moved." Shane's walking slowed down, and he cut his eyes as he talked.

"Why did they bully you?" It made little sense. Shane was thoughtful. Kind. The more you looked at him, the better he looked. Why would someone bully him?

Taking a deep breath, Shane cracked open a Yoo-hoo and took a large swig. "I don't know, really. I'm different here. Different than I was there."

"Do you miss Connecticut?"

Shane took a deep breath and tucked his long arms into his pants pocket. "Marcel does. He's always asking to go back and says there's nothing to do here. Hopefully, it'll change for him once school starts.

I miss the open space. Everywhere you turned, there was rolling green grass. I could think there."

"You can't think here?"

"Not with you here."

My arms brushed against Shane's and electricity shot through my body, rendering me brain dead. That's how it made me feel. Not an ounce of sense that God gave me left—except the parts that said Shane was a catch and I would never throw him back. We stopped and sat on a nearby park table which was sandwiched between two brownstones in the neighborhood and had a small kids' swing set. Someone took great care of the makeshift garden as I glimpsed tulips, lavender, and elephant ears planted all around the perimeter. The sun peeked over the top of the building next to us, and it landed perfectly on Shane's left cheek and created a halo around him.

"Yeah, I understand that." And boy, did I. Feeling misunderstood became an art form for me and I was a master artist. Licking my cone, I dug my sandals into the cool dirt beneath my feet. "It's hard when you think you know the real you, but people see you as something different. It makes it hard for you to believe in yourself."

At least that's how it was for me.

Shane nodded. "Boxing was good for me. It gave me confidence I needed at the time. That's why Mr. Fred and Mr. Dawson don't scare me. When you've had to pull yourself out of some dark places, you learn to embrace the light in every aspect."

I took a deep breath and embraced the light shining around Shane. His words hung heavy in the air. Did I pull myself out of a dark place? Or was I still languishing there—one Chase flashback at a time?

"We can rule out Ms. Gloria. She doesn't have the cane." I explained our conversation to him and how she could barely move around.

Shane removed a small notebook from his pocket and crossed off Ms. Gloria's name.

"Remember how we thought Mr. Fred might be doing this himself? Well, Mom conned her way into his apartment. She said it's absolutely filthy, not fit for a human being. But she didn't see his cane lying around anywhere."

"How did she con her way into his apartment?" I raised an eyebrow, amused.

"She told him she thought she saw a rat run under his apartment door. For as mean as he is, he was hopping around without that cane, running from an imaginary rat."

I cupped my mouth with my hands and giggled, imagining Mr. Fred running around his apartment. "So, who does that leave?" I looked around at the people walking by and wondered if any of them had ever stolen something from someone. New York was so loud, but when it was too quiet—I couldn't focus. Could we really be living amongst thieves? In our building?

Shane checked his list. "Jorge, Ms. Shanice, Mr. Dawson, and a few people on the fifth floor."

"That's still a good number of people. Something will turn up."

"Did you submit your application for the Teen Planter's Contest?"

With a bashful grin, I nodded. "Everything is in. Now we wait. Thanks for helping me pick out the perfect plants."

Almost like it heard us talking, a rat scurried under the bench we were sitting. "Ahhh!" I hopped onto the table and crashed into Shane. I was so close I could smell his cologne, and he had enough on, just like Gage. Must've been a man thing. "Did you see that?" My arms tensed and ears flared as I tried to sense where the rodent may be. I clutched to Shane's arm and trembled.

Shane's eyes widened in surprise. "Those rats ain't no bigger than the ones we have in the building." He cracked up laughing. "We should add that to our list of complaints." He pulled his notebook back from his jeans and wrote something down. We were leaned up against each other, crouched on top of the table— hiding from a rat in broad daylight.

Shane flipped his notebook shut and returned it to his pocket. "Besides, I got you," he murmured. He stared into my eyes, and I couldn't help but believe him.

He had me.

nine

. . .

"Nah, baby. He already took Marcel out for ice cream. If you hurry, you can catch them." Mrs. Walker shook her head.

"Oh, uh. Thanks," I mumbled. Shane took Marcel to get ice cream. Without me?

"Oh now, don't go thinking like that. It don't mean nothing. I know you got a little crush on my boy." She smirked and folded her arms across her chest, like she had it all figured out.

I gulped. "I don't have a crush on him. He's funny looking." I reared back and gave her incredulous eyes and tried to stifle back a chuckle.

"Girl, you crazy." Mrs. Walker burst into a smile. "I'll tell him to come down and see you when he gets back. Oh, and April. Thanks again for getting my plant together. You know—you really have a knack for these kinds of things, taking care and all."

Tears pooled in my eyes from nowhere, and I struggled to wipe them away as fast as they ran down my cheeks. That was the nicest thing I heard in a while. I backed away from Mrs. Walker's door with cloudy vision.

It was Friday and Friday was platter deliveries. I started on the first floor and worked my way up. Shane was getting ice cream with Marcel and didn't ask me to come.

Maybe he thought it was me who stole the cane?

God, don't let me spiral. I bit down on my tongue and prayed.

Homemade seafood soup, rice, with a touch of ginger, warm bread, and salad. Mom had stirred a humongous black and gray pot on the stove. She had complained that she didn't have room to cook—so Dad made Mr. Fred put in a larger oven a few years ago. She complained she needed more prep space—so Dad bought a new butcher-block dining room table and moved some of the humungous pots to the outside terrace. She complained she didn't have utensils and paper products. Dad got her some sort of subscription box, and soon enough—we had enough paper plates and forks mailed to the house every month to feed all of Harlem. Mom wasn't just an excellent cook; she was an artist. She had a whole business, right inside our kitchen. The only thing left for her to do was go back to school and make her culinary dreams official, but she always hushed away the thought when Dad brought it up. I wonder if having kids changes you like that. You start with having dreams and goals. Then you become a parent, and everything becomes about your child. You can't even imagine doing the things you *want* to do because you do the things you have to do. If that was what I had to look forward to—I could wait it out forever.

Did Gage feel the same way? He never seemed like he knew his next move, but he took his time when choosing. When it became about your kids, it was worth the wait; I guess. Some days, I wanted to roll in the dirt and play with my plants, and other days, I wanted to stay home and shave my legs. How did you decide to be just one thing all your life?

"Your mom said you were up here!" Ivy burst around the corner. She wore a crop top, camouflaged shorts, and cornrow braids straight back.

I glanced her up and down. "What are you doing here? Your mom let you come out of the house like that?" I joked.

"Smart ass. I came to visit and saw your boyfriend out front with his brother. I kindly thought I would come spend time with my best friend who I haven't seen in weeks and who, might I add, got the entire floor smelling like Red Lobster and Cheddar Bay Biscuits. And you have the nerve—"

My arm cramped, and I set the food down on the floor with a snort. "He's not my boyfriend. And it hasn't been weeks."

"Out of everything I just said, that's the part you remember? Mhmmm. Something is fishy in the state of New York and it ain't this soup."

Ivy and I cracked up laughing.

"I'm surprised Mr. Fred let you up here. He's been policing everyone coming in and out these days."

"Still with the *fucking* cane?" Ivy's mouth fell open. She grabbed a bag and looped it between her arm.

"Keep your voice down and stop all that cussing!" Feeling dizzy, just thinking about Dad popping up around the corner. Mom thought Ivy was hilarious and had personality, but Dad thought she had a nasty mouth for a girl.

"Girl, you cuss just as much as me! I don't care what these people think!"

"Yea, but you don't have to be so loud about it!" I rolled my eyes. "Anyway. Mr. Fred even gave Gage a hard time the other day. And Gage used to live here! Shane and I have been snooping to see if any of us took it so we can get Mr. Asshole his cane back, but no one is snitching. He canceled the Fourth of July bash. Mom and Mrs. Walker had to call the city to get special permission to hold it, anyway," I grumbled.

"Wait." Ivy stopped walking. "The party is still on, though, right?"

"For now, yes. But I think he's going to be pissed when he finds out they went behind his back and went to the city. We have to find this man's cane. My plants can't take it." I took a deep breath. "Hold up. Didn't you have a date today or something?" I recalled.

"I did. She stood me up."

"She did?" I raised an eyebrow. We walked down the steps slowly, slapping the stairs creating an awkward echo.

"I thought it was something." Ivy pulled her sunglasses from off her braids and onto her eyes. "But it's nothing."

I stared at my best friend hiding behind her sunglasses, but I saw *her*. Her deep copper skin was lotioned down. She wore a ton of bangles around her wrist—rainbow PRIDE inspired. Her clothes were always a silent ode to a life she had yet to fully embrace.

Ianesha Lane.

Named after Ian—a man she hadn't seen since she was born. When he left—Ianesha left—and became Ivy. Someone tangible that she knew. She didn't know Ianesha just like she didn't know Ian.

"Ivy. Don't you think it's time to . . . stop this." I approached delicately. "Just be yourself. It's okay if you like girls."

We hit the landing on the second floor, and Ivy turned to me with a crazed look. "I know you ain't talking. This Chase thing isn't serious—but you're still traumatized."

My face flushed. "I'm fucking not."

"Now who's cussing?" She raised an eyebrow.

"Ivy, I wasn't throwing shade. I'm just saying . . . Just be who you are. But you have to figure that out."

Ivy's shoulders relaxed, and so did her defenses. "My bad. I didn't mean to . . ."

"It's fine." I rang the doorbell. I shook off Ivy's words even though they felt like salt on an open wound.

And it was fine. Maybe I *was* traumatized by Chase. But Ivy was wrong about one thing. It *was* that serious, and there were parts she didn't know about that bothered me the most.

Jorge pulled the door open, and a fog of marijuana smoke

bellowed out so fast, I was sure the fire alarm would go off any second. "Hola, mi chicas," he sang.

"Hola, ladies!" Jorge's friend popped his head out from behind the door and rubbed his shoulder. "Come on in."

Ivy and I glanced at each other before ducking into Jorge's apartment.

"Hi. I'm Ivy, April's best friend. And you are?" Ivy glimpsed Jorge's friend up and down in amusement.

The Hispanic man smiled, and his dazzling smile and red tongue greeted us. "I'm Journey. Journey Love."

"Journey Love? Is that like, your real name?" Ivy squinted. "What kind of name is that?"

Journey cackled and put his hand to his mouth. He had a gold tooth in the corner of his right lip. "Well, I told the state of New York it was my new name, so it's mine."

"This is my life partner." Jorge turned down the music from the background and began counting out money to pay us for the food.

I dragged the food out of the warming containers and made sure not to spill the soup while pondering Jorge's words.

It was hard *not* to watch these two.

Jorge and Journey wore matching, silk candy-cane pajamas. Jorge wore about ten different Cuban Link chains around his neck and Journey alternated between two different wine glasses. They looked like extras straight from TLC's video, *Creep*.

"Are you guys celebrating?" I blinked around.

"It's Christmas in July. We have to celebrate every milestone. Every battle fought." Journey grabbed Jorge's hand and squeezed it.

Jorge searched Journey's eyes like they were the only two in the room. When he found what he was looking for he said, "And won. Every battle won."

"Okayyy, well, thank you for ordering. As always, I will see you next time." I collected the money and stuffed it into my pocket. These two were a Lifetime movie waiting to happen.

I couldn't put my finger on why, but mentally—I crossed Jorge off my suspects' list. He was in love—and probably didn't have time for petty crimes like stolen canes. I was a terrible investigator. I ruled people out solely based on vibes.

Ivy stared at Jorge and Journey. Her face held equal parts of longing and curiosity. If I was traumatized, she was grieving something that she didn't quite understand. I stared at her and wondered what she was thinking. Feeling. Like a giant Water Lily plant, one of Mom's favorites, Ivy could grow if only she believed she could. I hoped she knew the most interesting plants always grew in the shade.

ten

. . .

W hen I tapped on Shanice's door, a heavy thud made the
floor shake.

Ivy and I stole glances.

"Corey, pick up your baseball and stop playing in the house, you
hear?!" Shanice shouted. She unbolted at least three locks before
pulling the door open.

"Hi girls." She smiled with a touch of sweat on her forehead.
Moms always had a touch of sweat.

Ivy gasped, and my best friend instinct already knew what had
her salivating like a dog and sucking down hot, brownstone air.

Shanice.

She was wearing a tight, yellow sundress that came down to her
ankles and stood right above her pretty painted white toenails. Her
hips, waist, and chest were literally shaped like a number eight— and
her smooth, unblemished skin gleamed against the sun every time it
caught her smile.

She was gorgeous, and if anyone said otherwise—they were a
damn liar.

"Come on in. You can set it on the counter. Twenty, right?"

Shanice nodded. She wore an AirPod piece in her ear and bustled around the apartment.

"Yes, it's twenty," I breathed, peeling my eyes from her behind.

Ivy didn't move and watched everything on Ms. Shanice jiggle and sway. I nudged her back to life as she jumped in place.

"My mom loved that pasta dish you sent down Tuesday. She said it was time for you and her to have "fellowship." I shrugged.

Shanice threw her head back and laughed. "Fellowship, huh? She is right. We must get together and share recipes. The kids keep me so busy, and I don't have anyone else to—" and on cue, the bowling ball noise hit the floor again and Deja let out a chilling scream.

"What are y'all doing back there!" Shanice shouted. She turned back to me and shoved the money into my hands. "I have to go." She stalked off, shouting and sauntering her way down her dimly lit hallway.

Ivy's eyes were peeled to Shanice's backside.

"Pull up your bottom lip." I teased, closing the door behind us.

"Shut up!" Ivy finally muttered. She pushed me around the corner in the hallway, and I barreled right into Mr. Fred.

"What the!" He stumbled back. I felt bad for a second.

The way he fell into the wall and winced in pain told me he would benefit from having a walking cane. His clipboard and high-lighter went flying and crashed to the ground harder than he did.

"What y'all's asses doing up here!" He flared his nostrils.

I extended a hand to help Mr. Fred get steady. "I'm so sorry! I was coming around the corner and I didn't see you. We were just delivering Mom's orders and—"

"Delivering what? For your mama, right?" Mr. Fred snickered. "Well, I think it's about time we put an end to this ghetto ass fish fry. Tell your mama and your little boyfriend, until someone turns over my shit, everything they do 'round here gon' be hard! I should've done this a long time ago. And she don't even have a permit no way!" Mr. Fred leaned against the wall. His chest was moving up and down— his freckled face was littered with shiny sweat and disgust for us.

"Mr. Fred! The last order is yours. See, it says it right here. *Fred. Prepaid.*"

"I don't want nothing from none of y'all no more. I don't have to take this." Mr. Fred slapped his hand against the cinderblock wall and raised his voice. "You think I wanted to be a landlord? I fought in Korea and even Saudi Arabia. I collect my stamps and try to do right by y'all, but y'all come complaining all the time."

"Then why are you here?" Ivy crossed her arms and squinted.

"Why am I here? Why are *you* here? Don't nobody want your nasty-mouth self here, either, girl. Get on home!"

"That's not fair, Mr. Fred! I talked to my mom, and she said you can't do this!"

"So, you're going to argue with a bunch of girls?" Ivy shot Mr. Fred an icy look. She was ready for battle in her camouflage get-up. Ivy stood in front of me and stared down at Mr. Fred, just like she did Chase a few months ago in school.

"Until. I. Get. My. Shit. I'll. Do. What. I. Want." Mr. Fred enunciated every syllable to make sure we heard him. He was ready for the war.

Ivy stepped forward into Mr. Fred's personal space. The slight gesture must've meant an air-strike to him because his face tightened. "You don't even live here, ugly boy/girl! You can go home too!"

"Don't talk to my friend like that!" I shouted, and before long me, Ivy, and Mr. Fred were screaming at each other in the tight hallway and fish juice was spilling out of the containers trickling down the hall.

"Hey, hey. What is going on?" Shane's loud steps paced down the hallway with another voice behind him.

"Mr. Fred! I know you're not harassing girls in the hallway?" Mr. Walker got into Mr. Fred's face and towered over him. A vein was twitching in his head as he prepared for battle.

Marcel stood behind them holding two dripping ice cream cones, his eyes wide with fear. They probably heard the commotion from the stairwell.

My heart beat out of my chest while scared tears sprang to my eyes.

I didn't know what to do.

Frozen in place and time. It was like my body and my mind weren't one in these moments, and no matter how bad my brain screamed run, I froze and cried and cried and froze. People around me were fighting and even when I didn't want to be in the center of it —I seemed to be.

"Harass them? They assaulted me in the hallway! I'm a war vet. I don't harass anyone that ain't harassing me!" Mr. Fred roared and bucked up like he was ready for an army.

"Everything okay?" Shanice's voice was low and feminine as she poked her head out of her apartment. She shrieked and hollered moments earlier at her kids, but her voice cracked now surrounded by a group of men ready to duke it out.

"Everything is okay, Ms. Shanice." Shane nodded. "Just. Mr. Fred is mad that my mom called the city and got the Fourth of July bash back on, so he is screaming at girls in the hallway." Shane's muscle flexed and jumped through his t-shirt, and even with scared tears staining my eyes, I couldn't peel them away from him. He was so tall and loud. He demanded Mr. Fred hear him, and he did.

"You know, you're a funny looking knucklehead that can't tell the whole story to save your life. Ain't nobody mad about your mom calling no city. Party all you want, somebody will pay! I'll have to be extra careful next time new tenants move in, so it's not the likes of you," Mr. Fred sneered.

Shane stepped forward and clenched his fists. A vein pulsated against his forehead. "The-
the likes of me?"

Mr. Fred also stepped forward and poked out his puny torso

against Shane. Shane's bulky arms against Mr. Fred's Gumby pecks were a joke, but Mr. Fred didn't back down. "Yes, you. Ike Dawson is right. It's probably you who got my shit!" Mr. Fred reached over Mr. Walker's shoulder and took a swipe at Shane.

"You done wrote a check that your ass can't cash!" Mr. Walker's eyes widened as he shoved Mr. Fred

"Don't talk to him like that!" I shrieked. I kicked Mr. Fred's pre-paid food as hard as I could in his direction and the soup splattered out and all over his pants.

Shanice let out a blood-curdling scream and jumped in place. "Mouse! Mouse!" She shouted as Mickey scurried across the floor and circled around the delicious soup Mom slaved over all day. He stole a lick, then galloped into a small hole, disappearing behind a wall while Shanice squawked like he personally assaulted her space.

An impromptu floor meeting commenced as more tenants came out of their apartments to see what all the fussing and cussing was about.

Shane stood next to me and locked his fingers with mine as our brownstone entered a battle of soup, rats, and suspects.

eleven

. . .

I slammed the door behind me and stomped to the shower.

"Honey. Are you okay?" Mom turned off the stove burner and scurried behind me.

I tossed the money on the table, my tips included, and didn't say a word. The front door opened and shut, and I heard my dad's hushed voice. "Leave her alone, Caren. She's had a rough day."

"What happened?" She hissed in a not-so-quiet voice.

There were more muffled voices as dad tried to delicately explain the brownstone melee which left the walls coated in accusations—and her soup.

I turned on the shower water as hot as my skin could stand it, and although we were already in the middle of a heatwave, I wanted the water scorching.

Someone called Dad during the fifth-floor shit-storm and by the time he got there, he scooped me up over his shoulders and carried me home. Ivy and I were in full cuss-out mode, giving Mr. Fred our best four-letter words, not caring what adult was there. I was just so mad.

Snatching the shower curtain closed, I grabbed my shaver and shaving cream then went to work on my legs, underarms, and upper thighs. I scraped it over my cooch and winced in pain.

When Chase invited me to the Valentine's Day dance, I made sure I smelled good. Mom even pulled some old perfume out of boxes stuffed deep in her closet. Boxes she told me never to go in because that's where she kept her "good stuff." I peeked in a few times when they were gone and all I found were old lotions, perfumes, and some jewelry.

I had never been on a date before—let alone asked to the dance. A pimple-faced boy asked Ivy to the dance. As soon as he sent her a note in English class and made his intentions clear—she up and decided to stay home and sit this one out.

Chase and I danced and took pictures with his friends. Keri rolled her eyes in my direction, but I didn't care. I looked good, felt good, and smelled good. The trifecta. Even though my midsection poked a little and my chubbiness couldn't be hidden away entirely, Mom let me borrow her Spanx and it held me together like a strait-jacket.

I was channeling Shanice that night when I walked in on Chase's arm.

Pieces of Mom's jewelry shined under the twinkling lights and bounced off my caramel, cocoa bronzer. Whenever I thought about the events that followed, my stomach knotted. How did a beautiful night end so different from the picture I had in my head?

The shower water scalded my back, and I wiped angry tears from my face. Angry about the fight. Angry about Chase. Angry about my plants.

My *plants*.

I brought some of them inside from the terrace to protect them from the direct sunlight. They were doing well at first, but now, with the scorching heat and no protection against the sun, they were too exposed. Too much light and too much bad energy. Dad complained that the house and terrace were turning into a rainforest, and Mom complained gnats were buzzing around her head when she was cooking. Cinnamon helped with gnats, and so I pulled some from Mom's cabinet and gave a few shakes into each of my plants. The gnats went away, but now she complained I used all of her cinnamon and she needed it for the next platter sale. Damned if I do.

My mind drifted to Shane. He stood up for me today. . .Right? I was in the moment and couldn't remember exactly who said what. There were so many people screeching. But it wasn't what he said, per se.

It was a feeling. I felt . . .

Protected.

Like we were sitting on a park bench with a rat under our feet and everything would be okay. Because it *would* be okay with Shane.

I liked Shane. I expelled a large breath in the shower and rested my head against the damp wall. There. I admitted it to myself.... Now what the fuck should I do? I couldn't tell him; he could use it against me. That's what boys did.

That's what *Chase* did.

When I got out of the shower, I lotioned my entire body and paid special attention to my elbows and lower stomach.

My phone buzzed and it was Shane.

You okay?

I smiled at his name.

I don't know. I guess.

I pulled a fresh t-shirt over my head. It was 3 p.m. and I was drained from the day's events.

Meet me downstairs for a nightcap.

A night cap It's 3pm?

An afternoon ice cream run. What kind of guy do you think I am?

I coughed out a laugh and sent him a smiling face.

My mom tapped on the door with light fingers. "Honey, I know you're upset, but you have some mail here. I'll just slide it under your door. Oh, and I made some of your favorite chocolate-chip raisin cookies whenever you feel better." She slid an envelope under my bedroom door. When I picked it up, my heart stopped. My ears rang.

I scanned the letter, re-reading the same sentence over and over. *Congratulations. You have won the Teen Home Planter's Award and you have automatically been entered into the Teen Edition: NY Home and Garden Show taking place a few weeks away in August!*

I read the enclosed check. Five-hundred dollars. I won five-hundred dollars in the competition. I squealed and danced in place.

"Moommm!!" I shouted.

I grabbed my phone and double texted Shane.

Be there in 20 minutes!

I have something to tell you!

I tugged my shirt off my head and flung it back into my closet. I glimpsed down at my shaved, smooth legs and decided they needed to be seen. So much for hopping in the bed at 3.p.m.

The streets were calling!

Flipping through my hangers, I stopped when I found a yellow maxi dress. I pressed the soft cotton material between my fingers and wondered how it would look against my skin. It wasn't Shanice, but it was April. I took a deep breath and stared at it.

And maybe April was okay.

twelve

. . .

Corey and Marcel barreled from the Town House. "Rats, there are rats!" Corey screamed. Even though it was sweltering outside, I brought my jean jacket with me and wrapped it around my waist. I cinched it tighter to my hips as a small crowd formed and no one could stare at my butt.

Ms. Gloria poked her head from around the corner and her walker made a noisy shuffle.

"I wish they would do something about these rats. They getting bigger by the minute. I saw one the other day when Jorge was helping me to my house. It was healthy!" Ms. Gloria rested her arms on her walker. "Here. You boys take this $20 and go to the bodega and buy some traps. And then you take the receipt to Mr. Fred and tell him I want my money back and all sales are final."

"Can we get some ice cream too?" Corey eyed the twenty dollars, salivating.

"The Fourth of July bash is coming up. You hungry- hungry hippos can't wait and get your ice cream then?"

Marcel and Corey fell into a fit of giggles at being called hippos as they grabbed the money and darted off.

I smiled, listening to their conversation. Ms. Gloria could make me cry and laugh, all in one conversation too. I smoothed out my dress as I hit the bottom of the steps and took an uneasy breath.

When I came around the corner, her posture stiffened, and she did a double take. "Little Caren," she gasped.

My head hung low. Maybe I shouldn't have picked this dress to wear. It was so unlike me.

"Come here." Ms. Gloria motioned with her finger. Her eyes were wide, and her mail slipped off her lap and hit the floor.

I stopped down to grab the envelopes and handed them back to her.

"My April . . ." She breathed. "You looked beautiful. Just like your mama, girl."

"Really?" I bit my lip and ran my eyes over imaginary baby hairs on my arms. "You don't think it's too much? I'm just going to the bodega with Shane. I think I should change. Maybe—"

Ms. Gloria snorted and shoved me with her walker. "April! Stop doubting yourself. You look great. I've just never seen you like this. I see you. You got it, girl. *It.*"

I leaned against the wall, blushing.

"Don't let these rats and Mr. Fred ruin your fun. You go and have the best summer ever. Live your life. Wear what you want. Be who you want." Ms. Gloria gazed me up and down, and her eyes misted. "My girl is growing up. And go put on a goddarn slip! That's what's wrong with young girls today. Don't want to wear no panties." Ms. Gloria sucked her teeth.

My hand shot to my mouth as I giggled. A thought quickly found its way to me, and I wanted to kick myself. I didn't wear a slip the night I was with Chase. Was that the reason things ended so horribly? I wanted to kick myself for even thinking about him at this moment. Why was he always there? Assaulting my thoughts, invading my privacy in my mind. Every time I thought I might be happy; it came back to a cold Valentine's night when I became the butt of the joke.

"Whoa. April," Gage said. I turned around and Gage was walking into the brownstone entrance, carrying Milani in his arms. They wore matching daddy-daughter sunglasses that made me chuckle. I tugged at my jacket around my waist and goosebumps shot to my arms.

"Is it too much? And I thought you were still upstairs!" My eyes pleaded with Gage to tell me the truth. I thought I slipped out of the house unseen in *the dress.*

"You look great, little sis." He smiled. "One second. Hold your niece." He plopped Milani into my arms. She cooed and gurgled at me as Gage ruffled through his pockets.

"Here, take this," Gage said, shoving a twenty dollar bill my way.

"I don't need this; I have my prize money."

Gage shook his head and pushed my hands away. "Let me do this for my sister. Besides, any time a girl goes out with a man, she should have her own money."

"I have my own money." I loosened my grip on the twenty and held it like I was holding love. "And I'm just going to the bodega. This is not a date." My voice was barely above a whisper.

Ms. Gloria and Gage looked at each other and smirked.

"Hey, Ms. Gloria. How you feeling?" Shane's shadow engulfed me, and his scent made me swoon.

He put on cologne. Maybe this *was* a date.

"Oh, I'm okay, Shane. You know they say my sugar is acting up, but in no time I'll be fine. I'm going back to the doctor this week. Don't y'all worry about me. I'll be here a long time—me and the rats." She chuckled.

"Do you need anything from the bodega? I can pick you up something." Shane offered.

Ms. Gloria stared him in his face. "What a nice young man. I hope my girl can make an honest man out of you." She winked in my direction and then turned to my brother. "Gage. Help me upstairs and let me hold that baby. You know the babies love them some Aunt GG."

"Let's go, Shane." I put my hand to his back and ushered him outside before they embarrassed me any further.

"See y'all!" Ms. Gloria called from behind us.

Summer in Harlem hit me as soon as I opened the door. The cutthroat heat drowned the cool air condition out, and I started sweating immediately.

"You look great." Shane stared at me for a long second. He looked pleased; his mouth hanging ajar.

A fluttery sensation invaded my stomach, and I was pleased that he was pleased. "Thank you." My cheeks reddened. When Shane was around, smiles bought the farm and set up shop permanently on my face.

"So how you feeling?" He scanned my face. "After everything today?"

My neck tightened. "I'm okay, I guess. I'm just so angry. How can Mr. Fred blame all of us? Now we can't deliver food. My roses are suffering on the terrace. And he tried to shut down the Block Party. All while still blaming you. What's next?" I ground my teeth.

"I wanted to talk to you about that. Maybe it's Shanice." Shane stopped walking and moved out of the way for a group of kids. A Puerto Rican flag whizzed by attached to souped up bikes. They all had rims in the wheels and the one leading the pack had a small boombox attached to the back as Wisin and his reggaeton beats bounced around the neighborhood and painted the streets vibrant with kaleidoscopic colors.

"Shanice?" I gasped. "Why would she take Mr. Fred's cane?"

"Well, I ruled out everyone on the fifth floor. My mom went to Town House, and she said Shanice, Deja, and Corey were fussing about Mr. Fred. I guess he complained about all the noise coming from Shanice's apartment and threatened her with some sort of citation. Shanice went all Jamaican on him, cussed him out, and told him she was going to make him some *special spaghetti.*"

"And?" I squinted. The sun was shining in my face something terrible, and I pulled my sunglasses from my hair and popped them over my eyes.

"And? April, are you serious?" Shane cleared his throat. He paused, looked both ways for traffic, and extended his arm in front of me as we walked across the street.

"How does that mean she has something to do with it? Dozens of people were there for the fifth-floor fight," I held up five fingers. "Anyone could have an ax to grind at this point." I tightened my jean jacket around my waist.

"Well. Motive. Right? Corey is a little bad ass. I mean, I don't even like Marcel hanging out with him. He's always into something. Maybe she's tired of Mr. Fred coming to her about Corey, and she decided to get back at him."

I paused for a second, mulling over Shane's words. The city was loud all the time, and I had to make sure I was thinking clearly, hearing all sides of this story. Could Shanice be upset with Mr. Fred? He *did* come down hard on her about Corey. Child Protective Services even came to the house a few times about things he did in school or his behavior.

My chest felt tight at the thought of Shanice. Could it really be her? I swallowed. I didn't want to believe that, but it was someone— and that was better than we had yesterday, which was no one.

"I don't think it's her. Just a feeling." My jaw hardened.

Shane pushed the door open to the bodega. Marcel and Corey barreled out and almost ran us down. They giggled as they pushed past me with red water-ice rings around their mouths.

"Damn kids!" I scooted out of the way. Once inside, Shane and I went straight for the ice cream. He pushed the frost doors back to the ice cream, leaned in, and moved around a few bars until he found *the one.*

"Strawberry Éclair." He did a dance and presented it to me with a bow.

I giggled. "You are so crazy. Let me go grab your Yoo-hoo." I turned away to grab his drink out of the freezer, and his voice stopped me.

"April." He sighed.

The way he said my name made me want to gulp three Yoo-hoos.

"Yes." I spun around. My jean jacket loosened and slipped from my waist. It fell to the floor and so did Shane's eyes as he stared at my feet and roamed over my full-length body—not hidden behind my jacket. Standing still, I wanted him to see what I tried to hide from everyone else. Take in every inch of me that I worried was too much for others. This was a *moment*.

He took a giant step forward and his eyes never left mine. "You're so beautiful. You in that yellow." Within seconds, he was in my face; his nose and forehead touching mine. My hand went to its favorite spot, right above his scar. Shane squeezed the Strawberry Éclair. It squished between his fingers, and he licked his lips and leaned in to kiss me.

I closed my eyes and before his lips brushed mine, I heard, "Hey! Stop giving each other googly eyes back there. Buy and leave!" The bodega owner shouted.

With our trance broken, I noticed me and Shane being recorded on their security cameras. Shane was staring at me like I was the Strawberry Éclair, and I wanted to let him have a bite.

"Come on, let's go pay." Shane placed his hand on the small of my back and electricity shot through my body for what almost happened.

We strolled to the small park and carefully sat down on top of the table before searching for rats. They wouldn't catch us slipping again.

"So, what did you have to tell me?"

Shane's face always made me forget what I wanted to say. When it came to me, I snapped my fingers. "Look!" I pulled the mailer from my pocket and passed it to him with a grin.

"I won!"

He scanned the document, and his face broke into a wide smile. "This is great, April! And you automatically get entered into the NY Home and Garden Show? That's big time!"

"The NY Home and Garden Show is the first week in August! I hope I have enough time to figure out what I want to do before then. I have to get really creative. Do something . . . special." Part of me felt like I should be happy with just winning the Teen Home Planters contest, and that was enough. Who did I think I was to take part in the NY Home and Garden show? The entire state? In a few weeks, I would be sharing my love for plants with the world. If I wasn't ready, I had to *get* ready.

"No one is better with plants than you. This is one of those things you don't have to question. Just trust it. Your work speaks for itself."

"I'm not sure which plants I'll even use," I admitted. I mean, my plants *were* beautiful and cared for, but they are also now depressed and living on a terrace with bad energy. There was so much to consider. But yet, Shane was right. I was good. Real good, and I knew my shit.

Shane gave a confused face. "Not sure? April, this is who you are. There is no one half as good as you. We'll figure it out, I can help. Aren't you doing the centerpieces for the block party?"

I winked and shared a playful grin. "That I am."

"See what I mean. Who else makes custom centerpieces for a block party? My dad used to get free tickets from the NBA to the NY Home and Garden show because some players would make special celebrity appearances. I checked it out a couple of times and trust me on this one. This is so you."

"And who are you?" I challenged. "We always talk about me. What about you?"

Shane crouched under my words. He ran his hands over his head and sighed. "I don't know. What do you want to know?"

"Everything. I want to know everything about you." I stared into his eyes hoping he felt my intensity.

He grabbed my wrist and held it, palming the back of my hand, running his fingertips over the length of my veins.

And I did.

I really wanted to know everything about him and sit and listen to words spill out of his beautiful mouth. His truth, his life; told his way. I wanted to know it all.

Even if the rats came.

thirteen

. . .

Days later, Milani sneezed while in her playpen and I glanced her over. We filled her makeshift bedroom with centerpieces for the block party, and I hoped she wasn't allergic to any of my plants. Gage didn't have any space on the bed or floor and slept on the couch in the living room.

July, to me, meant bold, fun colors; and so I opted for a mix of vines, sunflowers, and roses. Each centerpiece for the ten tables were different, some big and some small. I clipped the extra stems and sprayed them with water, infused with a cinnamon stick inside the pail.

The block party was tomorrow, and Mom had been in the kitchen the past two days preparing a feast fit for kings while Shanice was upstairs doing her thing too. Dad got most of the meats from his job, as they always had extras left over from their deliveries. He sliced and jabbed into the chicken, cutting the quarters into smaller pieces. He helped Mom peel the membrane off of pork ribs and helped her stir a thick, burgundy barbecue sauce marinade full of heavy spices.

"Looking good in the kitchen, Dad," Gage joked and handed

Dad an apron. He pulled Milani from the playpen and her large, brown eyes took in all the action unfolding around her.

"Don't let your mom fool you. I can cook too."

"The difference, though. You can cook. But Mom can burrnnn."

"That is true, son." Dad nodded as he and Gage shared a laugh. Dad wiped his hands on the dish towel and outstretched his fingers for Milani. She broke into a large, gummy smile and whined for her Pop Pop, and that just about made a tear come to Dad's eye.

I washed my hands at the sink next to Mom and we grinned at each other. Block parties brought out the best in us, and we all needed a win.

"Mom, Dad, I'm meeting Shane at the gym. I should be back around 5 p.m."

"Are you asking us or telling us?" Dad bounced Milani on his hip, never taking his eyes away from her although his words were directed at me.

"Okay, let me try this again. Mom. Dad. May I go to the gym with Shane?" I asked again, praying they said yes. I did my chores, and I cleaned up the stems and leaves in Milani's room. Mom was on me about being more responsible, so at her insistence, I took my prize money and opened a bank account.

"Well, I needed you to help me get these pig's feet together before tomorrow."

"Mom! Please don't make me touch those things. I can't. I'll call the police!"

"Call the police for what? Girl, you crazy." She chuckled. "Fine, go to the gym with your boyfriend. Me and your dad got the pig's feet. And besides, they're special for Mrs. Walker."

"Now, Caren." Dad turned around and crossed his arms in front of Mom. "Don't go putting me in the middle of this. I'm not touching no pig's feet either."

"Gage?" Mom shot glances between all of us and landed on her oldest son with hopeful eyes.

"Ughhh, Mom." He scratched his head and looked away. "Something came up. I have to take Milani somewhere." Gage fumbled through his words.

"Fine! Bump all of y'all!" Mom shook a stirring spoon in our faces as we giggled. "April, be home by 5 p.m.!"

Minutes later, I parked my bike in front of the looming gym in front of me. Spying through the windows, men were in the ring, sparring with each other. I pressed my hands against the glass and cupped my hands to create a shadow. My head bobbed around until I spotted him. He was standing with an older man, wrapping his hands in tape, and slipping on his gloves. When he saw me through the window, he smiled and motioned for me to come inside.

"Hey you." He grinned and leaned over the ropes. He was in silky boxers and was sweating from every inch of his body. His chiseled chest screamed for me to touch it, and he had a trail of hair from the center of his chest snaking down to his belly button.

He was beautiful.

"So, this is all you?" I glanced around at the second place Shane would soon find solace in.

I hoped I was the first.

"Yeah. I've only been here for a few sessions since we talked about it, but the trainer knows my dad, so he's been letting me get some reps in, even when the gym is closed."

Men and a few women were in a large, industrial style gym. Small boxing rings made a tic-tac toe board around the space and people were grunting, huffing, and taking all their frustrations out on the bag, punching it as hard as they could.

"Aye, Shane, you up next or you flirting, man?"

Shane smiled at me. Sweat dripped from his skin and pooled into brown butter poetry at his feet. "I'm doing both." He pulled on his headgear and gloves as he danced his way inside the ring, squaring off at his opponent.

The boy at the other end of the ring looked like another teenager himself. He threw jabs and combinations with precision. He took his time and tested Shane, waiting to pounce in anticipation.

Shane was ready for him. His shoulders faced his opponent on an even line. He danced his way around the ring, making good use of every inch. His opponent chased him around, taking pensive shots that Shane ducked and skated out of. Shane batted and pushed the incoming hands away from his face. When he needed to protect his head from a high strike, Shane tucked his elbow up against his head in a triangle to take the incoming swing. After a few minutes of him throwing jabs that Shane ducked, his combos looked stiff and strained.

Shane noticed his opponent's change in intensity. His eyes darkened, and he narrowed his stance. Instead of dancing around the ring, he leaned forward on the front of his feet and tilted forward ready to spring into action. He almost leapt across the ring, barreling into his opponent with force. He found his rhythm and every punch he threw landed a body shot that I felt in *my* belly. His shots were crisp, and his form was more than decent.

Shane hit him with a right hook to the face and then came across his chest and aimed for the ribcage. He looked so powerful. His skin shined as sweat slung from his drenched body, and even through his headgear, I made out the squishy scar above his right eye. Shane moved around the ring with definitiveness, like he knew he was supposed to be there. His moves were meticulous and even though I knew little about boxing—the way his opponent's head flung back like a slingshot told me Shane *did this* shit.

Watching Shane, my heart swelled with happy feelings that shot through me like a firecracker. Shane was a boxer, and when he did what he was good at—it shined through every pore in his body. When he filled his own cup—the world benefitted from his overflow.

I thought about my plants and how they were my prescription. My remedy. My drug all rolled into one. They filled my cup and brought me the same cure boxing did for Shane.

We were becoming each other's medicine.

fourteen

. . .

The microscopic hairs on my legs were barely there. I turned my calf just right and let the sunlight catch hold of it. But they *were* there. I slathered more lotion on my legs, paying careful attention to my shins and knees.

Fourth of July bash.

Mama, Dad, Gage, and I lived in this same brownstone all my life. We almost moved to Brooklyn when I was in middle school, but Dad said no respectable man could raise a family in Brooklyn. Harlem would always be his home. Every year since I could remember, we came together to grill food, run in the streets, do the Cupid Shuffle, play Spades, and if we were lucky—someone would pop the fire hydrant and let the kids skip through water like we were washing ashore at the finest beach.

A knock at my door pulled me out of my worry regarding my hairy-not-hairy legs.

"April. Can you take this down to your dad and Mr. Dawson? He called and said he's ready for the meats and I'm still getting dressed." Mom poked her head in my room.

"Is Gage here? Did you get the hot dogs I like? You forgot them last time at the market." The lotion felt silky between my fingers so I rubbed them together.

When I stood, Mom's eyes roamed my body, and her mouth fell open. "When did you get these hips? And that sass? You more and more like your mama." She grinned. She ran her hands over her own hips and rested her palm on her tights. It was funny, when old pictures of my former self flitted from our hall closet, I stared at them in awe of how *great* I looked. But at the time, I believed I was overweight. If I was overweight, I was unlovable. And wrong. I was so wrong. And I didn't want Mom to look back at a time when she thought she looked better because she was the most beautiful thing in the world to me this day and every day.

"Yes, I got your favorite hot dogs. Yes, Gage is here. Now head on downstairs. You look great and when you look great, you feel great. Go be great." Mom glanced me over one last time.

I shuffled past her and into my bedroom mirror, catching a glimpse of myself and Mom in my body. "Mom. You look great too, you know. You go be great."

A tear sat in the corner of her eye that she quickly wiped away.

It was going to be a hot one, but I put on a light tinted moisturizer, some bronzer on my cheeks, and a little blush. I topped it off with strawberry lip gloss Ivy and I got from the hair store. Today I opted for a jean skirt and white tank top paired with my Air Force Ones.

I looked great and felt great.

Gage grabbed the food from Mom, and we walked down to the festivities.

"Where is Milani?" I asked. I held the door so he could maneuver the silver pans of food through the doorway.

"She's with her grandmom." Gage grunted, carrying the food carefully.

"How come LaToya doesn't come around anymore?" I questioned. When Gage lived here, they would be holed up in his bedroom for hours and she dipped out late at night. We never really got to know her. Now that he moved out, we saw more of him and Milani but less and less of LaToya.

"She . . . has to work. She's just busy these days. That's all." Gage looked surprised and waited for my response. I wanted to ask how they were managing her new job, but when we hit the sidewalk, scores of people were ready with tents, tables, and grills. Everyone brought their own furniture, and nothing matched— in New York fashion. Some people brought down their living room chaise chairs and plopped them under doily tents. Other people opened beach umbrellas with bright lounge chairs. Each block and family decorated their tent space with a different theme, and on days like today, the air smelled like many wonderful, peculiar things. Corey and Marcel laughed nearby, and I saw them hitting a baseball between the two of them.

Forget LaToya—it was about to be lit.

"Hey, April!" Marcel called out. "Shane is coming down soon!"

"You dummy. She didn't even ask about Shane." Corey giggled and swung the baseball bat.

"Here, come take one of these pans and give them to my dad!" I yelled to the boys. Mom's chicken marinated overnight in orange and red spices that tickled my nose and made me sneeze. Yellow and red peppers draped the meat and sticks of butter were already melting under the blistering sun, prepared for a fiery grill that Dad manned every year.

"Hey, son." Dad slapped Gage's back. He was on the grill and grinning from ear to ear. His brown face was flushed, drenched in sweat and sipping a beer.

"Hey, Dad. Do you need any help here?" Gage checked over Dad's work on the grill as the boys walked over with the silver pans.

Without waiting for an answer, Gage took a pitchfork and began turning meat over the open fire. Dad scooted out of the way and plopped into a lawn chair. He sipped his beer and directed Gage from his seat.

"Don't turn it too fast now. It has to sear," Dad instructed.

"I know that, old man! You taught me how to cook meat years ago. Chill—I got this." Gage placed his hand on Dad's shoulder and squeezed it. Dad looked him up and down.

"I'm not an old man," he grumbled. He watched Gage take hold of the meat, like a man was supposed to do in his mind. His shoulders relaxed, and he closed his eyes and took a swig.

I sat down at a table to catch my breath.

"You ain't even do nothing yet to be out of breath," Ms. Gloria remarked. She was sitting under a tent in the shade, sipping a soda. In the bright sunlight, her corner was dark, and a long, orange extension cord ran a massive fan to her tent that was blowing some mean air directly into her face.

"Hey boo!" Ivy plopped down next to me and popped her chewing gum.

We embraced, and I turned back to Ms. Gloria. "How you feeling?"

"I'm just fine, baby girl. Waiting for some real talent to come along so I can whoop some tail in Spades."

"Oh, here you go. Just because you used to play Spades with Moses and 'em don't mean you know what you doing. Can't even count books!" Mr. Dawson laughed. He stood between our table and the grill. He wiped his face with a washrag as my dad and Gage playfully argued, pulling the meat off the grill and slapped them into pans.

Mr. Dawson couldn't be taller than 5'3," and he looked so small standing next to my giant of a dad. When he was in a good mood like today, he enveloped others and told funny stories of his childhood that would leave us with tears streaming from our faces. When he was in a *mood*, he made sure everyone else was too. Each way, he talked more shit than a little bit.

"Ike Dawson, I bet I play better than your mama!" Ms. Gloria rocked in her chair, resting her hands on her big stomach. She had a plate full of barbeque chicken with the edges singed, rice, and corn on the cob. She never really ate, just nibbled on a little of everything and talked shit too. Days like these were important for moments like this.

Corey and Marcel sat down at the table with me, and we watched Mr. Ike Dawson and Ms. Gloria fuss and slap cards down on the table until it shook. My lips curled, and I tried to hold back my laugh. The boys couldn't resist watching, and soon they were holding their stomachs in a fit of giggles, making fresh memories.

"Oh wait, there she go!" Mr. Dawson leaned to the side of his chair so far that I thought he might tip over. He craned his neck and peeped at Ms. Shanice and Deja walking toward us with platters of food in her hands and a body so curvy that a pack of man-wolves sensed her pheromones and it stopped the Spades game altogether. Ivy was dumbfounded at her presence as Shanice moved through the sea of eyes fixated on her. Even my dad tried not to stare, but Gage's bottom lip was damn near to his chin. He cleared his throat and haphazardly moved the chicken around on the grill. She and Deja wore matching red, white, and blue knee-length dresses straight out of Old Navy.

It looked cute and wholesome on Deja.

It looked like lingerie on Shanice.

I wondered if I had the body to pull something like that off.

While we all checked out Shanice and created different thoughts about her in our heads—I held my breath.

Shane was walking up behind her and heading straight for me.

He was strong. Determined. A penetrating focus on me. Each

step told me he didn't see a Shanice. He only saw an April. I pursed my lips together and exhaled slowly. My eyes softened, and I was already wondering what he smelled like. He was two steps away from me when my already seated knees became weak, and me passing out surely had to be what followed.

"April." He looked down into my eyes when he descended on me. He grabbed my hands and pulled me to my feet.

"Shane." I looked up and searched his face. My lips spread and a knowing exhale fell out. There was too much space between us, and I wanted it gone. Steps became seconds, seconds became milliseconds, and the hairs on my arms stood when my fingers brushed against his scar.

My dad cleared his throat. "Uh, Shane. Can you get out of my daughter's face?"

Ms. Gloria cackled and coughed and coughed and cackled, and soon, so did Corey and Marcel.

"Shane, you know my girl's birthday is coming up. We usually spend our birthdays together, but since you're here, I guess I can relinquish her for the day." Ivy stood and stepped to Shane and play-fully jabbed him in the arm.

"You can come too if you want. If you don't mind being the third wheel." Shane held up his hands and smiled like he was waving the white flag.

Ivy looked Shane up and down, and her eyes rested on my favorite part of his face. That scar above his right eye. In the past when she looked at Chase, it was met with a permanent scowl. "I think we can make that happen." She grinned and looked back at me with a wink.

My heart leapt as I studied them and everyone around us.

My people. My family. My friends.

Dad and Gage stood shoulder to shoulder, frowning at me, Shane, and Ivy. More laughter and whoops spilled from Ms. Gloria's table, and when I looked back, Jorge, Mr. Dawson, and Shanice joined the party and cracked up at our expense.

Jorge pulled out his speaker and synced his music to the Bluetooth. Frankie Beverly and Maze poured from the speakers, and within minutes, Shanice and Mr. Dawson were dancing. Shanice really did the dancing while Mr. Dawson struggled to keep his eyes above her waist. Mom made her way over to dad. She changed into a white tank-top and matching shorts. Gold earrings dangled from her ears and waist beads adorned her hips. She looked like she used to have a Shanice body, but now hers was more womanly and the curves never-ending. Dad twirled her at the grill with hearts in his eyes. He slapped her butt as she sauntered toward him like it was 1995 and he was paging her over and over from the pay-phone.

Ms. Gloria bobbed in her seat as Gage took her hand and danced with her from her chair. Ms. Gloria grinned and closed her eyes.

From the corner of my eye, I saw Marcel imitating Mr. Fred walking without his cane, and I saw Mr. Fred, waiting, watching, and frowning at everything. His face was turned up like he smelled something rotten. For a second, I felt bad for him. Being the butt of the joke wasn't fun, and it was a feeling I wanted to stomp out and light on fire. Last year, Mr. Fred was right out here with us, enjoying the block party. Today he was alone.

"Don't worry about him," Shane said. "Come dance with me."

"But–" and before I got it out, Shane was shaking his arms and doing his best Stanky Leg rendition, and boy was it Stanky! I cracked up watching him move.

We danced next to the food, and the smells made my stomach want to reach out and touch. There were rows and rows of chicken, ribs, hot dogs, salads, fruits, and everyone's best rendition of macaroni and cheese.

I matched his movements for a while and then took a step back and did my thing. I twisted my waist and threw my hair over my head while I gyrated my hips.

"Oh, she's a plant lady and she dances. What else can she do?" Shane whispered in my ear while we jammed.

"She loves!" I yelled back over the music.

Shane placed a hand on my waist and raised an eyebrow. "What does she love?"

I looked around, taking in my favorite hot dogs on the grill and some of my favorite people. Up and to the left, I could see some of my plants on our terrace. I was nursing them back to health after they were evicted from their rightful home on the roof, but they were making it. So was I. I was making it.

"This." I panted. "I love this."

The next four hours were filled with sweltering heat, playing kickball with Corey, Marcel; me and Shane, laughing, joking, card games, and eating everything we could. The sounds of a Harlem block party littered the streets with shrieks and pure glee.

Dad was right. No respectable person would live anywhere else besides Harlem. Why would they want to?

Late in the afternoon, Shane and I sat in the Town House room to cool off. My feet were hurting in my kicks, and I took my shoes off and rested my feet across his lap. Shane grabbed my foot and rubbed it in the center ball.

"That feels so good." I bit my lip and crumpled into the seat.

"What in here feels good? Caught y'all fast asses!" Mr. Dawson barged in and beer from his can splashed on the floor.

Shane and I snickered.

"Y'all think I'm playing? I know what that young love feels like. I met me a love a time or two. I wasn't always alone." Mr. Dawson sat down. He had BBQ sauce on his chin and beer wet his chin hairs.

Shane and I shared an *uh-oh* glance, and my stomach fluttered at Mr. Dawson's words.

Young love.

Is that what this was? It felt old. Like I had it before and didn't know I needed it back.

"When I was stationed over in Ko-See-Vo, I had me a love. She loved her some me—and I loved me some her." Mr. Dawson ran his fingers slowly over the table like he was remembering something from a lifetime ago, but the memories from yesterday pressed him like they never wanted him to forget.

"I was going to bring her back here to the States but you see, she was white and well—you try to tell a white woman's daddy that you want to move his daughter to New York City to shack up with a Black man. He ain't want to hear it. I would have made an honest woman out of her. I just never got a fair shake. You young kids make sure you say what you need to say, and love who you want to love. You only get one chance, and don't nobody want to be wasting their time living without loving. Everyone needs love." Mr. Dawson nodded and stumbled out of the room. His words hung heavy in the air, full of truth and regret.

When Shane's dad called him back outside, I noticed Gage standing next to the door.

He heard Mr. Dawson's speech.

He whipped his head into the room as soon as Shane left out. "Funny seeing you here. And with a man licking on your toes, no less." His locs swayed from side to side.

"He was not licking my toes, asshole. Shut up, Gage!"

"Rubbing feet in broad day light. Okay sis, I see you."

I shoved him. He grabbed my head and stuffed it under his arm, twisting me into a headlock. "Get off, you're gonna mess up my hair, stupid!" I huffed and pulled away from him.

He turned me loose and cheesed as I fixed my hair. "I heard what Mr. Dawson said. About living without loving. Are you?" Gage crossed his arms at his chest.

"Am I what, ugly?!" I smoothed my baby hairs and dabbed at sweat on my forehead.

"You know, living without loving?"

"Are you? Do you love LaToya?" I shot back, annoyed. Out of

everyone in our house, Gage always wanted to search for the meaning of life and asked random ass questions.

"Yes. And no." His eyes softened. "Now you. Are you living without loving? Do you love Shane?"

My shoulders fell, and I straightened. "Yes. And yes."

fifteen

. . .

Shane walked back into the room. Gage winked at me and when he walked out, he was making a heart with his fingers and motioning to me and Shane.

Go away! My lips whispered a silent plea.

Shane and I sat down in front of each other with our knees touching. He paused and turned toward me, his eyes full of questions that my heart already knew the answers to. Some things didn't need to be spoken out loud to make sense. This made sense—whatever this was. We stared at each other for a few seconds, and I squeezed my thighs together at the growing sensation between my legs.

"April?" Shane hesitated. "Let's go upstairs."

"Okay." I leaned forward and stroked his cheek one last time.

Shane and I made our way to the rooftop, and I scoped out everything below us. It looked cold and barren without my plants up here. There was no life, no love. I gritted my teeth and swallowed my anger. Now wasn't the time for that.

The block party below was still in full swing. Jorge and Shanice were taking selfies, and Corey and Marcel were running around playing with glow sticks. Mom and Dad were laughing and roasting marshmallows over the grill. Someone must've dropped off Milani because I saw Ms. Gloria, Shanice, and Mrs. Walker smiling into her chubby, brown cheeks with Gage holding her.

I smiled, taking it all in. Our little slice of Harlem wasn't perfect and not fancy by some standards—but I loved it. I turned to Shane. "Do you like Harlem better than where you used to live?"

"I do. We've never had anything like this in Connecticut. This is really dope. And of course, because you're here." He stared at me and cleared his throat, running a hand over his head.

He was nervous.

"April. I want to ask you something."

"Yes?" I faced Shane, waiting for his words. His arms flexed in his t-shirt with every breath he took. Was he thinking what I was thinking? Feeling? This wasn't the same as Chase. Couldn't be. This was like trying to eat one potato chip, and I didn't want one of him—I wanted all of him. I couldn't get enough of whatever was about to fall from his lips in that gorgeous, chocolatey, funny shaped head of his. He was soul food to my heart.

"I wanted to know . . . Will you . . . Be my girl?" he stammered.

With a heart lighter than it's been in months, I grinned. There was no slow leak in this heart anymore. It was filled with truth, acknowledgment, and consistency. This was definitive. And those were a few of my favorite things.

"Yes. Yes, I will be your girl." I stepped forward and searched Shane's face. I ran my fingertips across his hair, eyes, cheeks, and scar. He took my fingers from his face, leaned forward, and kissed my forehead, then my cheeks, and finally, his soft lips landed on mine. His buttery tongue entangled with my lip gloss. We started slow and pensive, getting to know the taste of each other. Soon, Shane grabbed the small of my back, pulled me closer to him and kissed me with an intensity like he had found the last Yoo-hoo at the bodega.

On cue, fireworks lit up the Harlem night sky. Crimson, indigo, and amber colors radiated from the sky in noisy, holiday fashion. The noise scared the lightning bugs, and they buzzed around us, searching for their usual silence. Shane and I held each other tight and kissed under the luminous sky for what seemed like forever—but no time at all. He grabbed my hips and jerked me closer to him until there was no space between us. I used both hands to pull his face closer to mine. I wanted to be as close to him as possible. With the sky twinkling brightly around us, I heard more shrieks and laughter from below. Shane kissed my entire face, and I pulled my hands around his waist and held on tight.

I held onto what I already felt. Love. I knew it was love. I didn't have to question it. I was living and loving—and it felt damn good.

My stomach lurched when Chase invaded my thoughts once more. The truth about him would come tumbling out soon enough. Shane deserved to know who and what I really was.

"Shane. I have to tell you something." I untangled myself from his arms and stepped back. "You don't know me. Like really know me."

Shane scrunched his face. "What are you, an ax murderer or something?"

I chuckled. "No. When we go back to school in September, you're going to meet people. They will probably talk about me." I tugged at my jean skirt and vaguely made out my smooth legs. It looked like hair was already growing back and that added to the ball of fury spreading in my chest.

"What could they possibly have to say about you?" He grabbed my arm and pulled me toward him.

A loud popping noise followed by yelling interrupted our thoughts.

"What the heck?" I peered over the ledge. Mr. Fred was screaming at my dad and Mr. Walker. Corey was throwing pop rocks around them. "We have to get downstairs!" I barked and ran toward the rooftop door.

"Here, let's go!" Shane held the door as we ran down the steps. When we hit the steps, Mr. Walker was holding my dad back from Mr. Fred.

"I'm tired of talking about this cane!" My dad waved his arms. "Just buy another one. You can't keep making life hard for everyone else. It's just not right, Mr. Fred. Now we made you some food. I had my Caren set it aside, and if you want it, it's here for you. But you have to stop this." My dad swung the spatula around and baked beans fell from it. The music stopped. The annual block party was the one event with an unspoken rule: no drama, no guns, and no fighting. We never had so many disagreements until this summer and my heart ached watching our neighbors disband and rip at the seams.

Mr. Fred cocked his head back and smirked at my dad. "You all just don't get it. It's respect. I lived here for years, decades even. You think I didn't want to do anything else? You think I didn't want to *be* anyone else? When I got out of the service, all I had was this dumb gig given to me by my little sister's husband. Even after they passed, I've stayed here and taken care of this building. Taking care of you all. But yet I still get shitted on. It may seem small to you, a walking cane. But it holds my past. It holds where I was and what I done. I don't want another one. I want my shit back!" Mr. Fred shouted as a crowd formed around him.

"Oh, and Caren. Food deliveries are over. Like I said, you don't have no permit, and you ain't no real chef." Spit shot from his mouth and his eyes were fury red. The fireworks were in their finale and blasting off so loud, Marcel covered his ears and stood behind Mrs. Walker. The sky was bright with all different noises and colors that I wondered if Mr. Fred purposely timed his angry monologue to match the fireworks. He continued to spew venom to anyone who would listen, and people made their way in his direction to check out the commotion.

Mom was frozen against his words with glassy eyes that were lit up by remnants of angry fireworks; and *that* made me ball my fists and charge forward at Mr. Fred. How dare he? Mr. Walker saw me charging and slung his arm in front of me.

"Mr. Fred, I have a friend downtown who works in the Department of Housing. I can make a phone call and you won't have to deal with us anymore, since you seem to hate your job here." Working for the NBA was the right job for him because he was as tall as he was loud and he held me and all my fury back. My dad worked a regular, blue-collar job, but Mr. Walker commanded attention and stood like he knew he was important—and enough was enough. Mrs. Walker and Marcel fell in line behind him from tallest to shortest, letting Mr. Walker protect them with his presence and stature. A family man who didn't play about his family; he was tired of Mr. Fred's shenanigans and was ready to put an end to it all.

If that was who Shane would grow to be, then I would stand behind him any day.

Eyeing the small melee unfolding in front of me, tears sprang to my eyes. There was no way we could have an amazing community day and it end like this. Still flying high from my new boyfriend of a few minutes, a contest win, and entry into the NY Home & Garden show, that was overshadowed by a black cloud intent on raining on our parade. Needing a moment to myself, I backed away from the scene in the middle of the blocked off road and watched from the sidewalk. Where was Shane?

Corey whipped behind the group of people and zipped his bike at top speed. He was flying on the bike, not paying attention to anyone or anything happening around him. His lips were bright red from getting water-ice wasted and he was peddling fast.

He coming straight at me on the sidewalk.

I lost my footing and tripped over the curb, falling to my knees. I positioned myself directly in Corey's path. He was going too fast, and I fell too slow. His eyes were wide as he slammed on his brakes, but he was already coming at me full force. I squeezed my eyes shut and tucked myself into a ball, bracing myself for impact.

"April!" Shane pushed me out of the way as Corey slammed into him. Shane fell back onto the sidewalk and winced, grabbing his elbow, ankle, and head.

The adults stopped arguing. A hail of finished fireworks smoked out the crowded road and what went from a beautiful yearly event, now resembled a battlefield. Mrs. Walker gasped, and people crowded around a trembling Shane holding his knee on the ground.

"A- A-A April," he stuttered. "Are-are-are." Shane mumbled his words and the more he fumbled over them laying on the ground, I wasn't sure what he was saying. The words came out pressured and fast, but unintelligible. *What is he saying? And why is he talking like that?*

"Are you okay?" I crawled to his side, still on the ground from where he pushed me out of the way. My sneaker lay on the other side of the road and my t-shirt was ripped at the collar.

Shane grimaced. "Corey, you need to be-be-be-be-be c-c-c-c-c." Shane's words slipped through his mouth, but I wasn't under-standing what was happening. He was talking slowly, and each syllable painfully shot out—jumbled and muddled.

"Shane. Are you okay?" I repeated and inspected his face, arms, and legs for injuries. Did he hit his head? Ms. Gloria had a stroke a few months ago and when we found her, she was also talking crazy and vague, just like Shane was now. Was he having a stroke?

"My baby!" Mrs. Walker jogged to Shane's side, knelt down, and placed his head to her breast. "Come on, let's get you in the house. Corey, you have to be more careful!" she shouted with tears in her eyes.

"Corey, upstairs, now! I told you about that bike and it was not to be brought out today. Now you've ran over Shane and almost ran over April. Shower and then bed!" Shanice yelled. The block was eerily quiet with everyone watching our own fireworks.

"Ma! It wasn't even my fault. He was in the way giving googly eyes to April." Corey stomped his foot and picked up his bike. His tire was mangled, and the rim bent into a weird octagon shape.

"I said go!" Shanice shouted again.

Corey snatched a popsicle out of the cooler and ran inside the brownstone with his contorted bike.

"Let's get you up." Mrs. Walker took Shane's left arm, and I took his right.

"M-m-m-m Mom." Shane pressed through each word like it was painful as he rose to his feet.

"Shhh, honey. You don't have to speak. Let's go home." Mrs. Walker ushered Shane through the crowd. Her eyes were ablaze and she glared at everyone staring at her son, daring them to smile, or her fireworks would return.

Mr. Fred snickered at Shane like he was satisfied.

Dad eyed Shane with confusion.

Ms. Gloria watched Shane—with a sadness in her eyes.

I focused on Shane as he walked away with questions. So many questions.

sixteen

. . .

Two weeks later, Mom asked, "What do you want for your birthday?" She packed food into little containers and labeled them *prepaid vs cash on delivery*. Plastic bags were strewn across the table, and I stuffed them with a wrapped napkin and fork. "There's this spa on the east side. They have a professional sugar wax that I want to try," I said, keeping an even mouth.

It was delivery day. And I was helping her under duress. Mr. Fred already shut down platter sales. After Mom cursed and debated with Dad about what to do, she slept on it that night and woke up the next day and said she was doing what she had always done. Going to the market to prepare for platter sales. She didn't care what Mr. Fred said, and she was willing to poke the bear. I guess as her daughter, I had to poke with her.

The smells of parsley and basil filled our apartment since 9 a.m. and it made me want to give my plant babies extra love just for being in the same plant family. I wanted to give Shane extra love too—but he was being an asshole.

Since the block party, he wasn't speaking to anyone, and definitely hadn't uttered a word to me. Three days went by and with each passing day that I knocked on his door, Mrs. Walker gave me a strained smile and said he was sleeping or boxing at the gym. He wasn't responding to my text messages or calls. With me and Shane's birthday's coming up, I was looking forward to tasting his lips again since we were officially in a relationship. But were we? Really? Was he mad at me? I racked my brain coming up with reasons that he might be upset with me, but I came up empty. Everything happened so fast that night. I blinked, and we were both on the ground and he was having some kind of convulsion. Was he my boyfriend and was I his girlfriend? We seemed to come so close and had already lost it all.

Just my luck.

"A wax job?" Mom stopped labeling and stared at me. "You want a wax job for your birthday?" Her wig was a little lopsided and her apron covered with red sauce from the lasagna sauce she let simmer all day.

"Yea, sure, why not?" I tried not to make any sudden movements and prayed that Mom didn't ask any more questions. I didn't tell her about my secret—and I didn't plan to.

"You've been killing the Nair and running through shavers like it's nobody's business. Anything you want to tell me?" She stared at me, red sauce dripping from the spoon.

Streaks of heat washed across my face. I had been caught.

"No, Mom. There's nothing I need to tell you." I tied the plastic bags and piled them together. "I just like smooth legs."

"And what smooth legs they are." Mom shimmied her way from around the table and winded her hips in front of me.

Watching my mom shake her behind with pasta sauce and flour from homemade garlic knots in her hair made me giggle as I grabbed the bags and made my way out the door and out of this conversation. Explaining why I wanted—no—*needed* a wax job for my birthday was a conversation I didn't want to have.

I stopped at Ms. Gloria's house first and let myself in. She was sitting in the corner staring out of the window, people watching—

people judging. Twenty minutes later, I was wiping tears from my eyes, eating a spoonful of Ms. Gloria's lasagna from my mom, and rehashing the inner workings on my newfound but lost relationship.

"You can't just not talk to him!" Ms. Gloria instructed. Her window was slightly ajar, even with the air conditioner blasting. Her hair blew in the slight wind and a statue of Saint Michael sat to her left and Saint Expedite on the other. She was scooping heaps of pasta noodles onto her plate and licking her fingers. "You know, these young boys are funny like that out here. What's it called I hear you young people say all the time? Blocked? Cut off? You think he quit you?"

I choked back tears through a spoonful of lumpy ricotta cheese swirling in my mouth. Mom put her foot in this lasagna. "I don't know. I just hate how it feels. Everything was going so good and now he won't even talk to me."

"Oh girl, you ain't know him about a minute. But it's young love. Puppy love. And that's the most powerful one of them all. Gives you something to believe in and look forward to. Sucks you right in." Ms. Gloria made a swooping motion with her hand.

"What should I do?" My eyes pleaded.

"Well, first I think you should go down to the bodega and get me a Pepsi. I'm bout tired of these Ensures and my ankles done went down so I think I can treat myself. And two; I think you should do whatever it is you *want* to do. Whatever feels good to you. That's the point of this whole life thing, I guess. In order for you to get what you need—you have to do what feels right to you." Ms. Gloria leaned in and patted my leg.

A wave of disgust washed over me. Whatever kind of advice that was made no sense to me.

Before I left her place, I watered her plants, wiped their leaves with a terry cloth napkin, and sent them silent love.

I sent it to myself too.

I also sent it to Shane—and wished him healing for all the places he hurt that I didn't know about.

A few steps away in a different apartment, I repeated the story. I leaned against Jorge's kitchen cabinets and fought off a headache while Jorge and Journey folded their arms on either side and shot protective glances at me the same way Gage had done since we were kids. "Well, did you talk to him? Did you insist you speak?" They took turns firing off questions.

Snot dripped down my red nose. I turned around to wash my hands under the sink. "You think I should go up there again?" My chin quivered. "I can't just bang on the door and force him to talk to me!"

"Yes, you can!" Journey swung his neck around and snapped his fingers. "Jorge, remember when I thought you were messing with that guy, and I stormed into the gym?"

"Here we go." Jorge rolled his eyes and prepared for Journey's journey about their love gone wrong.

Journey folded his arms and continued. "I thought he was messing with another Papi, so I go to confront him at the gym. I had them call him over the intercom. They say, *Jorge! You have a visitor at the front.'* And when he come to the front, I lay into him like there ain't no mañana."

Journey was in full-blown story telling mode and acting out how he swung his fist at Jorge at the gym. I wasn't seeing the point to this monologue or how it would help me with my Shane problem.

"Give it a rest or get to the point, Journey!" Jorge frowned. He wore a red blazer with black slacks and velvet shoes. Journey wore a black blazer with red pants and the same velvet shoes. They were always in sync. I wondered if Shane and I could ever be like that, or if our moment had passed before it even began.

"Okay, okay." Journey stomped his foot. "I'll bring this *avión a casa.*" He waved his hands. "I'm saying. You go up there and get your man. Sometimes they don't always see a good thing right in front of them. Sometimes you have to go to the gym and bring the noise." Journey smirked at Jorge.

Jorge shook his head and tapped his fingers on the counter. "Done now?"

A few floors up, Shanice and I shared a garlic knot on her couch. She warmed hers in the air fryer and sprinkled some gouda cheese on top.

It was delicious. I had to tell Mom about this gouda cheese.

Shanice was a beautiful woman and I'm sure she had man problems. Didn't all beautiful women? Maybe she could help. "What do you think I should do?" I asked, after repeating my Shane woes for the third time that day.

Shanice pulled a notebook from her end table in the living room and started writing.

"Shane Walker." She scribbled. "We have to write it all down so we can come up with a tight plan," she coached. She didn't seem to hear the cries coming from her bedroom after I heard Corey tell Deja he would beat her like she stole something and then a big bang.

"I think you should definitely go up there and talk to him. Didn't he get hurt when Corey hit him? I saw him grabbing at his knee. That damn, Corey!" Shanice made a face and frowned toward Corey's room. "Make sure he's okay. That's your in. But you have to do it right, you know, feel him out." Shanice batted her long eyelashes and tucked a piece of hair behind her ear. She knew how to use her womanly wiles to get what she wanted. "Oh! Maybe we can bake him some cookies?" Shanice's eyes lit up as she snapped her fingers like she came up with a great idea.

"He likes cookies." I nodded and took a gulp of juice and tried to unload a thick piece of garlic knot in my mouth. Cookies were worth a try.

"Good. Men are dumb like that." Shanice feverishly wrote.

"Shane's not dumb," I huffed.

"I know, I know. I mean, not on purpose or nothing. They're just dumb." She shrugged.

"You can give him the cookies, then you will bat your eyes a little bit. . ." Shanice stood to her feet and slid across her living room floor. She leaned forward, her cleavage poking through her blouse, and she bounced on one leg, acting out her own soliloquy. "And then you could say. *'I made these for you. Do you have a minute to talk?'* And then he says, *'sure, you can come in, sweet thing.'* And then you can say, *'Well, where have you been? You left me hanging.'* Shanice tucked her notepad under her arms as she took turns acting out me and Shane's roles. I crept to the kitchen, snuck another garlic knot, and layered it with cheese as she perfected her acting chops about my love life.

Shanice was still giving her best Broadway performance when I ducked out. "Okay, Shanice. I'll see you soon and let you know how it goes."

I delivered the rest of my orders while avoiding Mr. Fred and crawled back home. I was dog tired from circling the building. I ran up and down the steps taking extra care to avoid Shane's floor or running into him. Mom and Dad were in the kitchen washing humongous pots with red sauce splatter everywhere.

"How'd everything go? Did Mr. Fred see you?" Mom wiped her sweating nose with sudsy hands.

"Ugghhh!" I growled, tossing the extra plastic bags and plopped down at the kitchen table. I cupped my chin in my hands.

"What's wrong?" Gage walked into the kitchen with Milani over his shoulder.

"I'm just tired. It's extra hot today," I lied.

"What time did you say you had to start that new job?" Dad interrupted, turning to Gage.

"It's third shift. I go in at 8 p.m. and I'll be done around 5 a.m."

"And you said LaToya can't watch the baby at all?" Dad cocked his head at Gage in a way that told me he didn't believe a word he said.

"No, Dad. She's working too. Is there a problem?" Gage pulled the cabinet open, snatched Milani's formula, and poured some into a bottle—all with a frown.

"We're just trying to understand, that's all. Gage. You're here all the time, now. We cleaned out your old room, but I think maybe we need to put it back together. We never see LaToya anymore. Sometimes you need us to babysit, which we're happy to do, but it's never planned, and it's always on a whim. We need to know what's going on, son. A baby needs structure. Routine." Mom leaned against the refrigerator in front of Gage. Our little kitchen was the epicenter of action in this apartment. Everyone had something heavy on their minds that could fit into those extra-large pots Mom and Dad scoured.

Gage shook the bottle harder as pale milk squirted from the nipple. "I'm trying to give her structure and routine. That's why I got this job. You know what? It's fine. I'll just go. I don't want to burden you guys any further," Gage said as Milani stirred in his arms. He ducked out of the kitchen and back to his room.

Mom motioned with her head for Dad to follow Gage. Dad disappeared down the hallway in search of his only son and straw on the camel's back.

Mom cornered me at the table. "And you. Is this about that Shane boy?"

Was it ever, I grumbled. I looked up at her with tired and befuddled eyes.

My mom knew just about everything a teenage girl could tell their mom, *except* for the full Chase story. I told her about Shane and how I *thought* we were building something. All the questions that followed the block party and the silence that accompanied the questions. Ms. Gloria's advice, Jorge and Journey's advice, and Shanice's advice. Mom listened. She grabbed a dish rag and wiped down the table and added in a few "mmmm's" here and there.

I *still* didn't tell her about Chase.

"What do you think I should do?"

Mom stopped wiping down the table and paused. She stared off into space for a second.

"Fall is my favorite season. You and your brother are summer babies. But I love the fall. We can learn so much in the fall. How to let go. How to grow. I would go up there, knock on that door again with a clear head, and say, *'Shane? What gives?'* And then I would be content with whatever the answer is. Whichever way this thing goes, you grow. So, help her grow, April." Mom placed her hand over top of mine. Her eyes were wet.

So were mine.

When Mom retreated to her room, Gage poked his head into the kitchen and whispered so mom and dad couldn't hear. "Do you have it?"

"Yes," I mumbled and pulled the last platter from my bag. The one I couldn't deliver.

The Walkers.

"Here's $5." I pushed a green bill into his hand as hush money.

"Keep your money, little sis. Just watch Milani when I need you. I'll take care of this." He shoved me hard in my shoulder and grinned, only like a brother would do.

seventeen

. . .

S haking like a leaf and with a thrust of my chest, I adjusted the warm plate of freshly baked cookies in my hand and knocked on the door.

"Hey, baby. Don't you look beautiful? You know, yellow is your color." Mrs. Walker surveyed my outfit when she stood in the doorway.

"Thanks." I smiled, looking down and checking out my clothes. I spent over an hour finding the right blouse to go with my white shorts. Settling on a yellow halter top, I pulled my hair back into a slick bun. I needed it out of my eyes today so I could see his face clearly.

I was here to get my man.

"Is Shane here?" I peered over Mrs. Walker's shoulder.

"No, baby, you just missed him. He left out a few minutes ago."

My face fell flat, and shoulders hunched. The cookies were searing into my fingers through the plate.

Sensing my deflation, she said, "It's okay, honey. Just text him, I'm sure he'll run right home for you. He's feeling better." She winked.

I thanked her and stomped my way down the semi-dark hallway. Why did I *ever* think showing up at his place would even work? That's what I get for listening to the ladies. Now his mom would tell him I came by, and he would think he won our one-sided cold war because I broke first. When I hit the second-floor landing, I didn't want to go home and explain to Mom that Shane wasn't home and the cookies we spent hours baking from scratch this afternoon were for nothing. I pushed the big door open to the brownstone and the bright sun stung my eyes. The cookies smelled delicious and burned like a bitch—just liked rejection. The trash can glowed and I itched to toss them inside. When I hit the corner, I lumbered straight into Shane's face.

"Ow!" I held my forehead.

"Jeez, April!" He frowned. His lip was busted and bleeding from our collision and literal meeting of the minds.

"What are you doing?" I stumbled over my own feet and held my head.

"I ran to the bodega. I was coming to see you, but I wanted to get that ice cream that you like." Shane shook a small black bag and I could see the end of an ice cream cone and a Yoo-hoo sticking out.

I stared into Shane's eyes with love and confusion. "You got that for me?"

"Yes. Did you break up with me that fast?" Shane rummaged through the bag and pulled out a napkin as dribbles of blood ran.

"Here, let me do that." I grabbed the napkin and began dabbing at his swollen lip. My eyes darted around, pleading to land anywhere but on his face. When I settled on his scar, I couldn't help but lower my gaze directly into his eyes.

He was already staring at me—busted lip and all.

After I cleaned his face, we crossed the street and sat down on our park's bench across from the brownstone.

I was perplexed by his words and actions, both of which didn't seem to align. Break up with him? I didn't understand it and I needed answers. "What gives, Shane? You ask me to be your girl and then don't talk to me for days!" My hands were shaking. I held onto the side of the bench to steady myself and keep an eye out for any rogue rats. The city was alive around us with people walking and music blasting, but no one saw the throws of our first fight.

"And your knee? Is that okay?" My hand itched and I resisted the urge to lean over and rub his leg where he was howling in pain days before. Not touching him was always hard for me to do. I fought to hold back against a nonstop, New York heat that beat down on us and forced out truths like an interrogation gone right.

Shane gulped from his Yoo-hoo for what seemed like forever. When he was finished, he belched and looked away. Silence.

"Are you serious?"

Silence.

Snatching the cookies, I sighed and pushed away from the bench ready to run home and shave all my skin off.

"Wait, wait." He pulled my hand back. "Sit down. My knee is fine. It hurt a little that night, but I'm good." Shane squinted his eyes like he was remembering something he'd rather not. "Remember when I told you about me boxing? And my scar above my head?"

"Yes." I searched his face and recalled what he said about his scar. He said. . . He got it boxing. Yea that was right. Boxing.

"Well. That was only part of it. . . ." Shane's voice lowered. His body stiffened when he leaned closer to me like he didn't want anyone else overhearing his secret.

I leaned in forward and held my breath so I could hear better. Whatever he was about to say, I knew he only wanted to say it once.

"I used to have a stuttering problem. It was bad—real bad. I couldn't get two sentences out without a tic . . . I used to get bullied a lot because of it. I got beat up something terrible one day in the bathroom at school. That was one of many times, but that one was the worst. My mom was worried and wanted to pull me out of school, but my dad insisted I defend myself and learn the art of boxing like he did. So, I did. I started boxing, and I also started seeing a speech therapist. The boxing gave me purpose. Helped me defend myself. Gave me confidence that I needed. Speech therapy helped me think about my words before they came out. It helped me slow down my thinking." Shane rolled the empty Yoo-hoo bottle between his hands and looked around recalling a time when he was him—*then*. "They both changed my life. Sometimes when I get nervous. . . or or . . . excited. My tics come back. And I stutter. That's what happened that night. With the argument and me and you making things official . . . It was just a lot."

"Were you excited or nervous that night?" I frowned.

"No, not really. But there was a lot going on. I didn't want you to get hurt and so I just reacted. It all happened so fast and I figured once you found out about me, you wouldn't want to be with me anyway."

My back softened under Shane's words. When I looked him over, his eyes were low, but his mouth was set in a tight, straight line. He tried so hard to be strong. Hiding himself behind boxing gloves and a never-ending smile that camouflaged his deepest fears.

Being seen. Being found out.

"Shane. Does that mean I wouldn't love you? Does that mean you're not deserving of love? "

Shane's entire body shook as he poked holes in his version of who he thought he was.

I cupped his cheeks and whispered, "Even you Shane, even you." I held his face between my hands and let him rid himself of what plagued him all these years. I could love him through it and I wanted to, but first I had to tell him what plagued me too. The sounds of Harlem faded out, as Shane and I held each other, and the brownstone loomed in front of us, shielding us from the harsh sun.

"Shane. I . . . I . . . I have to tell you something too. Something you don't know about me." I started.

Tears welled in my eyes, and Shane wiped them away before they even landed on my cheeks. "It's okay," he whispered. He sat on the back of the park's bench, and I stood between his legs with a hand on each knee.

"Last year. I went to the Valentine's Day dance at school with this boy. Chase. He asked me to go a few weeks before. I was so shocked. I didn't think he would ever look at a girl like me."

"Girl like you?" Shane frowned, not understanding.

"You know. Heavy-set. On the thicker side." The words felt strange slipping through my lips outside of my head and for listening ears other than my own.

"That night, we had a great time. I wore this black frilly dress that Mom and I took all day to pick out from *Macy's*. He asked me if I wanted to go with him to a motel. I already told Mom I was spending the night with Ivy. So, I went with him." My voice tapered off, and I took a few unsteady breaths. In the past, bits and pieces of the encounter played on repeat in my mind, but never, since that day had I pieced together the entire story, and not out loud. Shane brushed a few wisps of hair out of my face and squeezed my shoulder.

I continued.

"We were. . . kissing . . . and touching. I thought. This was it. This is the night I lose my virginity. I wanted it. I wanted Chase. I wanted to be wanted. When we laid together, it happened so fast and if it wasn't for the sharp pain—I wasn't sure we had really done anything. And then, that was it. He acted like I didn't exist in school. I called and texted him. I waited for him at his locker like normal. But nothing was normal anymore."

The events tugged at my heart, and I coughed and cried through my truth.

eighteen

...

"**G**et the fuck off me!" Ivy shouted. She was swinging in all directions and two of the school security guards were trying their best to pin her to the floor, but she was flopping like a fish, and they didn't have the bait or the stamina to catch her.

Hearing her loud pitched scream, I burst from my chemistry class along with students from other classrooms. "Ivy! What's wrong? What happened?" I shouted over a few basketball players who towered in front of me. A small crowd formed around Ivy, and everyone was locked so tight shoulder to shoulder that I couldn't get through to see what was wrong.

"You asshole!" she shouted. "Don't you ever talk about her like that again!" Ivy clawed at the tallest security guard. My blood ran cold when I thought about the trouble she would be in for fighting a security guard but when I focused on who she was glaring at, she was clawing her way toward.... Chase! She was crawling and screaming her way toward Chase who was standing behind the guard.

"Scuse me!" I scooched my way around the circle, trying to make my way inside. Chase. What was Ivy talking about? And why was she fighting? Ivy talked a lot of junk, but she wasn't a fighter. We had *study sessions and sometimes went to homework club after-school, for God's sake. We were good kids. Students had their phones out recording and now smaller duos in the hallway were knucking and bucking and ready to fight. The small hallway was packed with adrenaline filled teenagers and the excitement that came with an impending fight, a blind spot with no cameras, and not enough teachers to break it up. Our small school only had three security guards. They were older with big bellies, and only worked this job post retirement. Two were already here sweating it out, regretting their career choices, holding back Ivy, and the growing commotion, while shouting for help into their radios.*

"Chase?" I hissed when I caught up to him. I couldn't get to Ivy across the circle. I grabbed his shoulder and whipped him around to face me. He had a deep, red scratch screaming across his nose. "What is Ivy talking about?" I searched his eyes for an answer I knew he didn't have. He sucked his teeth and pulled away from me like he didn't know me, and I meant nothing. He didn't have answers and he didn't have me.

"Tell her, you piece of shit! Tell her what you were telling your friends in the bathroom!" Ivy clawed her way toward Chase. "I was walking by and I heard your name. I listened at the door and he was talking about you." The third security guard finally arrived, and when he did, two were able to lock both of her arms behind her back.

But her mouth.

Her mouth was lethal.

"I knew you weren't shit. I don't care if I get suspended or not! Every time I see you, I'm going to be two steps off your ass." Ivy squirmed and shouted, her face snarled into a rotten expression— all directed at Chase.

"Chase? What were you talking about in the bathroom?" My voice was so low I barely heard it. My face was as flat as I felt.

Chase looked around at everyone with their phones out.

Keri was one of them, smirking and licking her lips like she was entertained and held a secret that everyone knew except me. Salivating at my misfortune.

He rubbed his chin and chuckled. In a few words, he became someone I didn't know and never did. "I said you let me hit it the first night, and you don't shave. You know, a wolf-pussy."

"Ohhhhh," students around us shouted and laughed.

"So, she's a hairy one, huh, Chase?!"

"Yoooo, Chase is a wild boy!"

"City Girls down!" someone chuckled.

Students laughed and pointed in my direction, their lights from their phones flashing, illuminating me in every way.

My blood ran cold, and my toes tingled in my shoes. I couldn't breathe. I couldn't move. I felt like I was standing naked on a stage, and everyone was pointing at me and laughing.

Ivy was still clawing her way over the guard's shoulder and was looking at me with sad eyes. My best friend. Always ready to defend me, even when I didn't know I needed defending. I understood it now. It made sense now. I never meant anything to Chase. I was only something for him to do. A pawn in his never-ending story of girls and attention. The feeling settled into my bones with a dull ache that started in my heart but would surely infect the rest of me like a virus.

Minutes later, me, Chase, and Ivy were sitting in Mr. Hill's office, our vice-principal.

"So what happened here guys? Ianesha you were incensed. Did Chase do something to you? April, did Chase do or say anything to you?" Mr. Hill questioned. His eyes looked genuine, and he seemed like he really cared. He folded his hands together on his desk and his suit jacket crouched up around his neck. His eyes darted between the three of us and the clock on his wall that he checked every few seconds.

My thoughts were frozen. I couldn't speak and my mind raced a mile a minute. Nothing would come out and I stared at a blank space on the wall. A wolf-pussy? I didn't know girls shaved. Not down there. I didn't know I was supposed to do that. He told everyone that . . . that . . . I was dirty. Disgusting. Hairy. Was I?

"April? Ianesha? Really, nothing?" Mr. Hill pressed. A stack of write-ups loomed on his desk submitted by teachers for infractions ranging from chewing gum to fighting. Ours would be added to the pile, depending on what was said today.

"And Chase? Why was Ianesha ready to knock your head off?"

Chase leaned back in the chair rubbing his red nose. His varsity jacket was slung over the back and he looked smug and annoyed all at the same time. His scratch would leave a scab. He shrugged. He only seemed to speak when it benefited him.

"Man, just suspend me."

Mr. Hill's pale cheeks flushed, and he motioned to the stack of write-ups. He wrote a few sentences and slapped two more forms on the top of the pile.

"Ianesha and Chase, you two are suspended. April, you weren't a part of the fight, but something clearly went on here and I think you are involved. I'm giving you detention. And I highly suggest you find better friends."

He was wrong. I didn't need batter friends. I already had the best, and that was Ianesha.

What I needed was better judgement.

I swallowed and shut my eyes as I spoke. I sobbed and cried into Shane's shoulders.

"Shhh . . . shhh . . ." He comforted and rubbed my back. "It's okay. It's okay."

"I just wanted you to know because. I do everything I can to make sure I'm clean. At all times. And . . . And . . . I shave all the time. And I—"

"April. It's okay." Shane now cupped my face with his hands. We stared at each other face to face, nose to nose, shame to shame. "Have you told this to your parents?"

I snorted. "I could never tell them this. They found a movie on YouTube about the birds and the bees to talk to me about sex. But that was it. I could never." I scoffed. "When they called my mom and told her I had detention, they described it as *refusing to disperse during a fight*, I gave air quotations marks. She asked me about it when I got home, but I lied."

"April, Chase is a punk." Shane's voice rose. "And when we get to school in September, I'm going to beat his ass."

"You don't even know him!" I strained my voice and squirmed on the table.

"I don't need to know him. April, he didn't ruin you. You make it seem like you are damaged goods or something. Or less than. Girl —I like thick. I want cakes, not cupcakes." Shane looked me up and down with so much love in his eyes. "This happened when? Valentine's Day? So, for almost six months you've been torturing yourself thinking you're some gross, hairy girl?"

I wanted to nod, but hearing his words out loud made my actions so nonsensical. I leaned my forehead into his and muttered. "I know, I know."

"Listen to me." Shane grabbed my hips and pulled me close. "You are beautiful. The most beautiful chocolate, smart, creative, caring, funny . . . and did I already say beautiful? You are all of those things. And I'm not saying that just because we go together now— it's the truth. April, you are none of those things that he said you are. We've already wasted almost six months worrying about what he and his goons have said. Are we going to let the rest of the year pass while still holding on to his bullshit?"

"No. I don't want to hold onto it. I don't want to." A lone tear finally made its way down my face and Shane brushed it away.

"No more secrets between us, okay? We have to talk about things. Promise?"

I silently cried, letting my biggest shame disappear away. Carrying it for months was heavy and always felt like I was drowning. I didn't want to drown. I wanted to swim and grow.

"Promise." I breathed into his ear. Shane kissed my eyes, lips, face, cheeks, forehead. He brushed his lips against every inch of my face and washed away my tears. I turned around and my back faced Shane. He wrapped his arms around my waist. "I got you," he murmured and left a trail of Yoo-hoo kisses on my cheek.

Pulling opened the now half melted chocolate chip cookies, I handed one to Shane.

He stuffed it into his mouth and closed his eyes in chocolatey gooey delight. When he finished, he fed me one. His fingers lingered around my lips, tracing stains of chocolate across my jaw. He studied my face. He had me.

With the brownstone across the street halfway blocking the setting sun, it was a brilliant shade of amber. Against the streetlights, I made out my team. My support system, watching and peeping at us from the shadows. Ms. Gloria, Jorge, Journey, and Shanice spied us from behind their apartment windows and had front row seats to our love. That was the thing about the city. Even when you were alone—someone was always watching.

I didn't care. I had him. And he had me.

nineteen

. . .

"Have you thought about which ones you are entering for the NY Home and Garden Show?" Shane poured water from my lime green water pail.

Dirt surrounded us; my tights, ankles and toes. Our terrace landing was brown with speckles of white fertilizer, and some sat above Shane's scar over his eyelid.

His question— I wasn't sure yet. A leggy birds of paradise plant was always a showstopper, but a thick and playful monstera plant could turn heads. There were so many choices. I bit my lip, wiped my hairline, and quietly confessed. "I don't know."

Mr. Fred evicting my plant babies from their rooftop home came at the worse time. They weren't standing at their tallest and it pained me to think they weren't ready for the show because of this drama. Mrs. Walker let me use part of their terrace, but even between the three spaces—I swear my plants were drooping, and I didn't *do* drooping.

"Am I taking up too much of your time? Should I go home. You seem distracted?" He rested on his elbows and giggled. It seemed like that's all we did these days. Laugh. It was a wonderful feeling. Ivy came over a few days ago and hung out with me and Shane. She asked me how I knew it was real, and I didn't have an answer. It was something that couldn't always be put into words. It was a feeling. One that spread through my body and seeped out of every pore, determined to be heard and felt. It was demanding. Interactions with Chase left me perplexed. Mystified if what I thought I felt was what he felt, even though the constant stirring in my belly sending warning signals told me otherwise.

Shane answered all questions and made sure there was no misunderstandings just by his presence. To know someone wanted to be near you, simply because you were you. And *you* were enough, just the way you were. That was real.

"Now why would I send my water boy home?" I sprayed Shane in the face with my mist bottle.

He choked and swatted water from his face. "What do you think the Town House meeting will be about? Mr. Fred was insistent that we all be there."

I sighed. Town House was coming up and things were even more strained. Last week there was a new curfew instituted which had everyone in a tizzy. 9 p.m. every night, each resident had to be in their apartment, or they would be locked out of the building without re-entry until the next morning. Mr. Fred had a special keyless entry installed that denied entry to tenants even with their keys. "Your dad called the department of housing, right? Did he mention what they said?"

Shane frowned. "Dad said he couldn't even get through. No one was answering the phones, and then when he tried to leave a message, it said the mailbox was full. He ended up sending a few emails—but no one's responded yet."

We were caught in some weird trap in which Mr. Fred poked and poked at us tenants and because the people in charge were too busy to answer the phone, he was getting away with it. "I saw a number for the Channel 6 news on the table downstairs. Maybe I could anonymously call them," I suggested.

While Mr. Fred increased his attacks on us, Mr. Walker wanted to lay hands on him, and Mom spent early mornings cooking some of his favorite foods believing something tasty would calm him down. With summertime in full swing and love on my brain, I was feeling froggy and ready to take a leap at Mr. Fred myself.

Shane stood and his mouth fell open. "Calling Channel 6? Now that's what I'm talking about." His mouth moved a mile a minute and he excitedly shot out each word. "You know with my dad working for the NBA, he gets free tickets to the games and some of the summer league events. I can talk to him and see if we can get in front of the news or something, tell them what's going on."

"That would be great!" I reached up and brushed the dirt from above Shane's brow. "It's so cool your dad works for the NBA."

"Damn straight. I'm never leaving Harlem." He grinned so hard that my face involuntarily grinned back until only teeth and budding love were between us.

Mom yanked the sliding door open and stuck her head out. "The food is ready! Would y'all stop staring at each other and get out of this heat!? Shane, this will be your first time delivering with April, so April make sure you show him the ropes and y'all don't start another brawl in the hallway. And steer clear of Mr. Fred," Mom instructed. She wrote small notecards and receipts on each of the containers. "Shanice's food is on the house, and so is your moms, Shane."

"You don't have to do that, Mrs. Caren. My dad is loaded. He can pay."

My mom chuckled, and it warmed my heart to see her laughing at Shane. "Well tell him to leave a healthy tip, but the food is on me," she advised. "And you two have birthdays coming up. Any plans?" Mom shot a look between us.

Shane and I hadn't really discussed our birthdays yet. Everyday felt like a celebration so far, and it was getting easier to get used to this feeling of having something and someone to look forward to all the time. I looked forward to Shane, and all the days that came with him.

"Nothing yet, Mrs. Caren. But we'll think of something." He winked at me.

A dark shadow moved into the hallway behind mom, and I heard Dad's loud voice. "Caren. I keep buying stuff to unclog the bathtub spigot, but it ain't working. You and your daughter are gonna have to make some changes," He wore long, blue gloves that came up to his elbows, with goggles and one of Mom's old aprons. He was off work for the day and playing Mr. Makeshift Plumber, tinkering with the pipes, which he knew nothing about. Mr. Fred was the go-to for plumbing issues, but no one wanted to ask him for a thing, if they could help it.

"Now how do you automatically assume it's me and April that keep the tub stopped up, Kyle?"

Dad's eyes bulged. "Because Caren. I got real close. I even shined a light down the drain and it looked like those 'little hairs.'" Dad pursed his fingers together and squinted when he said little.

I could melt onto the floor right then and there.

"Mom, can you watch the baby tonight? I have to work at the club." Gage yawned and stepped into the kitchen. He leaned his head against the refrigerator and two brown rings circled his half-shut eyes.

I was never so happy to see my big brother.

"Didn't you work last night? When have you slept?" Mom side-stepped around dad, giving him a look. She passed an entire wall with pictures of me and Gage. Us as kids. Swimming, dancing, weddings. Every school photo from every grade. There were way more pictures of me than Gage. I noticed it and never thought to ask why.

Gage noticed though. And when he had the courage to ask why, he was met with tales of young, Black love. The type of love that didn't know what it didn't know, just yet. It learned on the fly and sometimes that meant as a parent, growing up *with* your child. Kyle and Caren. They were children, having children when Gage entered the world. By the time I came along—so did a little more wisdom. Our parents had raised me. But they *survived* with Gage. As I glanced my brother up and down, noticing his t-shirt bunched and loose at the collar, his pants sagging off his behind; I knew it was true. You could grow up in the same household with the same parents but be totally different from your sibling.

We were alike where it counted though.

"Ma, I'm okay. Just working a lot is all. Can you watch Milani?"

Mom bit her bottom lip and shuffled in place. She considered Gage's words, glancing him up and down. "Of course, I will watch my grand baby. I washed all her clothes in that special baby detergent and got her some new bottles, anyway. She is just fine with her grandma."

When my breathing returned back to normal from the 'little hairs' comment, I noticed Dad's chest rising and falling behind Mom's apron. "I want you to invite LaToya over for dinner too. Ain't seen that girl in months."

Gage's eyes shot open. "Why does she need to come here?"

Dad stared between him and Mom, his jaw twitching. A perfectly honest question he took as a challenge.

I moved out of the way and began gathering food and platters with Shane, knowing what was brewing in the Mays' household. Dad looked well-rested and ready to lace up his shoes and jump in the ring with Gage.

As usual.

"You are doing all this working, son. Where is she? I don't see her buying Milani anything or even doing her part. You sure know how to pick them; you can't just go laying down with any Toya and think things will work out. Be smarter, son. You're in and out, gone all hours of the night. I've had enough of this. It's time for us to have a family meeting." Dad lifted his chin, and his nose was a little too high in the air for someone he claimed he loved.

"Son, you have to know what you want to do with your life. You're a Black man in America and you always need a plan. If you don't plan your life, someone will tell you what to do, how many years to do it, and when you can stop. Get serious and get your head in the game." Dad put his hand on Gage's shoulder.

Gage pulled back and frowned, sizing Dad up with a scowl.

I packed platters faster into our cart. My cheeks reddened as Shane got a front row seat to the inner workings of my family.

Tough love for Gage was the only love my dad had to give, but it was a love that Gage never knew the language to. Gage never had the opportunity to play in dirt just for fun. He had to grow up knowing he was already behind the eight-ball.

Gage pursed his lips together like he was getting ready to say something that would sting all the parts of Dad that he thought made him a man. My eyes caught his, and I shook my head. *Don't engage, Gage. Don't engage,* I said with my eyes.

He gave me a blank stare, his face blank and tired. When Milani stirred in the back from his room, he sighed and retreated into the hallway. "Thanks, Mom. I appreciate you."

In a few minutes, Shane and I began on the first floor and worked our way up using the cart. I tugged it up the steps, leading the way and Shane lifted it from behind, making sure nothing spilled. We were making good time. "See. We work well as a team. Stick with me baby, we'll figure life out," Shane boasted.

He wasn't paying attention, missed the landing, and tripped up the stairs.

I burst out laughing, funny tears escaping my eyes. I needed funny tears. Heavy tears threatened to make an appearance from a few minutes ago in our apartment. "Boy, stop playing before we drop this food. My mom will have my ass!" I lifted the cart.

With my struggling plants on my mind, I said, "Have you ruled anyone else out for the cane?"

Shane's face fell. "No . . . no I haven't. It just doesn't seem like something anyone would do. My mom is livid about them accusing me. I hear her and my dad talking about it at night."

"Well, did you do it?"

Shane stopped on the landing and stared at me.

My face turned red. "You were outside when everything happened. What were you doing?"

Shane took a deep breath and leaned against the wall. "Honestly, April. I was staring at you."

"Huh?"

"You were on the roof, playing with your plants."

"Working—not playing," I corrected.

"Working, not playing," he repeated. "I was taking some boxes out to the dumpster, and I saw you leaning over the ledge, working on your plants. You looked so happy. I ju-ju-just couldn't *not* admire you."

I dropped my hand from the cart and pressed against Shane. "Why didn't you tell me that before?"

He shrugged and rested his head against the wall. "I don't know. I didn't want to seem like a stalker or something. I mean, we weren't what we are now."

I held his hand and pressed my thumb into his palm. I kissed his nose, cheeks, and the scar above his right eye. He closed his eyes and sighed.

"Take out your phone, let's practice a round in *Walkie Talkie* and get this food delivered. "

Shane took out his phone and opened the speech therapy app, *Walkie Talkie.* After Shane told me about his stuttering issue, we scoured the internet for something we could use to help him. The app was expensive, and he didn't want to ask his parents for the money. Parents, bless their hearts, worried about every damn thing.

We put money together and paid for it. The app enunciated words and phrases at an increased speed and pace. With each round Shane completed, he earned tokens for the next level. It was cool. Like a real-life video game, and oddly enough, it helped him practice his speech.

Shane sounded out each word carefully. He started slow like he was unsure of himself, but after three rounds in a few minutes, he moved through each sentence faster and with more confidence. Every day, we practiced his speech. The only way I knew how to get better at something was to do it over and over again.

So that's what we did.

We knocked on Ms. Gloria's door. When she opened it, she held the biggest grin and shot eyes between us. "So what's this here? The Black Chip and Joanna?"

Shane's shoulders shook first and we fell into a fit of giggles.

twenty

. . .

Town House meeting resembled a WWE match.

"What are you going to do about the rats? It's been a month and we're still talking about this cane, but yet the rats are running around here like they own the place!" Jorge shouted. He wore tinted yellow glasses and cooled himself with a Mother Teresa church fan. When I saw him earlier he still wore his work uniform—but the man could transform within minutes. Would I have to work a job that hid who I was? Only able to be myself once I got home and comfortable?

It sounded terrible. I looked over at Shane and hoped not. I hoped we could be happy and not hide our love.

"The management already laid down traps, called in exterminators and done everything we can. Someone must be feeding them because they keep coming back," Mr. Fred spoke plainly with flat, cold eyes. He was robotic and hunched over the table like it was protecting him from the people. His people.

"The management? You mean yourself? And now you're blaming us?" Mom scrunched her face and folded her arms in his direction. She made Mr. Fred every pound cake she knew how to make, but he rebuffed her free meals. He was a meat and potatoes guy. Disciplined. Controlled. All of a sudden, he couldn't be moved with the likes of a few delicious meals.

Mr. Fred sighed and wiped his face, and for the first time, I noticed beads of sweat forming at his head. He rubbed his temples like he had a headache—or he was tired of us. Maybe both.

I knew I was tired of him and by the looks of it, everyone was feeling the pinch.

Taking in my neighbors, I wondered if we really did have a thief among us. Things were quiet in our little brownstone and while we weren't perfect and had our share of disagreements, we didn't have a *thief* among us. Not until . . . the Walkers.

Not my Shane. We already squashed that. Maybe Marcel? Mr. Walker? His wife?

Nahhh, I brushed that thought from my mind. Marcel was just a kid. A weird one sometimes, but still—just a kid. And Mr. and Mrs. Walker didn't have a good enough reason. I already cleared Ms. Gloria and Shanice. Shane didn't suspect anyone from the third or fourth floor, but he didn't really know them. I've been living here just about all my life. I should know who the thief was before he would . . . right?

I grabbed the seat in front of me and crossed my legs. This damn cane had us accusing each other and I didn't like it. We had to tip-toe through the building delivering food behind Mr. Fred's back, and my plants were struggling to thrive in their new unhappy home. This had to end. Standing to my feet, I cleared my throat and rubbed my sweaty hands against my bare legs.

"Mr. Fred. I understand that you're upset about your cane. I know it means a lot to you and you've had it for many years. I've seen your stickers and the things you've decorated it with. I get it, I really do. But no one here has it. Can we please stop this and get back to enjoying the last few weeks of summer? I can go with you to the store if you want and purchase a new one."

Mom smoothed out the back of my blue dress as I talked. Her always-on-alert eyes shot up, and searched everyone's face in the room as I spoke. She stood up beside me and took a sharp breath. "I think April is on to something, guys. We've had no issues for years. If someone has the stick, please just turn it in so we can get back to peace. But if no one has it, Mr. Fred, please allow us to replace it with something else. Not better, but just different." Mom was careful with her last words, and they came out softly, like she was tip-toeing to a bomb.

The room swelled with bated silence as everyone searched Mr. Fred's face. It was so quiet, I only heard Ms. Gloria's noisy chest breathing from across the room and the clamoring air conditioner threatening to be heard at all times.

Mr. Fred took a shaky step back. "First of all, Caren, it's not a stick. And whoever thought they would call the department of housing on me, just know your days are numbered too. Did you think I wouldn't find out? I've done the best I could do because I cared, but the state of New York always sides with the landlords—not the tenants," he snickered, knowing he had us over a barrel.

Shane said the housing people never called back, but someone must've snitched for Mr. Fred to know.

"We're up shit's creek," I whispered to myself. When Mom heard me curse, she whipped her head around and narrowed her eyes.

Dad jumped to his feet and charged at Mr. Fred, invading his space in seconds. "You're taking things too far, Fred!" Dad took a swipe at his head.

Mr. Fred scurried from around the table, ready for a fight. He tripped on the table's foot and lost his balance.

Ms. Gloria gasped, and the room fell silent as Mr. Fred groaned, trying to stand without the support of his cane or his people.

Mr. Walker, who was sitting in the front row, knelt to help him to his feet.

"Unhand me, young man!" Mr. Fred yelped. He looked around

at everyone in the room, people he's known for years, some for decades. Contempt danced in his face and anger boiled in his eyes.

I spied Marcel and Corey in a corner, sucking on popsicles that turned their lips blue. Marcel watched everything happening, and his eyes were wide and fearful. His popsicle melted in his hands under his fright. Corey held a skateboard under his arm and wiped a few rogue tears from his eyes. When he saw me looking at him, he wiped his face faster. The two most carefree kids in the building were watching all the adults in their world argue.

An uncomfortable hush fell over the room. Watching Mr. Fred fall down *and* fall apart was unnerving.

Mr. Fred stared at Mr. Walker. "It was probably you who called the department of health, anyway. God himself told me. I think you and your hoodlum sons are in breach of your lease." He snarled and held his lip, which was busted in the corner.

I hoped Shane's dad really had access to news outlets. Maybe I *should* call them. The thought made my heart skip a step, talking to a camera and being stared at. But my home needed someone to do something; and it needed to be done soon.

With days remaining until my seventeenth birthday, and Shane's birthday a few days after mine—shit was fucked up. Ivy, Shane, and I were supposed to do something fun to celebrate. We didn't have any set plans just yet, but I knew I wanted to spend it with people who felt like the sun. How could I do something fun when my home was in shambles around me?

twenty-one

. . .

"Where are we going?" I peered out the train's window.

We were on the train and it was zooming today. Neighborhoods and murals whizzed by. I could see a thick haze of mean heat sitting right above the trees like it only did in New York when old man summer refused to give up his season.

"Chill, girl. We're gonna bring your birthday in right." Shane smirked and looked down the aisle.

"And then we'll celebrate yours." I snuggled closer to him and whispered in his ear.

His grip on the train's pole tightened, and I held his waist when we rounded a corner. I refreshed the weather app on my phone and even though it said there was a slight chance of showers, I was feeling bright and sunny today.

"Are you gonna blind-fold me or something? You know I have trust issues?" I chuckled. My mouth was near his neck, and I inhaled his scent. I closed my eyes to smell him, see him, hear him, and feel him. With each day we spent together, my thoughts of Chase decreased. I deserved this love because I was given this same love. This version of me was blooming into someone I liked.

"Ain't nobody about to blindfold you, girl. Just hush, we're almost there. Too bad Ivy couldn't come after all, I think she would've liked this too." Shane looked out the windows and his eyes darted between his phone and the windows.

"See what happens when you work during the summer? You have to go in when they call you and you have to skip out on the fun things." I shrugged. I was going to make my little contest money and tips from Mom's now secret platter sale last. I wanted to spend all my time this summer with Shane.

Once we got to our stop, Shane and I walked four blocks. I slowed my pace and took in the surrounding sights. We were in Yonkers and away from the big city noise. A few yellow taxi cabs littered the road, and the air smelled clear and sharp; like no one rushed around or had somewhere to be.

"Come on." Shane grabbed my hand and pulled me forward.

We rounded two more corners and hit a large farm. My mouth fell open when I saw the most beautiful, baby blue Wisteria trees sprawling through rolling green hills. All different shades of pink and purple roses surrounded us. Begonias, tulips, blush peonies, and yellow gardenias begged me to touch them and extended as far as I could see. Rows and rows of flowers lined the perimeter and they stood alert with a light mist sitting on their leaves. They were happy.

Food trucks and vendors were set up on the small strip of blacktop, and people were taking their best selfies around the exquisite mounds enveloping us and creating a canopy.

"What's all this?" I stared.

"It's a flower festival. Do you like it? I figured you could get some ideas for the NY Home and Garden Show." Shane searched my eyes and waited for my response.

I looked around, taking it all in. "You did this for me?"

"Of course." Shane pressed his thumb into my hand. "Anything for Selenas."

Shane and I roared out a laugh at the same time and people

whipped around and stared at us. We walked through the different rows and took in each color and flower species.

"Oh look at this one!" I ran to the tallest Wisteria tree at the festival. The trunk was fat and lush. It snarled and winded its way up in different shades of brown and green until the tree petals met the thick branches like a puzzle piece. "Take a picture of me!" I shrieked. "I'm getting so many ideas for the show!"

Shane smiled, grabbed my phone, and snapped a few pictures. "Just keep snapping," I said and moved around the tree doing different poses.

Shane circled me around the tree, and his tongue hung out of his mouth.

"Like what you see?"

"I love what I see." He got down on his knee and took more pictures.

"Babe, that's how I want you to take my picture. You have to get down on the ground like him." A girl next to us instructed to her boyfriend.

Shane was my boyfriend. *Mine.* Excitement surged through my belly, and I wanted to run to him while he was on the ground taking pictures and kiss his face.

That's exactly what I did.

"What's all this for?" His chocolate cheeks were red.

"Nothing. Just before I forget—thank you for a great day."

We strolled through the festival and stopped at a food truck. Shane ordered a popcorn and water-ice for himself, and I ordered a hot dog and milkshake. We sat at a nearby picnic table and woofed down our food.

"You know, I've been thinking about Mr. Fred and the cane. I think he's lying," Shane said, and popcorn shot out of his mouth.

"Lying?" I sat my milkshake down on the table and frowned. "Why? You said your mom went into his apartment and didn't see a cane?"

"It just doesn't make sense. I mean, we've ruled out just about everyone in the brownstone. There's thirty-five adults total, and twenty-seven children living in the building. Dozens of visitors in and out each day. Everyone is saying they haven't had these issues before until . . . until . . ." he stuttered.

"Go slow. Sound it out. You got it." I nodded.

Shane took a breath and started again, this time working to control his jumpy words.

"Until we moved in. But we know it's not us. I just think he made the whole thing up."

"But why?" Shifting in my seat, I eyed the clouds getting darker and the wind whipping by faster every few minutes.

"That part I don't know. He seems like he doesn't want to be the property manager. He almost does everything with a chip on his shoulder. Maybe this is his way out."

Shane lived in the brownstone for about one month and a half, and already picked up on Mr. Fred's permanent grudge. "Ms. Gloria says he's always been this way and she thinks him being in the service messed him up."

"Could be. But we still have to find a way to get to him. Show him we care."

I scrunched my face and fought back curse words. I didn't want to care. I wanted to lay back with Shane and explore all that young love had to offer. That was all I had capacity for. But once again, he was right. Regardless how it happened, Mr. Fred was an outcast and he was lashing out at everyone as a result. I hated that my plants weren't in their rightful home, and I hated that Mom was now stressed about her platter sales. She had me creeping around the building, slinging Styrofoam containers, peeking around corners hoping Mr. Fred didn't catch me.

"I do care. I know what it's like to feel misunderstood. I don't want anyone feeling that way towards me."

Shane's hands brushed my shin and moved up my leg. He

gripped my thigh and jiggled it. With every touch, I dreamed of summer days and ice-cream dates.

"These are nice." He smiled and stroked my leg.

"I didn't have time to . . . you know . . ." I shrugged and dropped my shoulders. Thunder clapped around us, and I jumped in my seat.

Shane scooted closer and put his arm around my waist. "You help me with my speech stuff. And we work on *this* stuff." He patted my legs. "I don't care what that guy said to you. It's not true. You hear me?" He cupped my cheeks.

I avoided his eyes and tried to look everywhere but him. When my gaze returned to his, he was still staring, daring me to believe otherwise about myself.

The thunder shouted again, and people darted under the nearby tents and stared up at the gray, swollen sky. When the rain finally spilled, so did tears from my eyes. "I know it's not true. But I have to make sure. I have to make sure." I repeated through clenched teeth and the same tough love my parents reserved for Gage, but I reserved for myself.

"How about you skip a day?" Shane stared at me and grabbed both my hands. "Instead of shaving and worrying about being hairy when you're not; how about you skip a day and shave every two days? That's a start. Right?"

I pondered Shane's suggestion. Even though I was convinced I was a wooly mammoth and an embarrassing misfit because of it—this pretty girl still rocked. This morning when Mom and I carefully picked out my outfit, she stuffed money into my pocket and said, *"a girl must always have her own. Just in case."* Life lessons she learned at a young age and passed to me. She stared at my waist and dabbed at my gelled down hair. She said, *"your skin is shining like the star that you are. You go have a great birthday, and remember, be who you want to be."*

I wanted to be free from the torment I placed on myself. About hair.

"Okay." I nodded to Shane. "Every other day. I'll try."

Shane smiled and stroked my cheek. "I love you."

The skies rumbled again, and rain fell around us. It pelted the Wisteria trees until their petals littered the grass and a sea of blue bewitched us.

"I love you too," I whispered. And I did. I really did.

twenty-two

. . .

"Give me a pair of gloves or something," Ivy fussed. "You better change that tone; my plant babies feel all the energy."

Ivy wiped her forehead with the back of her hand and pulled on a pair of planting gloves. "What time should I be here for the show?"

Dirt was everywhere on our terrace once again. "I was thinking maybe 5 a.m.? Shane said that should give us enough to pack the car and beat traffic."

"I bet he did." She smirked. "My girl is in love and I know what that means. You'll disappear and start waiting for him at his locker and wearing his varsity jacket and what not." Ivy fanned her arms like she was telling a story.

I giggled. "I am not that girl! No more varsity jacket wearing assholes for me. But . . . I told him . . . about Chase."

Ivy's smile dissipated and she stopped scooping dirt. "What did he say? Do I need to kick some ass, again?" She balled her fists and rested them on top of her legs. She wore ripped jeans at the knee and a cut-off rainbow t-shirt slouching over one shoulder. After the fight at school, Ivy was suspended for two weeks and her mom had to beg the school not to send her to the alternative school program across town.

"Honey, what happened in school today?" Mom said when I got home that day months ago. She was watching the cooking channel and cutting garlic into slivers.

"Nothing." I closed the front door behind me and rushed to my room. Each step was heavier than the last and my room looked so far down the hallway. I wanted to go in and never come out.

When I shut my door behind me, Mom was hot on my heels. "Mr. Hill said Ivy started a riot and you were there with her?" She crossed her arms and hovered in front of my window blocking the sunlight. I didn't need the sunlight anyway; my mood was dark.

I collapsed onto my bed and fell on my back. My bookbag was still on. My eyes fluttered from sheer exhaustion and when they closed, hot tears trickled from the corners and fell down my face and neck. I unhooked myself from my bookbag, pulled off my kicks, and climbed in the bed. I pulled my legs to my chest and burried myself under my dark blankets, and I cried.

"Shhhh . . . it's okay . . . it's okay," Mom whispered. She sat down beside me and patted my back.

Wolf-pussy. So many cameras. So many people laughing.

"What happened, honey?" Mom's questions were suspended in the air with confusion and love.

"Me and Chase are over." I sobbed. How could I tell her that I wasn't a virgin anymore? That me and Chase were now linked in ways I hated and I was sure she would be none too thrilled about either. We would always be tied to a cheap motel a few blocks away that we passed every week on our way to her favorite market. How could I tell her that Chase wasn't who we thought he was? Who I thought he was. Or maybe

who I had made him out to be? Either way, he wasn't him and I wasn't me. How did I tell her that it was the worst experience of my life, and I would never ever ever do it again?

Mom checked in everyday and didn't question me when I refused to go to school the rest of the week. I didn't leave my bed for days. I heard her whispering to Dad that young love was the hardest.

Thee hardest.

When I finally mustered enough strength to get up, the first thing I did was search all the razors in the house for the ones with the strongest blades. They ended up being Dad's. I stood naked in the mirror, searching for all the imperfections that Chase pointed out and then shaving every part of my body that hair even dared to grow, I felt like I was walking under water with weights. The only thing that pulled me out of my depression, was my plants waiting for me on the rooftop. My snake plant was my largest sprout, and I grew her from a pup; straight from the Farmer's Market. When I leaned in close, I saw a shoot creeping from the side of the plant. It was growing almost sideways, and I had never seen one come in that way. It grew on its own and was strong, even though it didn't seem to be hanging onto anything to bolster it. I scanned the sky, and it was a bright shade of blue and the clouds were extra thick. Squinting my way around, I adjusted to the intense colors of the world. My bedroom was dark, with me keeping the curtains drawn for days. Kids were racing each other down below and giggling. It was cold—and the chill caught in my throat as I inhaled fresh, new air. I didn't plan to do anything with dirt that day; I just wanted to check on them and then run back in my bed. Instead, I sat down, pulled on my gloves, grabbed some fertilizer, and did what felt right.

Snapping out of my stupor, I chose my words carefully responding to Ivy. Digging into the dirt slower, I said, "He said I was crazy to believe anything that Chase had to say. And that I was beautiful. And that he was going to beat his ass the first day of school."

"My man. See, I knew I liked him." Ivy grinned. "Girl—I am done with this dirt stuff, I'm just here for the tea and it looks like you have delivered." Ivy pulled off her gloves, dropped her shovel, and fell into the lawn chair in the corner like she had just worked a long shift. Her eyes glistened. "How did you feel?"

I stopped digging in the earth and stared at Ivy. Shane made me feel different emotions. It had been two days since we talked about me not shaving, and while tonight was technically my night to do the do—I didn't feel compelled to pull out my shaver and slice off hairs that weren't there. And I wasn't ugly if I didn't.

I was beautiful. Hairy or not.

"I feel seen," I murmured.

"Mmmm . . . seen." Ivy looked around the neighborhood in deep thought and nodded. "Seen is nice."

"I want you to be seen too. For you." I tilted my head toward the rainbow on her shirt.

She stiffened and avoided my gaze.

"Just talk to her," I pressed. "You think she doesn't understand, but you never know."

Ivy smiled, but it was a weak one. Her eyes were sad like she didn't believe any of my words. "Trust me. I know what I'm dealing with. My mom is not ready for this conversation."

Ivy thought she was being rebellious by dressing ambiguous. One day she dressed straight up like a man, and other days she was flirty, fun, and girly. The day of the fight in school, she was in full stud mode. Her mom worked long hours and didn't pay much attention to her, but when she did, Ivy was all girl and pretty in pink on those days. I didn't know what my mom would say if I was questioning my sexuality, but I hated seeing my best friend caught between who she wanted to be and who she presented herself as.

"Ianesha, April got you out here in this heat?" Mom pulled the sliding door open, interrupting our conversation. Mom handed Ivy a glass of lemonade filled with ice.

"This girl is crazy, Mrs. Caren. Got me out here sweating my tits off. Thank you!" Ivy gulped it down and patted her damp forehead.

Mom giggled at Ivy scanned my greenery. "Looking good, baby."

The floor was filled with different plants and flowers. The rules for the show stated that we had to bring ten different plants or flowers with proof that they were homegrown and not purchased. I wasn't sure how they could prove they weren't bought, but fortunately for me, I took tons of pictures of my plants, and Mom was bringing her iPad to display them digitally on the table. The show rules also stated that we were required to design and execute a custom piece displaying plants using their show theme of, *"It's a small world after all."*

Shane and I picked out the perfect green vines and created a vine hanging wall. It was partially finished taking up a wall in my room. We ordered a custom neon light to display right in the center of the wall, and it was set to arrive any day now. With ten days left until the show, we had enough to fill our display table. I smiled at my spread.

Things were coming together.

"Ianesha. You talk to your mom, baby. Okay? Give her a chance." Mom's voice was soft as she patted Ivy's hand and poured her more lemonade from the chilled pitcher.

Ivy turned her head, and her high cheekbones and brown skin shined against the setting sun. A single tear trickled down her face. She didn't say anything, but she squeezed my mom's hand back.

Moms just *knew.*

Ivy said, "What are you doing for Shane's birthday? I still can't believe your birthdays are three days apart." She gulped her lemonade and expertly changed the subject.

"There's a basketball tournament downtown. I got us some tickets." I gulped from Ivy's lemonade cup.

"Oh! That's dope. You're already doing all the thoughtful, girlfriend, things." Ivy gushed and faked wiping a tear from the same eye a real one just fell.

"I told you, baby—these boys like girls with some meat on they bones nowadays, Little Caren." She sparkled as she shimmied in front of me and Ivy.

"Mrs. Caren. When are you gonna get yourself a food truck or something? Especially with Mr. Fred acting like this?" Ivy asked.

Mom's cheeks reddened. "Oh, I don't know. I got a good thing going here. Well, at least I did before Mr. Fred. No need to rock the boat. Besides, I don't know if I want to be responsible for an entire business." Mom laughed nervously. She gulped down a swig of lemonade from Ivy's cup too, her thirst hitting her under the weight of Ivy's questions.

"But Mom—Ivy is right. People rave about your food. You said yourself you were tired of cooking in our little kitchen. If you think this is hot, try frying chicken in the middle of July." I turned to Ivy.

"You think I could do that? Be like . . . a businesswoman or something?" Mom whispered the words like she was hearing and understanding them for the first time and how they related to her.

"Are you serious? Don't be silly, woman." I smirked. She had repeated the same phrase to me earlier when I asked her if I looked okay in this dress I was planning to wear for Shane's birthday.

Mom plopped down next to Ivy in the lawn chair. "I don't know if I would be good at all that stuff. I just like to cook." She crossed her ankles under the chair and clasped her hands.

"Mrs. Caren, don't take this the wrong way, but they got you effed up." Ivy pointed a finger at Mom.

"What I told y'all about that swearing!" Mom slapped Ivy's knee and they giggled together. "And who got me effed up?"

"I'm sorry, but seriously, Mrs. Caren. The world. The world has you effed up, or whatever has you thinking that you can't do this. Don't sell yourself short. Sometimes these things happen to us and they end up being a blessing in disguise."

Mom's body melted into the chair, and she tapped her nails on the armrest. She stared up into the warm, falling sun and closed her eyes, letting the rays settle into the creases of her face. A face that spoke of acceptance. A knowing of what she was supposed to do. Maybe she just needed the confirmation, and Ivy gave her just that. A face that resembled so much of mine, just with more rings around the trunk. More stories. More problems. More love. More love for me. For Gage. More of every feeling you could have when you realized, maybe it was you whose been standing in your own way this whole time.

She was a woman who brought your best friend lemonade on a hot summer day, and left with courage.

She was sensational.

twenty-three

. . .

Rain pelted the windows and debris whipped by our screen door on the terrace.

It was July 27th; Shane's birthday, and a freak storm stole his thunder and raged for the past five hours. I planned our day so carefully, making sure we took the right train to get us closest to the basketball tournament. When I got an email that the tournament was canceled due to inclement weather—I cursed under my breath. Shane planned an amazing birthday for me and now I couldn't reciprocate.

"What are you kids going to do now?" Dad licked a spoon clean. He and Mom were sitting on the couch sharing a bowl of ice cream, watching tv with her legs sprawled across his.

"I don't know, Dad!" I rolled my eyes and stomped past them in the living room.

"Don't get testy with me Miss Mays. I didn't want you alone all day with that boy no way, pitching woo."

"Oh hush, Kyle. Leave that girl alone. Always messing with her." Mom swatted at Dad's protruding belly and shoved another spoonful of butter-pecan into his mouth.

"Oh, you want some too, Caren?" Dad grabbed Mom's hands, pulled them behind her back, and kissed her in the crook of her neck until she yelped and giggled. Sweet trails of sticky ice-cream moistened her skin.

While they loved on each other like two teenagers, Gage stormed into the house and slammed the front door. He was panting and he had a deep red scratch on his face.

"Baby, you okay?" Mom hopped up from the couch and the ice cream toppled to the floor.

"She's gone for real! For real! She left!" Gage paced around the living room floor so hard, I thought he would wear a hole into the carpet.

"Who is gone?" I took a step forward into the room.

"LaToya," Gage muttered. He half fell onto the couch. Black stress rings sat around his eyes giving their best racoon impression.

"What happened to LaToya? Where is the baby?" Mom questioned him like Judge Judy and didn't leave him room to actually answer. She shot worried glances between me and Dad.

"Son, I think you better start talking." Dad's hands were on his hips when he stood to his feet. He and Mom wore their favorite weekend attire—matching pajamas. She wore the top t-shirt, and he wore the bottom flannel plants.

Gage dropped his face into his hands and blubbered. "No, no no, what am I going to do now?" His body shook like he was cold. It was one of those colds that you felt down to your toes when everything was out of your control. I had been freezing cold before and knew it well.

"Son!" Mom shouted. "Where is the baby and LaToya?"

Dad knelt in front of Gage and shook his shoulders like he was shaking him awake.

Gage looked down at Dad with red and tired eyes. "She's with LaToya's grandmother. LaToya left. She said she needed to find herself outside of being a mother. She's gone for good."

Mom gasped.

The rain rampaged outside and as Gage told his truth, the clouds spilled out there's.

"She left about a month ago. She had an interview at the courthouse but it didn't go well, and they didn't hire her. She left then. She didn't want to work at the courthouse anyway. She was only doing it for us and because her cousin, Tina, worked there and said she could get her in. Humph, some cousin she turned out to be. She called me crying. Said she hated every minute of the interview, and instantly knew she couldn't do it. She wouldn't. To be turned down for a job she didn't want anyway was too much, and she needed to figure out who she was outside of us. So she left. She said she would be back once she figured some things out, but she called today and said she wasn't coming back and didn't want to be with me anymore."

"And where have you been staying? What have you been doing all this time??" Mom searched his eyes and clutched her hands together at her heart.

Gage rocked on the couch and he licked his lips. His chest grew and fell as each breath was more shallow than the last. He looked so much like the boy in those photos in the dining room wall, and I didn't like that I just noticed right here, in this very moment that he *always* looked worried.

Did family do that to him?

"I couldn't afford the rent without her, so I rented me and Milani a room. We stay there on the days we're not here," he whispered. "I got LaToya's grandmother watching Milani too. But only when she's not here with you guys. She's older and can't move around too good, but she good people, love her some Milani, and don't charge me that much."

I sat down next to my big brother on the couch and pulled a pillow to my chest. Gage dealt with so much and he kept it inside. Just like me. Just like Mom. And Dad. We were four sides of the same coin, plastering armor on to keep others from seeing our soft spots. Was it a family trait or human nature?

"This doesn't make any sense, son. Why didn't you just tell us that? Why didn't you say something? We would've helped." Dad was furious. Maybe at Gage. Maybe at himself. His forehead was sweating, and he paced around the living room.

Gage hopped up from the couch and squared off with Dad. "Ask for help? You lecture me all day about what I do wrong. You kicked me out of the house after LaToya got pregnant and I had nowhere to go! The only reason I told you now is because. . . because . . . shit. I don't know!"

"Watch your language in my house, son. You were irresponsible with that young lady. You had to learn to be a man, and that had to happen outside of this house." Dad folded his arms and set his face in the tightest parental I-am-right-and-you-are-wrong stance.

"Irresponsible? I told you I strapped up, Dad! I used protection and did everything you told me to do. I can't help that it broke!" Gage shouted; a vein in his head pulsed.

Mom's hand covered her mouth and she leaned against the living room wall. She faced the terrace and the wall of rain pounding what seemed to be only our apartment. I didn't want to hear about Gage strapping anything up and I'm sure she didn't either.

But maybe we needed to hear about life from Gage's experience.

"You never give me the benefit of the doubt about anything. Anything! Why would I come to you for help? I'm sorry I lied—but I figured I would handle things on my own until LaToya got back. But she's not coming back," Gage cried. He was carrying something heavy in his spirit and we added to the load. Gage didn't see a safe space within us. When he was down and out in his time of need—he didn't want to call on us.

The lights in our apartment flickered against the storm raging outside.

"You don't like LaToya." Gage took a breath as he stammered

through his truths for the first time. "You always seem mad at me. And Dad; do you even like me?" Tears formed in the corners of his eyes.

Dad dropped his folded arms to his side. He grabbed Gage by the shoulders and yanked him up from the couch. "Son. I . . . I . . . I didn't know you felt like this. I thought I was showing you how to be tough. How to be a man. I wasn't upset with you when Milani was born. I was upset with myself." He stared into his first-born's eyes. "I thought I failed you as a father. I thought it was my fault." Dad's voice cracked as thunder boomed right above our heads.

Dad and Gage's shoulders shook as they embraced and choked out their lifetimes worth of apologies. Mom and I gazed at each other from across the room. She wiped her face and cheeks, dabbing at her eyes. I released my grip on the pillow and exhaled. She mouthed to me across the room, *I love you.* I wasn't crying before, but for some reason—I was now. My face broke into a smile, and I mouthed back, *I love you too.*

The drama in our apartment quieted down, but the rain still demanded it's time and attention.

What the heck were Shane and I going to do today?

Another yellow dress laid across my bed. Mom and I decided yellow was my color of the summer, and we went shopping for more bright outfits. Yellow didn't seem to be the fit for the day against the torrential winds outside. But then again, we weren't going anywhere.

Taking a long sigh, I did the most uncomfortable thing ever— and I pulled my two-day old, unshaved legs into the yellow dress. After I lotioned up and pulled my hair back into a bun with a sock, I glanced myself over in the mirror. I looked good.

When I stepped out of my bedroom, Mom and Dad stared me up and down.

"Where did them hips come from? Caren, she looking like you these days. No, she ain't going nowhere with that boy. No, she ain't going." He shook his head.

"The girl is seventeen now, Kyle. What do you expect? She's growing up." Mom assured. "Baby, you look beautiful. I made you something special for today. Go check in the fridge."

I paddled to the kitchen, and when I opened the fridge, my heart swelled. Mom had baked a small personal sized cake in the shape of an "S."

"Mom, he'll love this! Thanks!" I beamed and ran to the living room to hug her.

She smiled and looked so pleased with herself, and I wanted her to be. I don't know how other teens complained about their parents, mine were everything and more. So was Gage, my big brother.

A few minutes later, I nervously rapped on Shane's apartment door.

He swung it open and grinned from ear to ear.

"Happy birthday!" I shouted and pushed the cake toward him.

"For me? I can't believe it?" Shane feigned surprise.

"We were supposed to go to the basketball tournament but you know, the rain," I explained. "I didn't know what else . . ."

"April, it's okay. As long as you're here." He pulled me inside the apartment. He pushed me up against the wall and kissed my forehead.

"Where is everyone?" I looked around and sat the cake on the table.

"My parents are coming back from getting food. My mom said since we couldn't go out for dinner, we were going to make something here."

Thunder clapped around us and the lights flickered again. "I hope the power doesn't go out." I leaned my head against their kitchen window and peered outside. It was really coming down out there.

Shane's front door jiggled, and his parents walked in carrying large take-out bags. They were soaked from head to toe and Mrs. Walker's sandals squeaked with every inch she walked. As soon as they shut the door behind them—the power went out.

"Perfect timing!" Mr. Walker huffed.

"Y'all go get some candles and the flashlights in the junk drawer," Mrs. Walker instructed. "We'll have to eat by candlelight until the storm passes."

Shane and his dad headed in the direction of candles and lighters, and I walked around the table and helped Mrs. Walker set out the food. They had bought bacon, sausage, French toast with strawberries and cream cheese, potatoes, grits, and orange juice. We set out plates and utensils while Shane lit small candles and placed them around the table. The perfect brunch.

"Did you wake up your brother?" Mrs. Walker asked.

"You know he likes to stay up all night and sleep all day. A regular summer vacation," Mr. Walker interjected.

"Shane, go wake his behind up." Mrs. Walker sucked her teeth as she arranged the candles on the table away from anything flammable.

A few minutes later, me and the Walker family sat around their kitchen table illuminated by food and candle flickers. Sitting next to Shane and watching his happy birthday face tickled my stomach. I wanted to reach over and touch him. I placed my hand on his thigh under the table, and he shot up straight in his chair. I tried to keep a straight face as he squirmed in his seat.

"April, are you excited to go back to school? I wonder if you and Shane will have any of the same classes?" Mrs. Walker poured herself a glass of orange juice.

"I hope so. I'm looking forward to us, next school year." I lied. I really wasn't. Part of me wanted things to stay exactly how they were right here. The power could stay off, and it could rain all damn day and night for all I cared.

Life with Shane seemed to get better every day and I didn't want to change a thing.

And when did that ever happen? When could you actually say that life got better every day? I was used to it getting worse. Or so I thought it was worse. But with Shane, there was no worse. There was only hope.

"You know, Shane has had a rough go at this school thing. Has he told you?" Mrs. Walker asked.

Mr. Walker's jaw clenched.

"Yes, he's told me some things." My hand rubbed Shane's thigh back and forth as he sat quietly while his mom did what moms did best. Tell their kid's business.

"Shane has been through a lot," Mrs. Walker continued. "Making friends has been tough for him. Because of the stuttering." She leaned in and popped a few pieces of bacon in her mouth. The ultimate mama bear rearing her head. "But our boy is strong now. We want to make sure you have good intentions for him." I wasn't sure whether she was serious or not until a smile crept across her face.

Soon, one spread on mine, too. "Good intentions for him? Did he tell you my mom and I slaved in the kitchen to bake him a cake from scratch? From scratch! No Duncan Hines over here," I joked.

Marcel was sitting quietly at the table with red bags under his eyes. Probably from being up all night. He giggled at my comment and soon everyone at the table was laughing.

"I highly doubt you cooked anything. Stick to the plants." Shane smirked and shoved French toast into his mouth.

We sat and talked, laughed, and shared stories from Shane and Marcel's childhood for hours. We were hungry again, and the candles were burned all the way down to their wicks until Mrs. Walker found more. We only found one birthday candle in the house. We lit it up and sang happy birthday to Shane in almost complete darkness.

Even though the day was rained out and we couldn't do what I had planned, I'd never seen Shane smile more.

Shane and I retired back to his room. The house was quiet, and his parents and Marcel were napping. The power was still out and rain pelted our brownstone, softer now. It had waved the white flag and was tapering off after raging a war against our plans. For a moment in time, I knew happiness and it damn sure knew me. There was nowhere to go and nowhere else to be. I was right where I was supposed to be—and what a beautiful feeling that was.

"I didn't know the speech thing was as bad as it was," I said quietly, rubbing Shane's head and recalling his parents' comments.

"It was. I had to change schools a couple times before I found boxing. Bullying and stuff." Shane shrugged.

"You seem so different now."

"I am different now. I will never be in that situation again. I can take care of myself, my dad made sure of that." Shane punched his own chest, and although he was trying to be funny, I saw a sadness in his eyes.

"But how are you, here?" I pressed my hand against Shane's heart and felt the heat of his skin.

He crumpled under my hand and his face softened. "Here is good. So good." Shane placed his hand on top of mine on his chest. "And what's this little dress you have on? Let me look at you?" He looked me up and down, his eyes shining in the darkness.

I stood and did an awkward dance in front of Shane until we both giggled.

He rubbed my leg and caressed my skin. "Your skin is so soft. So smooth and soft."

"Really?"

He nodded. "You are truly a beautiful girl, April. You bloom, just like your plants."

My eyes filled with tears. I wanted so badly to believe Shane.

Actually, I did believe him. But why was so much of who I was, tied to something Chase said?

"I didn't even want to really do it that night," I confessed softly. Lightning clapped as the storms surge returned with vengeance. The candles flickered around us. "The girls at school were always talking about how it hurt the first time, and so I thought, let me just do it and get it out the way. It didn't last long at all, but I remember his face. He looked at me like he was disgusted with me. My body. He said he never had a "thick" girl before, and he said it like I should be happy that he chose me. And I *was* happy that he chose me. That was the sad part. I was happy to be chosen. After the fight with Ivy, I went into the locker room later that day for gym. That fast . . . that fast . . . someone had left a razor in my locker with a Post-it note that said, *"Shave your cooch, hooch.* Tears tumbled down my face and with each word, Shane wiped them away.

"I should've said something. I should've stood up for myself, or . . . or . . . I don't know." I crumpled my face in my hands.

Shane placed his arm around my neck and pulled me in closer. The rain settled outside, but now I cried inside.

"One thing I learned in boxing is you are what you say you are. I say that I am a boxing phenomenon and no one can beat me. No one is quick with their hands like me." He raised his fists and jabbed at the air. "That's what I tell myself, but I had to learn that. You are more than what Chase or any of those hoes have to say about you. Half of them don't even know who they are—but have so much to say about other people. But you have to believe that. How do you feel? How do you want to feel? If the two don't match up, then do something about it. We have to do things that support how we want to feel," he whispered in my ear. "We'll do it together."

"I'm learning that." I nodded through blurry eyes. Shane pulled me in even closer, and my face rested in the crook of his neck.

Shane saw me, and I saw him.

Hair—just like my plants— grew from love. Nourishment. Nurturing.

 I was love.

Right then and there I decided that when I got home, I would throw away some of my razors. Not all—but some.

I was blooming.

twenty-four

· · ·

What's it called when it looks like something won't work? Can't work? Impossible?

Faith. It's called faith.

Shaking in my boots. That's what I was doing.

Mom, Dad, Shane, Ivy, and I got up at 5.a.m. and loaded up the car. That's where the problems began. Dad couldn't figure out how to load the vine wall into the trunk, and for thirty minutes we ran around the car figuring out the easiest way to tie it down from the top. The entire car was filled with greenery of all shapes and sizes, and quite a few gnats. I re-fertilized them a few days ago and gave them a nice neem oil spray down, but the dead fish mixture smelled putrid. I was used to the smell, but with all of us sitting in the car together, it made everyone's eyes burn. Ivy coughed the entire way to the event.

Shane and I were up late, clipping teeny tiny brown edges off the plants. I never lost a plant before, never. One never died on me, drooped, or turned brown until they were moved from the rooftop.

The NY Home and Garden Show: Teen's Edition was housed at the Javitz Center in Manhattan. When the event staff showed us to our table, I looked around in awe. Teens from different nationalities, makes, and models were here, bustling around getting their tables setup. The table next to me had a strobe light and I wasn't sure where he was going to put it. We were in a large open space with rows of tables set up as far as I could see. Someone was blaring out table assignments and directions to the bathroom over the loudspeaker. An entire family wore matching t-shirts a few tables adjacent to ours. They laid down a custom-made carpet in front of their table, and their table skirt had the same matching emblem.

"They have a Bromeliad plant! That's an exotic! It's not even indigenous to our area." I croaked. My underarms started to sweat. *What am I doing here? Am I ready for this?*

Ivy walked in front of me and laid her hands on my shoulders. "Look at me. Cut it out. Don't even do that to yourself," Ivy commanded. "You are here because you deserve to be."

How did she know what I was thinking?

"You're ready for this. You're prepared for this. No one is more prepared for this than you. You earned the right to be here just like everyone else, and you have a bomb ass vine wall that we strapped to the car, and Shane held down with one hand all the way across the Verazano Bridge."

"I sure did!" Shane chimed in. He placed his hands on my shoulders from behind.

"You're ready for this." Shane and Ivy both nodded at each other like they were already in agreement and I was the one who needed to catch up. With Shane having my back, and Ivy protecting my front, I took a deep breath and started to set up.

For the next three hours, I moved around the table fixing plants, spraying them with water, and saying silent prayers for any drooping leaves.

After going back and forth for weeks, Mom and I settled on a large vine wall with dangling pothos. Pothos didn't need much attention and their deep green and silver-gray color were striking and unique. They hung from a display wall mount that Mom and I found at the crafting store. We had a custom neon sign made that sat in the middle of the vine wall and it resembled the Manhattan's skyline. The neon phrase was bright pink and under the Manhattan's skyline it said, *"better together."* As I stared at my favorite people around me; supporting me, loving on me, I knew. We *were* better together. Sticking to the theme, it indeed, was a small world after all. And New York was my world.

We made flyers with my name and a short bio about my love for plants. Dad snatched them off the table and handed them out to people walking by. Mom hopped up and worked the other side of the table, handing out small sample sizes of her famous seafood salad with every vote for my table.

"My, what growth they have." A woman stopped in front of our table. "What do you put in them to make them grow?" She took out a small notepad and waited for my answer.

I took a deep breath. "The usual stuff. Fertilizer— filtered water. But I just love on them." I turned to Shane. "Love is a journey, and it's one we have to walk together in order to grow."

"How fearless you are." The woman smiled. She scribbled in her notebook and walked away.

Mom and Dad sat down behind the table watching the happenings throughout the room.

"My girl said she grows her plants with love. Ha! Bet they ain't heard that one before. They don't want none of us!" Dad rose from his stadium chair and clapped super loud like we were at a basketball game.

"Dad, be quiet!" I hushed him as my cheeks flushed.

Shane and Ivy manned the vine wall, making sure it stayed upright and was refreshed with water. "Are all those people for the bathroom?" I craned my neck at a long line of people standing next to our table behind the vine wall.

"No, girl. They're for you! They're for the wall!" Shane whispered in an excited tone.

I paused and gazed at the massive numbers of people in front of me. They couldn't all be for us. Everyone had their phones out and were taking selfies up against the vine wall.

"Hey y'all. How can we help?" Gage popped up with a smile. He wore Milani in a baby holster strapped to his chest and the baby bag was over his shoulders. Milani bounced up and down and giggled when she saw Mom.

"Give me my grandbaby!" Mom shouted and cut through the line of people waiting to take a picture with the wall. She shuffled to Milani and in a quick motion, unhooked her from Gage's chest and snatched her up with kisses.

Mom had herself a new best friend, and by the looks of Milani's laughs and cooes, she felt the same.

"Gage! I didn't know you were coming!" I ran around the table and hugged him.

"You didn't think I would miss your big moment now, would you?" Gage waved to Ivy and dapped up Shane.

"Hey, son. I'm glad you're here." Dad grinned. He pulled him in for a bear hug, and my insides got warm. Ever since Dad and Gage had it out in that freak storm days ago, they were hugging and talking more. It started slow at first—Dad adjusting to not critiquing everything Gage said. With each inch Dad gave Gage, he matched him with an inch. Gage was coming around a lot more and Mom seemed happy.

"What can I do to help?" Gage looked around.

"You can help man the wall. As you can see, we have a long line of people waiting to take selfies in front of it." I swept my hand in front of the line. *They are really here for me.*

"I'm on it, lil sis." Gage nodded and saluted me like he was in the army.

Two hours later, I was running on fumes and sweating. I had a headache. My feet were hurting and I ran out of flyers. Mom, Dad, and Milani were slumped in their chairs and dozing off to sleep. Milani's bottle was hanging from her mouth but she never dropped it. Shane, Ivy, and Gage were still manning the vine wall although the line was dying down.

Tap tap tap . . . A woman beat on the mic at the front of the room. There were so many people that I couldn't see her but I heard her. "Ten minutes everyone and we will be announcing the top three finalists to close out the show. We would like to thank all the participants as today's event was the best we've had in a long time. It was a hard decision, but I think we really found something special."

"We can start packing, guys." I tapped my parents on the knee to wake them.

Dad was lightly snoring and looked startled when his eyes popped open. "What you say now, April?" He rose his voice.

"Keep your voice down," I giggled. "I said let's start packing."

"We have to wait for the results, April," Shane frowned.

Looking around at the dozens of participants, I wasn't sure if I was even a contender against all the talent in the room, but I was still grateful to be there. "I don't think I'm gonna win," I whispered.

"You don't know that," Ivy said in a hushed tone. "Let's just wait and see."

"April, what are you talking about? Half of this entire room took a picture with your wall. We are not going anywhere until they read those results." Gage picked up Milani from Mom and rocked her in his arms. He scrunched his eyes at me like I was being ridiculous.

"What's wrong with the girl, Caren? We came all this way and she talking about she ain't gon' win. We going home with something today. We leaving here with something. I can feel it." Dad stood and guarded the table so no one could start packing it up.

The mic tapped one more time, and the same voice came back on.

"Okay everyone, we are ready! Thank you for everyone coming out to the 15th Annual NY Home and Garden Show: Teen's Edition. This event started with the NY Times Home Planters for Teen's Contest. We chose our favorites all across the city, and they advanced to this round and competed against teens all across the state of New York. The grand prize is $1000 and of course, bragging rights," the woman chuckled into the mic. "We want you to know you are all winners in our books, and we hope to keep this event going for years to come. Are we ready?" she yelled.

The crowd cheered and my nervous nelly insides made my teeth chatter.

"3rd place goes to . . . Truman Wilks with his Bromeliad plant!" she shouted.

Everyone clapped and the crowds parted so he could walk to the stage, pick up his trophy, and take pictures.

I plopped down in a chair and waited.

"2nd place goes to . . . Shirin Clearwater with her Jungle plant display." Shirin's family roared, and the crowd parted again so she could walk to the front and accept her award.

A hush fell over the room.

"Okay everyone. This is the moment we have been waiting for. This was a hard decision, but we give points for creativity, uniqueness, and of course, genuine effort. 1st place in the NY Home and Garden Show: Teen's Edition, with advancement to the national competition taking place next February in Disney World goes to . . ."

I held my breath.

"April Mays with her vine selfie wall!!"

"Ahhhh!!" everyone around me erupted.

Shane pulled me to my feet and screamed, "You did it!! You won, you won!!"

"That's my girl! That's my daughter!" My mom and dad shouted and jumped in place.

"That's my sister!" Gage hooted and hollered, cheered deep from his belly.

Milani burst into tears at all the noise.

The crowds parted again and this time—it was for me.

When I made it to the front, I couldn't tell the announcer's voice, but when I saw her, I blinked away tears. The same woman from earlier in the day with her notepad. They placed a check and a large trophy in my hand, and I cried and cried. I cried for my old self. I cried for my new self. I cried for who I thought I was and who I grew to be. I grew to be this person with love, and I flourished.

A large camera stopped in front of my face, and a man pushed a microphone my way.

"April Mays! Congratulations on your win! Please tell the people about your journey."

I froze. I wasn't comfortable being in the spotlight, but this was where love brought me. It opened doors for me, and I wouldn't close them on myself any longer.

Mom, Dad, Shane, Gage, and Ivy stood front and center with their phones out hanging on to my every word. Love and excitement spilled from their faces.

"My journey? My journey starts at home." I gushed and looked at them. "We all live together in a brownstone in East Harlem, and that's where I learned about love, family, friends, and community. I try to treat my plants the same way and give them love and community. That's how you grow." I looked at my parents. "Sometimes the community goes through things and it changes them. People can go through a metamorphosis too and we figure it out. We keep growing. Just like my plants. When their circumstances changed, they were still able to grow and transform into something fascinating. You can't grow love until you know love."

Mom and Dad held onto each other and watched me as their eyes sparkled with tears.

Shane smiled at me with a sloppy grin on his face and love in his eyes.

I changed the game. I thought plants were my quirky thing. I thought it was something a silly teenage girl was into, but as I looked around the room at all the enamored faces hanging onto my every word, I realized everyone had their thing. Shane boxed; and his face lit all the way up when he talked about it. Mom had cooking—and she made people happy with just one bite. And I had my thing too—only it wasn't quirky or weird. It was mine. I cultivated a new crop and that crop was me.

April showers really did bring flowers.

twenty-five

• • •

August rounded the corner, and it was hotter than ever. I was anxiously awaiting my school schedule to come in the mail. I hoped me and Shane had classes together.

Mr. Fred and I stared at each other.

My parents always taught me when interacting with adults, it's always yes sir, no sir— and you definitely didn't look them straight in the eyes.

"Mr. Fred. I'm moving my plants back up to the rooftop. I don't have the space for it on our little terrace. I know my dad told you about the contest that I won, and they gave me even more plants and things to start growing. I need the space. You said I could have the rooftop, and that's where I'm going." The top landing of the stoop stood higher than Mr. Fred at the bottom landing. Even though it was only three steps—I towered over him and felt powerful. I *was* powerful.

"I heard about your little speech you gave in front of all those cameras for the world to see. What you think? You can just talk bad about me and what's going on here?" Mr. Fred inched closer, his eyes red and incensed.

Confusion ran across my face. "Mr. Fred, I didn't say anything about you or anything going on here. I don't know why you think that, but either way, I'm moving my plants back." Out of the corner of my eye, I caught Shane walking from the bodega. When he saw me and Mr. Fred, his pace hastened, and he hustled across the street. When he made his way toward us, he was like a cat ready to pounce.

I spoke directly to Mr. Fred. "I respect you. I know you've worked hard to take care of this place, and you feel disrespected. I know how that feels."

Mr. Fred's eyes softened, and for a second, I saw it. The alcohol he became best friends with. The anger he let shield him. The memories he couldn't forget from faraway places that changed him. He was a man who had nothing and only wanted one thing that felt like something. His cane.

I continued. "I know it's not what you want. But, I really would like to help you find a replacement cane. I can go with you to the store. I have a friend from school; you know her, Ivy. She is creative and can make stickers and badges and other trinkets on her mom's Cricut machine. She's actually coming over in a few with her machine to hang out anyway. We're making t-shirts. If we pick out a new cane, we can decorate it together. I'll help you." I nodded. I hoped he saw the sincerity in my eyes, in my heart. My home needed peace, and instead of my neighbors all being suspects and Shane and I running around trying to figure out who was responsible; we needed to move past this and heal together.

Mr. Fred peered at me with curious eyes, and he shifted his weight to his left leg. He really didn't look like the same person without his cane, and if he wasn't the same person—we weren't the same people. People needed to be who they were—but they needed it under the right conditions.

"Mr. Fred . . . I-I-I." Shane stood next to me and tried to speak.

I patted his back and nodded at him to take his time. He needed healing too.

He closed his eyes, cleared his throat, took a deep breath, and started again.

"Mr. Fred . . . April and I have been trying to find out who took the cane all summer. It's the truth. I know you have your reservations about me, but I didn't do it, and I don't think anyone here has. Please—let us make this right." Shane interlocked his fingers with mine and squeezed my hand.

With a long sigh, Mr. Fred closed his eyes. His breathing was shallow and ragged, and his eye twitched like he was battling with himself. "Okay," Mr. Fred grumbled. "We can go buy a new—"

The front door to the brownstone shot open and it pushed me forward off the stoop.

Shane caught me as I almost tumbled down the short few steps. Mr. Dawson's eyes were red. He smelled of beer, anger, and a late-night poker game broken up by Mr. Fred—which only added to his fury. Shane told me that part early this morning.

"What is going on out here, Fred!? Is Shane stealing again? I've had enough of this shit! I'm going to get my gun!" Mr. Dawson turned on his heel and dipped back into the building.

The softness I saw in Mr. Fred's face seconds ago flashed away, and the rage returned.

"Ike Dawson, you ain't pulling out no guns in my building! Move out the way, girl. This old jack is cruising for a bruising!" Mr. Fred pushed me to the side, hobbled up the steps, and followed Mr. Dawson into the brownstone.

Town House was filling up for our meeting, and eyes were shooting back and forth watching the showdown. "You better not go get no gun, Ike Dawson! And Fred! This is enough, y'all cut this out, now!" Ms. Gloria shouted from her wheelchair.

Mr. Fred had a one-track mind and he stomped his way toward Mr. Dawson's apartment.

Mom, Dad, and Shane's parents rounded the corner and Mr. Fred pushed his way past them with a scowl.

"What's going on?" Dad frowned and eyed everyone suspiciously. He fixed his shirt from where Mr. Fred pushed him.

My chest was on fire. Worry sat on my heart for what was about to happen. I couldn't get the words out fast enough. "Mr. Dawson said he's sick of this shit and he's getting his gun!"

"Watch your mouth, April!" Mom glowered.

"Getting a gun? Shane, it's time to go home!" Mrs. Walker insisted.

"But Mom, we have to—"

"Let's go!" she repeated. Her hands were shaking.

Hearing the commotion, someone in Town House screamed *gunnnn*, and tenants who had lived in the building for years—and never had an issue here—ran for their lives to take cover.

Mr. Dawson and Mr. Fred's voice boomed down the staircase. Mr. Dawson was coming down the steps from his apartment with extra pep in his step.

Mrs. Walker's eyes widened. "Shane, get upstairs and call the police! Take the emergency exit stairwell!" She grabbed Shane's arm and he pulled in the opposite direction of Mr. Dawson.

"No! I'm staying with April." He tugged at my arm and away from his mom.

Mr. Walker and my dad stood guard at the bottom of the steps, trying to calm down Mr. Dawson. As people scattered throughout the room, I saw Marcel crouched in a corner. He was shaking like a leaf and scowling, shooting worried eyes at everyone. He looked so oddly out of place. I pushed my way through the crowd. Someone bumped me hard, and pain shot through my right shoulder. I winced in pain and lugged my way across the room to Marcel. "Are you okay?" I knelt down.

"I just wanted to play with it. That was it. I'm sorry, I'm sorry. I don't want anyone to get hurt!" He pulled his knees to his chest, tucked his face, and cried.

twenty-six

. . .

"Marcel!" Mrs. Walker exclaimed. "What are you talking about?"

Marcel tightened his grip around his legs and hugged his chest. He squeezed his eyes shut and cried as a small crowd formed around him. I held my breath. Marcel . . . it was Marcel this entire time. I thought about all the times I saw him playing outside by himself. He was always around listening, waiting, watching. An onery little boy—that's what I took him for. He was never on the suspect's list. But then again, I was too busy noticing his big brother.

Oh, *brother.*

Mr. Fred scurried to Marcel's side and towered over him. "Well, where's my shit, young man? Unhand it!"

"Calm down, Mr. Fred. Let us figure this out." Mr. Walker put an arm in front of Mr. Fred.

"Calm down? Calm down? I knew from the beginning it was a Walker boy! I just had the wrong one. Shane, I apologize for accusing you—but I know'd it was one of you!" He wagged his finger in Mr. Walker's face.

Mrs. Walker placed a hand over her mouth and eyed the crowd.

Everyone had scampered out of the room, but now they were slowly trickling back in to meet the brownstone's thief, Mr. Dawson and gun in hand—included.

"Marcel, where is Mr. Fred's cane?" Mr. Walker asked with a pinched voice. His jaw was tight.

"It's in the walls. In my hiding spot."

"In the walls? This boy is crazy! They getting evicted for this!" Mr. Fred pranced in place and yelled to anyone who would listen. Fortunately for him, and unfortunately for Shane and his family, Mr. Fred had an audience while everyone watched on in shock. Mr. Fred was in rare form; he was a Black man vindicated.

"Did you have something to do with this?" Shanice pressed Corey. Her, Deja, and Corey stood off to the side and Shanice shot dangerous your-ass-is-mine mom daggers at him.

Corey's eyes bugged and he shook his head no so fast I was sure his neck would break. "No, Mom. No!"

I looked at my phone and checked the clock on the wall. Ivy was supposed to come over after the meeting. She walked through the door right on time. "Psst!" I whispered and motioned to her.

"Excuse me. Excuse me." She scooched and scooted toward me. She carried her large Cricut machine through the room, unaware of the melee that was our brownstone.

"What happened now? It's always some drama here, girl," she whispered as she got closer to me. I noticed a passion mark on her neck as she turned her head to survey the scene. I would talk to her about that later.

Mr. Fred heard Ivy's comment and scowled looking at her crafting bag. "I saw you sucking face with that girl down at the rec center the other day. You can go home too. We don't have time for your arts and crafts today. This ain't the YMCA."

"Mr. Fred! Enough! Let Marcel speak so we can get on with this nonsense. I have to get upstairs to take my pressure pills; y'all about to have my sugar up," Ms. Gloria clamored.

"Well let's call the police," Jorge interjected. Him and Journey were standing side by side with matching beret hats and their arms folded. Jorge worked nights and was missing sleep to attend our meeting. He was physically tired and tired of *this* shit.

Someone gasped behind them, and the room hushed.

"Call the police? He's just a boy." Mrs. Walker knitted her brows together. The Walkers stood together in front of Marcel, shielding him from an angry mob that wanted answers while he held his knees and furrowed his head.

Shanice scrunched her face together and looked at Corey. She was probably thinking the same thing I was thinking. It could have been Corey they were threatening to call the police on. In a brownstone filled with Black and brown families, when someone threatened to involve the police, it wasn't taken lightly, and you better be damn sure that's what you wanted to do.

Mrs. Walker knelt down in front of her son and stroked his face. Her voice was low but stern. "Marcel, honey. What does that mean? In the walls? In your hiding spot?" she clarified.

Marcel was shaking. Dozens of eyes stared at him and his words caught in his throat. His dad extended a hand and helped him climb to his feet. "I'm sorry. I just thought it would be funny to take it after Town House. I wanted to check out all those cool stickers. And then everyone started arguing and fighting. I just couldn't say it was me after all that, so I kept it."

"Well why didn't you just leave it in front of Mr. Fred's door? Or leave it somewhere where you knew someone would find it and return it back to Mr. Fred?" Mrs. Walker asked.

Marcel shrugged and scratched his head. He was a ten-year-old, scared boy—and his mischievousness didn't mean he had all the answers or thought this thing through.

"Marcel. Where is this hiding spot?" Mr. Walker's voice and eyes were soft for Marcel, but he grimaced as the crowd swelled behind him demanding answers.

Marcel dropped his shoulders and looked at the floor. "It's in the walls, with the rats."

"With the rats?" Ivy inquired. Even *she* needed answers.

"The rats. They're my friends. They have a secret hiding spot in the walls where we hide all of our treasure."

"Rats? Treasure? What is this child talking about! You know what—you're right, Jorge. Someone call the police," Mr. Fred lamented.

"Wait, I'll show you." Marcel wiped his cheeks where streaks of scared tears stained his brown face. A path parted in the room, and he walked through like he knew exactly what to do and where to go. Marcel walked out of the room and across the hall, over to a utility closet next to Town House. I had never been in the small closet and only saw the maintenance crew in there every now and then. *What is back there?*

Marcel wiggled a panel and a tiny, crickety sliding door creaked open. "It's in there." He pointed.

"And you go in here often?" Mr. Fred's head disappeared inside the dark hole as he peeked in.

"Yes, it's my spot. This is where all the rats go. I give them some of Ms. Caren's food and they love it and keep coming back."

"Myyy God." Mom shook her head.

"So, you have been stealing from your neighbors and keeping the rats fed and happy?" Shanice rolled her eyes between Marcel and Corey. Corey lowered his head, and I wasn't sure Shanice wasn't sure Corey didn't have anything to do with this. Marcel and Corey were two peas in a pod these days.

"Wait—" Mr. Fred paused. "There are tunnels back here and they've been sealed up for decades. The brownstone was used as a safe haven for The Underground Railroad back in the

1800's, but I didn't think they were still accessible." Mr. Fred stuck his hand behind the door panel to see if he could feel anything. "Ouch!" He yelped and pulled his finger back. He was bleeding.

"Here, come get a Band-Aid. I keep em' with me at all times." Ms. Gloria opened her fanny pack and pulled out Band-Aids, gauze, and Neosporin.

"Ms. Gloria, why do you have all that stuff?" I eyed her makeshift emergency kit.

"Mind your business, my dear. You never know when you'll need stuff. Don't we need it now?" she said and motioned for Mr. Fred to come to her.

My dad peered inside the wall panel where Mr. Fred felt around. He tapped on the wall and some parts sounded low and dull. He tapped again and another part sounded hollow. Dad kept tapping where it felt hollow and with a big bang, another sliding door popped open. The sound was jarring and people in the room gasped.

Dad ducked his head into the hole. The room was hushed as everyone waiting for something. Anything.

"What do you see, Dad?" I inquired and tried prying over his shoulder. "Marcel, what's in there?" I looked over my shoulder at him.

"I only stay in the first tunnel. I didn't know there were others. I never opened that door," Marcel said and pointed to the door Mr. Fred had just cut his finger opening.

My dad didn't say anything, but his breathing changed. I heard the faint sound of rats scurrying and my skin itched.

"Well, what is it?" Mr. Dawson said, annoyed. His gun gleaned on his hip.

Dad said nothing but I watched his grip tighten around the door until his knuckles were white. He took off his work jacket and handed it to Mom. "Hold this please," he said.

"Kyle, be careful!"

Mom stood right behind him like she was watching his back. She tossed his jacket off to the side and peered behind him into the dark hole. He stepped inside the small tunnel and crouched down. It was tiny, and my dad looked humongous trying to fit inside. It was definitely made for a child's size. He rummaged around for a few seconds while we crowded the hallway in the light with bated breath.

Shane held my hand and squeezed it.

I love you, I mouthed to him.

He grinned and mouthed, *I love you too.*

"April, come here!" Dad yelled, but he sounded far away. I dropped Shane's hand and inched closer to the hole. From the darkness, Mr. Fred's cane emerged—perfectly intact. I handed it to Mom behind me and like a chain, the cane was handed down the line to Mrs. Walker, Shanice, Jorge, and finally . . . finally . . . once the Band-aid was carefully wrapped around Mr. Fred's finger—he was ready to receive his prized cane. When it was placed in his hands, his face lit up like a Christmas tree.

"I got this from my daddy. It was the only thing he ever gave me. Thank you." Mr. Fred hugged the cane. His eyes were red again, but this time it wasn't because of alcohol. This time it was pure emotion.

I turned back to my dad as he descended further into the tunnel.

"Kyle, don't go too far!" Mom shouted, worry all over her body.

Dad didn't say anything.

"Kyle?" Mom repeated. She side-stepped me and peered into the hole.

No response.

"Kyle!" Mom shouted.

Silence.

"Hold my stuff, I'm going in." Mom handed me her purse.

She placed her hands on either side of the wall and was ready to hop in when dad popped his head back out. He was breathing fast and his eyes were wide.

"Mr. Fred, I'm glad you have what you need. But Jorge was right. We're gonna have to call the police."

"Why? What's in there?" Mr. Fred and his cane waltzed to the opened wall.

Dad's face was ashen.

twenty-seven

· · ·

When Dad crouched even further into the crawlspace, he grunted and struggled to pull something. Mr. Walker moved to front of the wall, knelt down, and said, "Here, let me help."

Dad yelped and lifted something heavy, and when he placed it into Mr. Walker's hands, we all gasped.

The large, square shaped painting was shrink-wrapped tight and manila tape secured it in place. Hidden behind the walls for years, it was covered in dirt and cobwebs. The rats were louder now, squeaking and zipping past eachother with their lair exposed to people and the light.

Mr. Fred pulled a pocketknife from his pants jacket and began slicing into the bubble wrap. Dad and Mr. Walker grunted and sweated as they pulled more paintings from behind the trap doors, all bubble wrapped.

The room was silent while the men removed painting after painting from the walls.

"That's all of them," Dad said, climbing out of the crawl-space and back into the light. He had cobwebs in his hair.

Nine I counted. There were nine paintings.

As each painting was unwrapped, someone new in the room gasped. When they were all finally opened, nine paintings depicting various scenes from what looked like the Civil War era were displayed in pristine condition. I checked them over for marks, dings, or imperfections and saw none. They must have been preserved behind the walls for years.

"Where did these come from?" Mom asked, astonished.

"Ms. Caren, I'm not sure what this is." Mr. Fred sat in a chair next to the hole, and he rubbed his eyes. He knelt on his cane and he didn't seem so small. I eyed the corner of the paintings and saw the name Edwin Forbes.

"It says, Edwin Forbes, Dad. Who is that?"

"Siri. Who is . . . who is this Edwin Forbes?" Ms. Gloria spoke into her phone. I was grateful I taught her how to use Siri. It would come in handy today.

"Edwin Forbes was an American landscape painter and etcher who first gained fame during the American Civil War for his detailed and dramatic sketches of military subjects, including battlefield combat scenes from the late 1800s. His rare collection can be found in the Smithsonian Art Museum, although some of his pieces were stolen and never recovered," Siri said.

The room was silent again as we put together the clues.

Never recovered.

Until today.

"We have to call the police," Mrs. Walker said quietly. Her hand was to her mouth in shock.

"Indeed, we do." Mom nodded.

"Why? We found it—not them!" Mr. Fred's cane dropped to his side as he hopped in place in excitement. Funny, any other day he was limping around, whimpering about his cane, but today he was limber as could be.

"We did find it, but they're clearly stolen. We can't just board the wall up and act like we didn't see this."

"And what if there's more in the building?" Shanice chimed in. She held a fist to her mouth in disbelief.

"I have a friend who teaches art at the city college. I can call her," Ivy offered. She glanced between Mr. Fred and my dad.

"Please call, Ivy." Dad gazed around at the canvasses.

Ivy smiled, happy to be needed, and excused herself to the back of the room as she made a call.

"9-1-1. We have an emergency," Shanice spoke into her phone. The room was quiet with a few murmurs full of questions lingering in the air. "We found something . . uhhh . . in the walls of our brownstone. And . . . can someone come down here please? Yes, that's the address. No, this is not about the cane again." Shanice shot a glance at Mr. Fred. "Thank you," she said, and ended the call.

"They're coming."

"Well, what do we do now?" Jorge placed a hand to his chest in disbelief.

"We wait." Dad pulled up a chair in front of the paintings and looked them over.

Ivy excitedly skipped to the front. She was out of breath. "Hey y'all. I just talked to my friend. She's a professor at the college and teaches Art Appreciation 101. She said this Edwin guy is bigtime, and that all of his stuff is famous, but nine unique pieces were stolen from the Smithsonian over eighty years ago. She said there's a big reward."

"Well, I can appreciate that," Ms. Gloria exclaimed. She slapped her legs and hoo-haaed.

A few minutes later, the police arrived along with Channel 6 News. How did the news get here so fast? Word surely traveled fast because within minutes of their presence, a crowd formed outside and police blocked off the front stoop with crime scene tape.

"We found it. It was right there in the walls. We thought there was going to be a shoot-out but instead, we found treasure!" Jorge illustrated to the neighbors who had walked in late on the action. He held Journey's hand. Before the cops got here, they both ran upstairs to change their clothes and came downstairs in matching sleeveless frayed jean jackets and bronzer on their faces to talk to the news' crews.

Shanice argued with an officer. "I have to take my kids to their dad's house. I can't stay!" She crossed her arms and cocked her head to the side.

"I understand, ma'am, but this is an active investigation. We have to talk to everyone who was in the room by tonight. No one leaves. No one is allowed in or out."

"This is bullshit!" she shouted. "I don't know anything. Mr. Fred and Ike were about to argue, Ike went and got a gun. That boy over there confessed to stealing Mr. Fred's cane, and then they found the paintings. That's it. That's what happened."

"Gun?" The officer scrunched his face. He placed a hand to his hip and his finger twitched." Who had a gun?"

Out of the corner of my eye, I saw Mr. Dawson back out of the room, and he was promptly sent right back inside by another police officer standing guard at the Town House door.

"That's not the point here. What this fine lady is trying to say is —you can't keep us hostage like this. It's getting late and we need to go home," Mr. Fred said.

"I'm sorry, sir. I have been given strict instructions not to let anyone leave this room until more information is obtained." The officer chomped on gum.

"Everyone sit down. Sit down at this table, now." Ms. Gloria tapped the table. She rested her arms on her walker. "Let's let these people do their job and maybe we can get out of here faster. Ain't nothing we can do but just wait, so let's calm ourselves down."

"Ms. Gloria, but don't you need your medicine? It's getting late?" I checked the time.

"I'll be just fine, April. I'm not missing none of the action." She flashed her eyes. "Now how about you tell us all about your big win at the Home and Garden Show the other day? How are y'all planning to celebrate?"

I took a deep breath as dozens of eyes turned toward me. It hardly seemed like the right time to talk about my big win.

Shane nudged me. "Come on." He smiled. "Tell them, big money."

For the next hour, I relayed my day at the show. I told them how nervous and worried I was about my plants because they had been on the terrace for so long and not in their usual place on the roof.

I cut my eyes at Mr. Fred when I told that part.

I told them how the other participants displayed exotic plants and wore matching t-shirts. I told them how Shane had to hold down the vine wall that we made and strapped it to the car roof.

They cracked up at that part.

"I don't want a big celebration or anything." I shook my head. "Just winning is enough for me."

Jorge and Journey came in from their primetime interview with Channel 6, and they sat down at the round table and listened to me. Everyone listened to me. In school, I was weirded out when I did projects talking in front of people. I chewed on the inside of my lip and sometimes swayed side to side out of sheer nervousness. In our past brownstone meetings, I hated being at the table and feeling like I was being watched. But today and after I won the show; I talked about what I loved. When I did, the room shifted and made room for me at the table. I talked about what I knew. What knew me and what loved me.

My plant babies.

With each word, I relaxed. I talked about my plants, and I used their official names, never dumbing it down or disrespecting them for anyone.

English Ivy

Boston Fern

Variegated Snake Plant

I talked about them all and why I chose them. Why they chose me.

"It was just love. They grew from love." I finished. I looked around the room, and some of the police officers had walked inside. They had their hands on their waist, and they were watching and listening intently to my story. Mom had tears in her eyes and Dad grinned from ear to ear.

twenty-eight

. . .

Four days. It was four days since a razor touched my skin. I studied the hairs threatening to lift on my legs. Peeking around the corner, I spied Shane waiting in the living room with a towel slung over his shoulder and sunblock plastered on his nose. I inspected my inner thighs for hair.

I didn't see any.

I tied my bathing suit straps behind my back and pulled a sheer camisole around my waist to cover myself and any possible hairs that decided to spring up within the next three hours.

A day with Shane at the rec center pool was just what the day called for since our brownstone was crawling with police and news wanting to catch a glimpse of the treasures discovered in the walls at our place.

I wanted to slither back in my bed and hide. I wanted to peel off my bathing suit and wait and tuck away under the peace and warmth of my blankets. I also wanted to leave Chase in the dust. With each smile, kiss, and confirmation from Shane, I wanted to evolve. With each passing day, looking at my body didn't give me so much angst. But today—in a bathing suit with my melanin out and on display and the news circling outside like a pack of seagulls at the beach—it was a rough one.

Taking a deep breath, I exited my bedroom and met Shane in the living room. He licked his lips when I rounded the corner.

My shoulders relaxed and I instantly melted.

"Don't be ogling my child, Shane. I know you don't want a knuckle sandwich. And why you ain't got no clothes on, anyway?" Dad scowled at me in my bathing suit. His feet were slung over the coffee table, and he was fanning his long toes.

"Kyle, hush! And put those creepy crawlers away; we have company. April looks amazing. Look at that body." Mom grinned. She wore a long mu-mu that came down past her knees and her breasts hung and swung low. By the pleased look on her face, I knew I reminded her of what she once looked like.

"Listen, here's some money so you kids can get some snacks. You have my girl back by a decent hour. The news people should be gone by then." Dad handed me some cash and I stuffed it into my bag with no complaints this time.

Outside, the sun was blazing and by the time we made it to the front stoop, I was already sweating. Thank God the rec center pool was only four blocks away. We stopped at the bodega and grabbed some snacks. A Yoo-hoo for Shane, and an ice cream cone for me. We crossed the street and hustled down the busy four blocks.

"We never go past the bodega." Shane laughed. "We make one big square and come back around."

"The subway and everything we need is in the opposite direction. Including your gym." I shrugged.

"That'll be our next adventure. Ohhh what's beyond the bodega?" Shane held up his hands and arms like he was a ghost.

I giggled. "Have the police talked to your parents yet?" I surveyed the pool scene once we arrived at the rec. It was filled with kids splashing each other and doing cannonballs into the water. I didn't see anyone from school.

"No not yet, but they're supposed to come tomorrow. I just can't believe all of this. Who would've thought, you know." Shane shook his head, pulled his t-shirt over his chest, and placed his clothes down at a lounge table. The police had already interviewed each person in the brownstone, but they wanted to specifically re-interview the people who were in Town House when the discovery was found. I thought the story would quickly die down, but days later, they were even further from figuring out who stole the paintings and placed them in the walls to begin with. The news' crew set up shop and refused to leave—wanting to be the first with breaking news about stolen war artifacts, as they were calling it. People were saying they were worth millions. Millions.

Shane's flat abs and smooth brown skin were show stopping. I stopped and stared while he pulled sunglasses over his eyes. With temperatures already searing, watching him move around the pool so cool and calm—had me scorched.

"I've lived here all my life, and I never thought there was anything special about the place. The entire time, there was treasure in the walls!" I lifted my camisole over my head and pulled it from my sweating skin. I immediately grabbed the towel and placed it around my waist so no one would see.

"What do you think the police are going to do with all of it?" Shane walked down the small steps, dipping into the water.

I was frozen in place. Shane sounded like he was under water, but he wasn't. He was standing right in front of me, waiting for me to immerse myself into the cool water with him like we planned.

I couldn't.

I wouldn't.

I held a death grip on my towel wrapped around my waist and squeezed it—afraid to let go. The summer was a hard time for girls struggling with their bodies, and I constantly felt like I walked the plank. Picking out clothes and bathing suits left you in a perpetual state of "does this look okay? Do I look fat? Hairy?" Fear had me in its clutches. I was afraid that people would see what kept me staring in the mirror at myself before we left. My body was on display, and so was my self-esteem.

"Move!" a little kid shouted as I stood in his way. He didn't see me mustering up courage and battling with myself. He ran around me and cannonballed into the water. I jumped in place as the water splashed me and left cold streaks on my warmed skin.

Words were caught in my throat, and my heart was pounding. I blinked a few times, feeling faint. I heard kids around me screaming and having fun—but I swore they were staring at me. When I looked at them, it felt like all eyes were on me—judging me, pointing and laughing at hair that wasn't there.

In a flash, Shane hopped out of the water and was standing directly in my face. He grabbed my cheeks and held them. "Hey. Hey," he whispered. "You are safe. You are loved. You are wonderful and fascinating beyond words. Physically and mentally. Fuck Chase and anyone else who has anything to say. Some days you're like the river and you'll move slowly and softly. Some days you'll feel the need to roar and crash like the ocean. Both are beautiful—because . . . b . . . b," he stuttered. He closed his eyes and found the words. "B-b, because you are. And I love you."

Kids laughed and splashed around us. Grownups paid them no attention as they applied sunblock, read books, or talked on the phone. Tears streamed down my face amongst all these people, and they were none the wiser of the internal battle that raged inside of me that Shane constantly calmed.

"I love you too." I breathed.

"It's me and you. Just call us Yoo-hoo." He smirked. He placed his hand on my chest and my beating heart slowed. "Breathe. Just breathe," he coached.

Taking in gulps of alir and staring into his eyes, I released the vice grip my hand had on my towel, and I let it fall to the ground, crumpling around my feet.

Shane picked it up, folded it, and sat it next to his clothing on the lounge table. He walked back into the water, slowly this time and extended his hand for me to follow.

Carefully, I stepped into the cool water. It felt so refreshing against my skin. Shane held my hand and pulled me closer. I wrapped my legs around his waist under the water and hugged his neck. He murmured into my ear, "You won."

"Huh?" I frowned.

"What you just did right now. You slayed a dragon. Baby, you won."

With a grin, I tilted my head up to the smoldering sun, and I let the rays warm my face.

I won.

twenty-nine

...

"How's Marcel?" I asked.

Shane's jaw tightened. "My parents really laid into him about that damn cane. They signed him up for some sort of therapy, and they ask him a ton of questions now. He still feels guilty everything came out the way it did. He'll be okay, he's just scared. He thought taking it would be funny, and look at what it's turned into." He rolled his eyes.

"Are you upset with him?"

Shane paused for a second and looked around like he hadn't considered how he felt.

"You know. At first, I was. All this time Mr. Fred was coming at me, and he had other people convinced too. I guess I'm just used to people making me out to be something I'm not, so I let it ride. But Marcel, he's different. He thinks everything is funny. Everything is a joke, until it's not. My parents need to do something. He needs discipline."

"Is that right?" I chuckled at Shane's parenting advice.

"When I had issues, they put me in boxing and it ended up being a good thing for me. He needs something to do. He can't just hang out with Corey all day long. I'm not sure about the two of them together."

I nodded and didn't say anything. I wasn't sure about Marcel and Corey together, either. Even though Corey still swears up and down he had nothing to do with the cane, he and Marcel were a perfect elixir for a bromance gone wrong.

"Where do you want these funny looking ones?" Shane held up one of my Snake plants.

"First of all, don't call them funny looking. YOU are funny look-ing." I rolled my neck.

Shane put one hand up and feigned shock. "Whoa whoa whoa."

Gazing around the rooftop, it hadn't changed much, but yet it did. I was putting my plant babies back in the rightful place on the roof with full sun. With some of my competition earnings, I bought a large makeshift greenhouse, complete with a roof, door, and skylights. It was a bitch to put together and took me, Shane, and my dad hours. When it was finished, I stood back and stared in awe. I had endless space to tend to my plants, house all of my supplies, and let them flourish against any rogue sun or wind.

Mr. Fred was extra nice to residents these days. He even apolo-gized to Mom for canceling her platter sales, even though they were never really canceled.

He still didn't know that part, thank God.

We were in the home stretch of summer break, and it felt anything *but* a break. I moved around the roof, placing my old and new plants strategically for the ones that needed more sun, and the others that preferred shade but high humidity.

Shane saw me standing there looking around and placed his hand on my shoulder. "You ok?"

I sighed. "I was waiting for this day when I could put them back up here, but now with so many cops and news reporters downstairs and all over the brownstone, I hope they don't get in the way of this." I swept my hand.

Shane was quiet. My Shane—who always had an answer for everything— was quiet. He knew like I knew. It had been almost ten days since the paintings were found, and cops still roamed the building. At first Mr. Fred and Mr. Dawson shut it down. Anyone coming in and out of the building who didn't live here, they watched guard at the door and gave them a hard time since it was private property.

The paintings were just the beginning.

In addition to the cops, now there were scientists, historians, and construction workers taking the walls apart and searching for more goodies. They combed through every inch of the building, and the tunnels weaved together a story of survival, love, truth, and freedom. They were finally able to confirm that the building was used as a safe haven for the Underground Railroad, and with that —the city deemed it a historical site, and no longer private property.

It was property of the state of New York.

They were determined to search every inch of the building at all hours of the night, regardless of who complained. Some of the tenants were even taking off work and just hanging out in Town House. Everyone wanted to be around just in case they missed the action.

The police put up crime scene tape that led up to the rooftop stairs. Mr. Fred snatched it down and told me I could put my plants back up there and he didn't care about no police and no paintings. I smiled when he said that—and Mom gave him extra oxtails when I dropped off his Friday platter of food.

Shane finally cleared his throat. "I'm curious about this big meeting tomorrow. What do you think they will say?"

I shook my head. "Who knows. It's like we're prisoners these days. It's hard getting in this place and it's even harder getting out. I hope they're going to say all of this will end soon. I feel like I'm sneaking to see them."

"Them?" Shane scrunched his face, but it soon dissipated. "Ahh.

The plants. Them." He playfully slapped himself in the head. "I thought you meant me."

I giggled. "Come here." I wiggled my finger.

Shane dropped the planting shovel right where he stood and barreled to me. "You rang?" He got into my face.

"Kiss me," I demanded.

Shane grabbed my cheeks and pulled me in for a long kiss. When we finally came up for air, Shane said, "Remember when we kissed here at the block party? "I didn't even want to—but you insisted that I be your boyfriend. I mean, you are fine and all, so I said yes."

"What?!" I threw some dirt at him and laughed out loud.

He dodged the dirt, grabbed the water hose, put his finger on the opened tip, and sprayed me with the water.

"Ahhh!" I yelped and ran around the rooftop. Shane chased me until we collapsed on a bench in the corner, laughing, and cooled down from the water hose.

"April."

My stomach fluttered. The way he said my name did something to me that I couldn't put into words.

"Yes?" I stared at him.

"Me and you, we got something good here. We're good for each other." He grabbed my hand and held it.

"I couldn't agree more," I said, stroking his knee. And even though there was a swarm of people downstairs in the walls. Even though Harlem was extra noisy and mean today with people clamoring to get inside our building. And even though Shane and I were still figuring out our places in the world. There was nowhere I'd rather be in this moment—than right here with him.

thirty

. . .

The chicken wings were golden brown and filled with specks of pepper.

"Make sure those are wrapped tight. You know how people feel about my chicken," Mom advised. "And wrap six extra pieces and set them to the side. I'm going to give those to the news crew outside the building."

The aluminum foiled ripped as I hugged it closed around the steaming food. "I got it, Mom. You know I've been doing this with you for years. Did anyone ask you to cook?" I questioned. It wasn't our usual week for platter sales.

Mom shook her head. "No, I just figured folks would like something nice to eat, since so much been happening around here. Food is the only thing that can bring people together in times like these."

The air in our brownstone was thick with contempt of police. They still roamed the building and the more they made their presence known, the more antsy the residents became. Especially the male residents of color.

Home was supposed to be a safe space that was tucked away from bullish eyes of the law. When your safe space was invaded with the very man you had been born and bred to fear—no one was comfortable. With the initial excitement dying down, the energy was thick with people on their last nerve and fresh out of patience.

Shane rounded the corner, pulling the handcart we used to tow the food for deliveries. Mom cooked a full spread for our emergency brownstone meeting, and he helped load the food and set up.

"Shane, baby. Can you cook?" Mom asked.

"Can I cook? I sure can. My specialty is mashed potatoes!" Shane grinned. He looked proud of himself and that made me smile.

"Mashed potatoes!" Mom exclaimed. "Everyone can cook mashed potatoes!"

"Hey, mashed potatoes are an art form. You have to get the butter to milk ratio just right. A lot of people can't do it." Shane waved his hands and explained.

Mom and I giggled as we loaded the food into the cart. A few minutes later, we made our way downstairs for the meeting. Dad was already there conversing with Mr. Walker. They had stern looks on their faces and their arms were crossed. I wondered what they knew, when they knew it, and how it would affect us.

Shane and I set out the food across the large round table. We spread the plastic utensils and paper plates. Ms. Gloria and Jorge arrived first and began leading the pack, loading up their plates down the buffet line. They thanked Mom along the way as delicious aromas wafted through the room. More people made their way to the table and grabbed a plate. Mom was right. Food did bring people together.

"This is right on time, Caren. You know I love me some fried chicken. The young kids want to eat that funny stuff. Chipotle this, and rasta pasta, that. Me? I'm an old-fashioned meat and potatoes kind of girl." Ms. Gloria happily nibbled on her chicken. "You know, before my husband passed, he had a dream to be a bodybuilder. You know, one of those strong men with the baby oil on them. I used to tell him, 'I can be a body builder too, I got me a body built. Just not the one you're talking about.'" She cackled and food shot from her mouth.

"Seeee." Shane nudged me in the side and hissed with a smug look. *"Potatoes."* He raised his eyebrows.

Jorge was right behind her and scooped a large spoonful of rice onto his plate.

"Jorge. Where is Journey?" I handed him some napkins for his food and rolled my eyes at Shane.

His face fell. "My love has decided to leave me."

"What? Why?" I said in a hushed tone. More people were coming into the room and began loading up their plates. I moved out of their way and tried to keep my voice down.

Jorge shrugged. "His father came back into town. He is a very stern and proper man. He didn't know . . . about him . . . about us." Jorge swallowed. "He is trying to be someone he is not."

I understood that as my thoughts turned to Ivy. Damn, I understood that. Journey and Jorge were older. Not *old*, but older than me and Ivy. I wondered if that's how she felt. To be their age and still hiding behind the façade of who people want you to be.

Mr. Fred sauntered into the room with a man I'd never seen before. He was without his cane, and he had a new pep in his step as him and the man strolled in together like long lost friends. I still couldn't believe everything he put us through, and now that our place became ground zero for a treasure hunt, all of a sudden he didn't need his cane. He even had a new haircut.

One of my favorite plants was the Dieffenbachia; that was its official name. It was a temperamental plant but if the conditions were right—it could grow to be six feet tall. Unofficially though—its name was a Dumb Cane plant. While the room hushed and Mr. Fred began to speak, I realized all the conditions were right and this turned into the perfect storm.

All because of a dumb cane.

"Mr. Fred, where's your cane?" Mom asked.

Mr. Fred cleared his throat. "It's home. I'm going to get a second one to take out with me that's not so . . . important. That one should stay home."

Umph . . . wait til I tell Ivy this shit.

"Tenants, this is Mr. Ayala, and he is a Historian and an art broker from the Manhattan Art Auction." Mr. Fred changed the subject and introduced his well-dressed and tight-assed friend.

"Hi everyone. I hope you are all well amidst the flurry of activity that has happened in your home." Mr. Ayala smiled. "Like Mr. Fred mentioned, I am here representing the Manhattan Art Auction. They're working with the scientists and a few other historians, and they've authenticated the paintings as the original lost artwork from the famous Edwin Forbes. Nine pieces were stolen 80 years ago, and nine pieces were found in the walls of this building."

Someone in the room gasped, but otherwise it was so silent you could hear a pin drop. I faintly heard Mom's business laugh as she walked back into the room from handing out plates of food to the news crew outside. She sat down next to Dad, and they gripped hands under the table. I grabbed Shane's hand and clasped his.

"What does this all mean for us?" Shanice jumped up from her chair and put her hand on her hip. "We have to get on with our lives and these people are still here every day banging inside the walls. Mr. Fred and them have taken care of the rats finally, but what about the news crews still hanging outside? And the police? My son is afraid of the police! When will all this end?"

The crowd grumbled and many people nodded their heads in agreement with Shanice.

Mr. Dawson stood and I swore I saw an imprint of a gun in his hip waist. "Now I don't mean no harm around these parts here. But it seems to me like we are all due what is owed unto us. I mean —we *were* the ones who found it. And y'all people said there was an outstanding reward, right y'all?" Mr. Dawson eyed everyone in the room.

Tenants nodded their heads in agreement and fanned their faces with pamphlets.

Mr. Ayala cleared his throat. "Everyone, I understand your frustration. I can't speak to the issues with the police or the news crews. I can't even say that it will get better or even worse anytime soon. I just don't know. I will defer that to Mr. Fred to handle." Mr. Ayala turned to Mr. Fred to confirm.

"Yeah, yeah, now get to the good part." Mr. Fred licked his lips and shooed on Mr. Ayala, not addressing or confirming anything.

Mr. Ayala cleared his throat and continued. "Um, okay. Well to answer the first part of your question Mr. Dawson, that's what I'm here to talk to you all about today. The company that I am representing is very interested in purchasing the art pieces. We have reviewed the bylaws and what legally should happen in these types of unique situations. As a result, the company is prepared to offer every family who was in the room at the time of discovery a substantial cash reward offer— in exchange for dropping all claims to the paintings."

"Cash reward?" Dad's eyes widened.

"Substantial? Ohhh I know what that means. Hot damn!" Ms. Gloria shouted from her wheelchair. She hopped so high, I hoped she wouldn't fall to the floor.

"Mom, are you okay?" I looked her up and down. Her face was flushed red.

"I'm fine, honey. I just need to sit down. I did too much today. This man said a cash reward. Water. I need water." She plopped into a chair in the front of the room and Dad began fanning her face and feeding her ice chips.

The room was abuzz with activity and chatter. Shane squeezed my hand under the table and winked.

"Well how much will it be?" Shanice interrupted. She wore a long white one-piece jumpsuit that hugged her body. Whenever she used to walk in the room before, Mr. Dawson ogled her behind.

Today, when it was about money—he disregarded her and ogled Mr. Ayala.

Everyone in the room hushed and turned to Mr. Ayala, waiting for his response that could change their lives.

Mr. Ayala pulled a piece of paper from his pocket, grabbed a pen from his coat's lapels, and wrote something down. He pushed it across the table to Mr. Dawson.

Mr. Dawson coughed and his eyes watered. "And this would be per household for whomever was in the room at the time of the discovery?"

"Yes, that is correct." Mr. Ayala nodded. "We would like to make this process smooth for everyone. You have to understand, this was quite a rare find. The compensation is substantial," Mr. Ayala spoke animatedly. His eyes were soft and excited. He was rooting for us; the underdogs.

Mr. Dawson passed the note around the room until all the adults laid eyes on the number. When I leaned over Mom's shoulder to check it out—my eyes bugged out of my head. It was enough to buy all kinds of exotic plants, expensive shavers, and a new kitchen that Mom always complained about.

"Well, we just can't be won over by money." Mrs. Walker stood. "I don't know if my family and I even want to live here anymore, after what you accused my oldest son of, and then what you put my Marcel through."

"Calm down, honey. We'll talk about it later." Mr. Walker placed his hands on her shoulders and guided his wife back to her seat.

"No, no!" she shouted. "Mr. Fred, you accused my oldest boy of being a thief. I tried to let that go, but I can't. And now you walk up in here all calm and smooth, without your damn cane that you called the police on my son about. Do you know what that does to a teenager? And now you think that some money will make everything better? We would like an apology, at the very least."

"Mom, it's not that serious," Shane grumbled. He shrank down in his chair and crumpled his face in his hands.

"Uhhh, Mrs. Walker. I'm confused here. It *was* your youngest boy, Marcel, who kicked all of this off. Honestly—if it wasn't for him taking it in the first place, we wouldn't have found what was beyond the walls." Mr. Fred stood tall, the tallest I've ever seen him without his cane.

"I'm sorry. I am. But are you saying you don't want the money?" His eyes weren't red, and he wasn't swaying in place. He was sober, alert, and apologetic.

Even he could grow.

Mrs. Walker clamped her mouth shut and was in full momma bear mode. "I'm not worried about the money. I would like an apology to my son—not me" She stared at Mr. Fred. Mr. Walker pulled up a chair next to her and began whispering in her ear and patting her leg.

Mr. Fred eyed Shane up and down, finding the words to put an end to this witch hunt that had put Shane at the center of it all. Technically he was right, all along.

It *was* a Walker boy.

"Shane, I apologize for accusing you of stealing my cane. You and your family moved in right around the time it went missing, and I just assumed. . ." Mr. Fred trailed off.

Mr. Ayala stared between Mrs. Walker and Mr. Fred. "I see this has affected everyone in different ways. Mrs. Walker, your family doesn't have to accept the money if you don't want, and you can petition the courts for ownership of the paintings. It could be a lengthy process. I'm not sure what occurred here, but hopefully it can help ease some of your angst. If you all agree, the process will move pretty quickly. I can have the NDA's and checks ready for signing and printing within the next ten days."

"Ten days?" I could be a millionaire in less than ten days?" Ms. Gloria smiled bigger than I've ever seen her smile.

"Yes, potentially," Mr. Ayala explained. "Depending on what you do come tax time." He winked.

"Why do we have to sign an NDA?" Mr. Walker rubbed Mrs. Walker's back and frowned.

"Well, this matter is quite delicate. For right now, the news is reporting found treasure inside a brownstone complex, but that is all. The New York Police Department and the Department of Housing don't want people ripping into their walls, searching for buried treasure, and potentially getting hurt. A lot of lawsuits could come with that. They would like this matter to be as contained as possible. They don't want anyone discussing exactly where the paintings were found."

So when Mr. Walker called the department of housing to report Mr. Fred, he didn't hear from anyone, but when there was 'treasure' involved, all of a sudden they didn't want a scandal and copycats tearing into their high-rises?

Cash rules everything around me.

"I think we all need some time to think about this," Mr. Fred chimed in. He stood next to Mr. Ayala but kept his focus on us.

"That works for me. Here's my card, and once you guys make a decision, we can get started."

Once she got herself together from the shock of the number, Mom walked to the front of the room with a warm Styrofoam container filled with chicken to make everything better. "Here, Mr. Ayala. This is for you. Thank you." She pushed it toward him and smiled.

thirty-one

. . .

The water can tipped and I let it fall over my plants. *Drink up, time to grow and glow,* I said to myself. They were doing amazing since being moved back to the rooftops and in their new greenhouse. Things had slightly died down and now it was easier to get upstairs and check on them.

Moving around the perimeter, I checked on each of them for gnats, yellow leaves, and molding. Having found none, I sat down pleased and just stared at them and what I grew with my bare hands.

The roof door opened, and Mr. Fred waltzed in. He stopped at some of the plants closest to him, leaned down, closed his eyes, and smelled them.

"You're doing a good job up here," he admitted.

"Thanks." I beamed. That was better than any compliment I could receive.

Mr. Fred stood next to me and cleared his throat. "You know, April. I apologized to Mrs. Walker for accusing Shane, but I also wanted to apologize to you. I made things hard for you here." He sat down in the lounge chair beside me and rested his head on the back of the chair. "I thought I was important with my cane, and when someone took it, it just rattled me. Then when I saw you on the news at your competition, you looked so confident. So smart. I had never seen you look like that. Not that you're not confident and smart, but it was different. These plants really bring out a different side of you." He nodded and looked at me like he was really seeing me for the first time. "I felt like you were talking shit— I'm sorry. Talking junk." He placed a hand to his mouth. "Talking junk on me and on the brownstone. I don't know why my mind went there, but it just did. When you get to be my age, you don't know what to believe and if you still see things as they always were. I talked to Ms. Gloria that day, and she called me a crazy old man who needed a life." He chuckled.

I snorted; Ms. Gloria was so crazy.

"I had big dreams too. Mine wasn't plants, but I wanted to make rugs. Beautiful, hand-crafted rugs. I learned how to tuft them when I was stationed in the service in Marrakech. My cane reminded me of those places and when it was taken, it was like my memories were taken."

"But they weren't," I interjected.

"I know that now. I see that. I was being a bully. Plain and simple. You know, my daddy gave me the cane on his death bed. I was always a little guy, as you can see." He extended his arms and swept his body up and down. "He told me to walk strong; even though I was a little guy. So I did. I walked tall with my cane. But I realized through this whole ordeal, I can walk strong without it. I was too dependent on it. What a crazy thought, huh?" He laughed deep from his belly, his shoulders shook. "You and your family have lived here a long time, and we've known each other for even longer. You didn't deserve that, and for that, I apologize."

Tears welled in my eyes, and I tried to stop them from falling. "Thank you. Thank you, Mr. Fred," I said through sniffles. "What are you going to do with your share of the money?"

"I wasn't sure at first. I wanted to make sure everyone else was taken care of. You know, I have to redeem myself, after starting all this mess. But now that everyone has accepted the offer, I think it's high time I go and make me some custom-made rugs. With custom patches, of course." He gave a toothless smile. Pride washed over his face like it did only for a man with a master plan. Putting his own happiness first.

I grinned and, in that moment, the sun shifted and shined right on Mr. Fred. He looked young and healthy against the rays. The lack of drinking booze was doing wonders for his skin. It seemed when the police disappeared and left our home, so did Mr. Fred's drinking.

"That's great!" I exclaimed.

"You know, you have a lot of courage, girl. It'll take you far in life. Keep it up." Mr. Fred smiled. He lifted himself from his chair and strolled back to the rooftop door.

He walked strong. Without a cane.

thirty-two

. . .

I vy and I lugged Mom's big cart filled with Styrofoam meals down the lit-up hallways. It was funny, the hallways were dim, and that was one of the things people complained about during our Town House meeting. Now that there was money and important people roaming the halls, they were lit up with the brightest lights that made my eyes squint and wince.

Ivy wore a black ball cap backwards, an oversized men's flannel shirt and extra-large jeans shorts that hung down past her knees. There was something different about her I couldn't quite place yet.

"So, what's up with you and ol' girl?" I rearranged the platters cart so they wouldn't tip over as we hoisted them up the steps.

Ivy smiled and turned her face away. "Oh, you know. A little of this and that."

A little of this and that, I mocked.

Ivy giggled.

"You never did say who put that passion mark on your neck. AND you were spotted at the store with someone. What's going on? Since when did we start keeping secrets?"

Ivy sighed and helped me lift the back end of the cart. "It's not a secret. I just . . . I don't always understand how I feel. You know? Sometimes I feel like I really am trapped, and no one understands me, so I have to hide certain parts of myself. Other times I want to let my freak flag fly."

"Freak is the right word. Remind me to never drink after you." I nudged her as we walked toward Jorge's apartment.

"Drink after me? The way you and Shane be slobbing each other down these days? I know you ain't talking!" Ivy put her hand on her hip, and we laughed.

Before I could knock on the door, Journey swung it open. "It's about time, you heifers showed up, we're starving. Come on in." He waved us through.

Journey's presence surprised me and I frowned. Jorge was in the living room stacking boxes. There were so many I bumped into them trying to pull the cart through the hallway.

"What's all this?" I looked around.

"Me and Jorge are going to live our dream. We're going to make clothes." Journey jumped up and down.

"Make clothes?" I said, and pulled their food out of the cart and sat it on the table.

"Yes ma'am!" Jorge placed his hand to his chest and his eyes softened. "Working in a plant—some factory— is not for me. I want to make designs. Fashions for people to wear. For people like us." Jorge nodded at Journey, and then he turned and nodded at Ivy. "I know a blessing when I see one. Those paintings and that money they gave us is nothing short of a blessing. And me and my love have decided to stay together and dream in color. We won't let the man, or anyone else tear us apart." Jorge took Journey's hand and held it while they exchanged lovey dovey eyes.

Ivy stared at Journey and Jorge, their feelings on display and in color, while hers were muted and stuck in a sunken gray area. "That's beautiful." She nodded, and I saw tears in her eyes. "What are you guys going to call the clothing line?"

Jorge and Journey cut their eyes at each other. Journey cleared his throat and said, "My birth name is Michael David Humbert. But my life, and our love has been a journey. It's taken us awhile to get here, to this place. No, money doesn't make someone happy, but it can damn sure start. It can even level the playing field a little." He held Jorge's hand, and together in their matching teal tracksuits and man flops, Journey said, "We're going to name it after me. Journey Love. Because our love has been a journey."

Jorge winked at me and our conversation days earlier replayed in my head. He almost lost Journey because of Journey's dad, and his fear about what people would think of him and their relationship. Money didn't help the situation, and they still had mountains to climb. When you worked all the time doing what you hated, dreaming became obsolete.

Ivy plopped down onto their couch and put her head in her hands. Jorge knelt down in front of her and spoke softly. "Ivy, your mom will still love you. Give her a chance. You can be whoever you want to be. Do you know who that is? Don't wait too long like I did; suffering between who they wanted me to be, and who I really was. Don't waste your life." He looked up into her eyes and studied her face.

A single tear dropped from Ivy's face. The room was quiet as Jorge comforted her. Journey gave me a half smile and pulled me in for a one-armed hug. "Help her help herself. Help her grow," he whispered to me, and I wondered how many times he had to repeat that to himself before he believed it.

Clearing my throat, I knelt down on the other side of Ivy, and I knew exactly what to say. It was the same exact words Ivy had uttered to me after the Chase debacle when I was considering switching schools. "Ivy..." I started. "Do you want to do in five years what you are doing now? If you were talking to your former self, what would you teach her about herself? About who she is?"

Ivy placed one hand on top of mine and the other on top of

Jorge's. Journey leaned on the wall and a lone tear found its way down his cheek too. Ivy said, "I would say, your name is Ianesha Lane. Not Ivy. That was your safe name. Your name is Ianesha. You are a Queer woman. And that's okay."

I hugged Ianesha's neck. She was so brave, and I was proud to be her best friend. We would dream in color.

"Do you think friends can fall in love?" Ivy pulled away from me with misty eyes. "Not like, romantic love, but like best-friend love?"

I held onto Ianesha's hand and squeezed. "Girl, you became my soulmate the moment I saw you swing on Chase in school."

We chuckled together at the memory and wiped our faces. We had finally, finally hit a moment in time where we could look back at the situation and laugh. And that meant progress, and progress was good. A few minutes and tears later, Ivy and I made our way to Shane's apartment. I knocked on the door, dying to see Shane and he flung it open. His face was contorted and eyes ablaze with sadness.

"What's wrong?"

"We're moving." He gave a blank stare.

"Oh shit," Ivy muttered with widened eyes.

"Oh shit, is right," Shane uttered.

My words were caught in my throat. Nothing would come out, and even if it did, I didn't know what to say for the moment. I just found him—and I was losing him already. How was this fair?

"Why?" I managed through clenched teeth. My hand clutched the food cart behind me but I wanted to toss it to the side.

Shane shrugged. "My mom says she doesn't like the way our family has been treated here. She asked my dad to put in for a transfer, and that fast—it was approved and my dad was reassigned to their southeast division. We're moving to Florida in two weeks."

"Two weeks?!" I shrieked. "That's the week of school! But your dad wanted you guys to live in Harlem!" The walls in the hallway closed in on me, and I panted and leaned up against his door frame.

"I know. I know. Come inside." He waved his hands.

"We have your uhh . . . food." Ivy managed a weak smile. She searched through the mountains of Styrofoam containers while I plopped down at Shane's dining room table, stunned and unable to work.

Shane kneeled down before me. "April, we'll be okay. We'll just have to figure it out." He rubbed my back.

"How will we figure it out? You'll be clear across the country, and I'll be here. You won't have time for me in your big Florida adventure." Every bone in my body was tense, and a pain already pulsated through my shoulders.

Shane was quiet. My Harlem renaissance—by way of Connecticut—now turned Florida love who always had the words for every moment didn't know what to say. And that made it even worse.

"Where are your parents?" I sniffled.

Shane rose to his feet, pulled up a chair and sat next to me.

"They had to run some errands. It all happened so quickly. The day of the Town House meeting, Dad put in a transfer request. Honestly, I didn't think it would be this far away and his last transfer request didn't happen this quickly. I was thinking maybe somewhere along the East Coast. But I guess the NBA can put you anywhere a recruiter is needed."

"So, you knew?" I glared.

Ivy was quiet as she sat forks and spoons wrapped in napkins on the table. She sat them down gently so she didn't make any noise.

Shane was silent again. He leaned back in the chair and shut his eyes. When he opened them he said, "Yes. I knew that day at the meeting. I overheard them talking beforehand about not feeling safe and there being too much action in the brownstone now with the paintings, and the police, and everything. Mom said with the reward money, at least we could relocate somewhere her Black sons weren't accused of theft. I didn't know how to tell you, but I knew I had to tell you today."

"But he *did* take it!" I banged my hand on the table. Ivy and Shane jumped at my outburst. "This is all Marcel's fault," I grumbled. "If he hadn't of taken that dumb cane, you wouldn't be leaving me. Leaving us." My hands were shaking and clammy. I clasped them together.

"I agree! It is Marcel's fault. I'm pissed off at him too. Do you think I want to leave? I want to stay in Harlem too. I want to start boxing here. I want us." His voice rose.

"Don't yell at me!" I shouted.

"I'm not yelling at you!" he shouted back. He grabbed my hands to settle them from shaking and I noticed his were shaking too. We stared into each other's eyes, the same way we did the past three months. There was already a far away, not gone, but not mine to keep—look. How many more times would I have to look at him like this?

The tears came instantly. "This is happening so fast, Shane. It's just not fair." I sobbed. I couldn't see him through my tears, and they fell onto the table right onto the Styrofoam platter.

"Hey uh, guys, I'm gonna head out. April, I'll deliver the rest of these platters and drop what's left to your mom."

"Okay," I grumbled. The door quietly shut as she left, and I didn't look back.

Fuck them platters. My man was leaving.

"We'll figure this out. Just give me some time to think about it, okay? I don't know how we'll do this, but we aren't over. We just aren't." Shane grabbed my arms and held them as he stared into my eyes. "April, I love you. And I don't care where I am, that love won't change."

"I love you too," I whimpered. And even though I meant it, I knew better. This was one of those times when love wasn't enough.

thirty-three

· · ·

The ceiling stared back at me. I tossed and turned the entire night, replaying me and Shane's conversation. Maybe if I talked to his mom . . . maybe if I got my mom to talk to his mom . . . I grabbed my notebook by the side of my bed and wrote down all the possible scenarios so Shane and I could continue our relationship, but nothing seemed to make sense. We both had just turned seventeen and there was no way we would make a New York-Florida long distance love work.

I slammed my notebook back onto the table and balled myself into my blankets. Life could be so cruel. I wanted me and Shane to go to school together. I wanted to see him in the boxing ring. I wanted people to see us together. I wanted Chase's face to meet Shane's fist. I wanted our love to have a chance to grow roots. To develop into something that lasted.

"April, honey?" Mom knocked.

Before I said come in, she opened my door. "April, it's almost noon. Let's open these curtains up and get some sunlight in here," she said softly.

"I don't want to open the curtains and I don't want to get out of bed." Pulling the covers over my head, I hid myself from her. From the world. From real life.

She sat on the side of my bed and patted me. "I remember my first love."

"Moooomm, I don't want to hear about you and Dad, that's disgusting." I moaned and turned over on my side.

"I was a whole woman before I married your dad, and me and these hips lived a good life, thank you very much." She cocked an eye at me. "His name was Ray, and he was foine."

My pillow was already stained with my tears, so I flipped it over to the cool side and turned over to listen to Mom, annoyed. "And what happened?"

"He taught me so much. We went to school together too. Actually, it's not that far off from you and Shane. We lived in the same neighborhood after he moved in with his dad. We hung out as friends, but we were both dating someone else. When the summertime hit, we started spending a lot of time together and fell in love. It was the summer of love, that year." Mom got a faraway look on her face as she remembered her own memories. Years may have passed but you never forgot how something made you feel.

I sat up in my bed, tucked my knees under my chest, and listened.

"You see. I thought I was an ugly girl at that time. I was thick and back then thick wasn't the thing to be; not like it is today. They used to call me Caren the whale, and I used to beat their asses. I got in trouble a lot." She chuckled.

"He was the first person who really paid attention to me. To me." She pointed at herself.

"He made me feel like I was someone. He told me over and over how beautiful I was, and how my beauty was internal *and* external. We even got into a fight together once." She laughed. "Some lowjack tried to trip me when I was walking home from school. I wasn't no punk though, so I pushed him, and he pushed me back!" Mom recounted. "I was nervous in that moment because I knew I was a big girl and could hold my own, but can't no girl beat up on no man. So, I thought once I pushed him back he was gonna whip my tail. But don't you know, Ray came around that corner swinging. And together, we beat the brakes off that lowjack." Mom laughed, and her stomach shook.

"Lowjack, Mom?" I stifled a giggle.

"Shut up, girl! Anyway, after that, I brought him back to the house, and I cooked him some turkey legs and rice. He finished that meal and asked me where Mama was because if I cooked like that—then he was going to ask her for my hand in marriage, right then and there."

"So what happened?" I sat up in the bed.

"He moved away." Her eyes drifted off. "One night, he knocked on my door. It was late too; Mama was watching *Unsolved Mysteries*. His dad was parked in our driveway with the car running. I knew that wasn't a good sign. He said, '*give me your address?*' I said, '*for what?*' He said, '*my mom got custody of me and my brother. We're moving back home.*' My entire world crumbled, in that moment. In the blink of an eye, my life was over. Or so I thought. We kept in touch here and there. We did what we could, but we were young. Eventually I met your dad, and we fell in love. But I don't think I would have been able to appreciate your dad and the man that he's been to me, had I not experienced love from Ray. Sometimes people come into our lives to teach us things, to show us something we need to learn about ourselves, and then they leave. I see the change in you. How you've come alive these past few months. I think Shane had something to do with that, but remember Little Caren, it's still all you."

Angry tears. Worried tears. Sad tears. They made my eyes puffy. I didn't know my mom loved anyone before Dad. Or that someone else had experienced her cooking and empowered her in a way that helped her make it a strength. Her strength was cooking, but so was I, and so was Dad. When you love, *really* love, it doesn't make you weak—it makes you strong.

My love for Shane made me strong.

"If you need to dock your boat for a little while, honey, you do that. You dock your boat. But don't stay docked. Not when you finally realized the beauty that comes with stepping away from the shore and swimming on your own."

"Thanks, Mom." I wiped my face and pulled myself out from under my blankets.

The room was still dark from the closed shades. Mom patted my leg and said, "Anytime, honey. Now you get yourself out of this bed and go spend the last few moments you have with Shane." She had tears in her eyes.

The front door opened and shut. I heard Dad's keys and noisy steps making his way toward us. When he stepped into the dark room, he found me and Mom, both with tears in our eyes. He stood in the doorway and shot half concern- half smirks between us.

"What's this? The heartbreak hotel?"

A few hours later, I pulled the covers over my head as Nas blasted from Gage's room. I banged on the wall. "Turn it down, Gage!" When the music got louder, I flung the blankets off and stomped across my room to Gage's room.

With my plants back on the roof, Dad and Gage were in his room setting up a crib. Pampers, bottles, a car seat, and pink clothes were all over the place.

"Gage is officially moving back in. This is his home and it'll be his home until he gets on his feet," Dad said it so matter-fact as he swept up marijuana seeds off the floor. He clenched his jaw, closed his eyes, and pretended not to see them.

Gage saw them and stood in front of Dad.

"Dad," he said. "I'll smoke on the terrace from now on. My bad."

Dad took a deep breath and whatever was sitting on his tongue, ready to be said to his Gage, he held back. "Thanks, son."

"Yes, son. Thank you." Mom appeared next to me in the doorway, rubbing my back. She nodded at Gage and handed him a glass of iced tea.

"Oh, I don't get no iced tea. Just Gage?" Dad huffed. He dabbed at his forehead with the famous rag all men his age carried to wipe their sweat.

"Yeah, none for me either?" I joked.

"Well, if you would come out of your room you can have all the iced tea you want." Mom wagged her finger, walked into the room, and opened Gage's curtain. "Gage," she said. "I know you like it dark in here too, but a baby needs light. My baby girl needs light," she instructed.

"I got you, Mom." He smiled. He smiled like there was nothing stopping him from wanting to laugh and joke with his parents. He smiled like people did when they were starting over. And we were starting over. This time honest and hopeful.

"Back under the same roof again, huh, big brother?" I smirked.

"Kiss my whole ass!" Gage pinched my shoulder and playfully shoved me.

"Y'all and this language! Can't y'all let the good Lord use you for something good? My gracious!" Mom fumed.

"He started it." I fixed my hair he mushed out of place.

"So, Gage, me and your dad are going to watch Milani overnights while you work at the club."

"Mom, you don't have to do that. I still have Milani's grandmother I can use."

Mom paused, mulling over his words. "Maybe so, but I ain't fully met the woman so I don't know if I trust her just yet. Besides, I gotta make sure Milani ain't fussing and cussing like you kids. And she gotta learn to at least stir a spoon and stuff some deviled eggs by four years old."

"Deviled eggs, Mom?" I asked incredulously.

"Honey, I'm going to get you some iced tea." Mom breezed out of the room, not answering my question, or turning around as we laughed at her. She hesitated in the doorway.

"And Gage. We're glad to have you back. I love you, son."

"I love you too, Mom." His lips curled into a silly grin.

thirty-four

. . .

I pulled my bedroom door open just a crack. Shanice and my mom were in the living room talking in hushed and excited voices.

Grabbing my housecoat and slippers, I fumbled my way into them. It was the only thing I had to wear today, and I didn't care. My hair hadn't been washed in a few days and my edges were curling up from the late August heat. My dirty clothes were stacked in the corner of my closet and my room looked ransacked. When I looked around, it resembled exactly how I felt. Disheveled. All over the place.

"What are you guys in here talking about?" I plopped down on the loveseat across from them. My housecoat was warm, but I wrapped it around my waist tighter.

"Well hello, Ms. April. Finally, out of bed this morning, are we?" Mom cut her eyes at me. "I thought I was going to have to go in there and snatch you out of bed." She tossed some papers on the coffee table.

"The Shane thing?" Shanice mouthed to Mom as if I wasn't sitting right there.

Mom nodded. "My baby is in the throes of young love." She nodded and looked at me with longing eyes.

"Mommmm." I groaned. "Stop telling my business."

"I'm not telling your business; I was only telling Shanice how upset you were about Shane. But alright, alright." She waved her hands. "I hope you showered today, don't be sitting on my couch growing potatoes out of your ears."

"What are you guys doing?" I looked down at the mountain of paperwork sitting on the table, ignoring her last comment.

Mom and Shanice grinned at each other. "We got a vendor's permit. Me and Shanice are going to open a food truck. Your dad said since we now have money from the paintings that we should invest in something. And I was thinking about what you and Ivy said. A business. For us. Doing what we do best." Mom smiled at Shanice and searched my eyes, waiting for my response.

Mom had been cooking her whole life, and this was how she showed her love for people. The brownstone knew that every other Friday Mom had a fierce menu, and she would come through with something delicious. Shanice was an added bonus, and when I looked at her also waiting for my response. She looked hopeful.

They were women who were unsure of themselves and needed approval. I guess we all did in some ways. They knew they were good at something, and it could take them far, but they still needed a reaction from people closest to them.

"That's great you guys!" I exclaimed in a pitch and tone too high for my liking. I wanted to be sad about Shane, but I was so excited for them. "This makes perfect sense. Ivy was on to something." Shuffling my feet around, I swallowed and felt guilty. I meant every word I said. I knew they would make it. People loved them and their food, so together they would be unstoppable. But Shane had been that for me. He had been *my* approval, *my* partner. Mom and Shanice were combining forces and using their talents to create something that really had steam. But what did I have? I had my plants, but without Shane there, it didn't seem so important.

Shanice pulled me out of my thoughts. "You really think so?" she questioned. She was wearing a white t-shirt with no bra and navy-blue tights. Her hair was pulled back under a bucket hat, and her lashes were done with each of them accentuating her smooth cocoa skin and cheekbones. Sitting down, I could see her hips spreading into the seat. Even dressed down— Shanice was something to look at.

I tugged at my ratty old housecoat and felt the overwhelming urge to run to the shower and shave. "Yes, Shanice. You guys are made for something like this. The news crews are still posted up outside. You could make a killing just selling to them." I softened my eyes. "There's just one problem."

Mom squinted at me, and Shanice grabbed a notebook and pen off the table and clicked the top, ready to take notes. She leaned in forward waiting and anticipating me exposing a kink in their plans.

"Does this mean I'm out of a job?"

Mom and Shanice giggled, and soon, so did I. The three of us sat chuckling for a few moments. When I looked at them, I saw their excitement, their nervousness, their anxiousness. No, they didn't race to the bathroom and check for hair obsessively like I used to, but they had their own fears and insecurities. And they charged forward.

And so would I.

"Of course not, girl. I was hoping you would help us take orders and work the register. You know you young kids are good at stuff like that. Can you believe it, April? Us–a register. A business!" Her and Shanice shared another excited laugh.

"One more thing," Mom said. "We're having a small going away party for the Walker's in three days. Catered by us, of course." She smiled at Shanice. "I think it'll be a nice way to end the summer, and what a crazy one it was. By the way, you have some mail on the counter I think you've been waiting for, and some other mail that looks quite interesting." She wiggled her eyebrows around in a playful manner. "Go check it out. Oh, and go upstairs and see Shane. He came by here asking about you, but I told him you weren't up to it."

Shuffling back to my room, I tossed dirty and clean clothes all over the place until I found something semi-presentable. I grabbed a long black cotton jumpsuit. It was hot as hell and maybe black wasn't the best choice, but it was the only thing I had that was clean and besides—I *was* in mourning.

I grabbed the mail off the counter and tore it open. My stomach did flops as I read it. I grabbed my keys and took the steps two at a time up to Shane's apartment. After knocking, I waited nervously.

He opened the door and his low-cut waves, crisp white tee, and dazzling smile made me want to collapse into his arms and beg him not to leave. Instead, I closed the space between us and dove in for a kiss right on his lips.

"Hey you." He held me and closed the door behind him. His smile never left his face, and if our brownstone could talk, it would speak of fireworks from my home to his, from my heart to his.

"Hey, Mrs. Walker." I waved. She was in the living room putting items into boxes. I checked out her peace lily on the patio terrace behind her. It was healthy and thriving, even in just a few short months.

"Hey, April." She rolled a long piece of tape over a cardboard box and wrote on it with a permanent marker. "You keep your lips off my son now, okay. I'm too young to be a grandma."

I giggled and Shane's face turned red. "Ma, do you mind if we go in my room?"

"Sure, just keep that door cracked." She cut an eye at us.

"What's that about?" I sunk down onto Shane's bed.

He shrugged. "She knows if she wasn't here, I'd jump your bones. Especially you in all that black." He eyed me up and down.

I swatted Shane's arm and blushed. "Is that right?"

Shane sighed and stood with his hands on his hips. "I'm going to miss this."

I cleared my throat and prayed that tears wouldn't fall. "Miss what?"

"Joking. Laughing. Walking to the bodega."

Swallowing away the lump in my throat, I said quietly, "Me too."

"Don't go missing on me again, okay?"

"It was just a day or so."

Shane stopped to count his fingers. "Three days to be exact. But don't go missing on me. Let's make the time that we have left count."

Shane was right. After he told me he was leaving, I holed up in my room and let my thoughts get the best of me. "That's a deal." I promised. "I'm sorry. I just. . . this is hard for me, you know."

He nodded. "It's hard for me too. I keep thinking about how things would be different if Marcel hadn't done what he did. It makes me so mad when I think about it. But at the same time, everyone seems so much happier with the money."

Shane stared at me and grabbed my hand. "I want to see you every available moment. When I went to your apartment earlier your mom said you weren't up for company. I was going to go to the roof, scale down the wall, sneak into your bedroom window, and say, *what gives, woman! You breaking up with me?!*"

Shane and I burst out laughing, and it felt good to see him laugh. It felt good for me to laugh. It felt like us. No drama, just love.

"I have some news." I whipped out the mail from behind my back. "I got my school schedule." I pushed it toward him.

He got up from his bed, rummaged around on his desk and pulled out the same envelope.

"I got mine too."

We examined our schedules and sure enough if Shane was staying in New York, we would have had three classes together and the same lunch. Tears welled in my eyes. "We didn't even get a chance to be great." I hung my head.

"You're right." He frowned. "But we are still great. You and me. Us. This." He pointed a finger between us. "This is great. No matter what happens."

"I have more news." I pulled the second letter from behind my back, and I gave a sheepish smile. "The NY Home and Garden Show wants to do a special segment on my win. They want to come to the house and check out my rooftop."

Shane's face broke into a huge grin. He jumped up, swept me off my feet, and hugged me so tight I couldn't breathe.

"That's great, April! See I told you. People see the greatness in you. You have to see it. You have to believe it. I've always seen it. I see you." He locked eyes with me.

"I see you too." I reached up and ran my hand across his scarred forehead.

"We need to celebrate. How about a trip to the bodega?" He grinned.

"Ice cream cone and a Yoo-hoo?"

"Sounds like a date!" He wrapped his arms around me from behind and I closed my eyes and enjoyed the moment.

thirty-five

. . .

"What do you want me to do with them all?" I stared at her.

Ms. Gloria scrunched her face. "What do you mean, girl? They're plants. I want to pay you to take care of them."

"But why?"

"My heart isn't in it. This is your thing, anyway." Ms. Gloria sat in her favorite corner in her favorite chair, and she wore a fanny pack around her waist and compression socks all the way up to her shins.

She smirked. "Besides," she said. "I took your advice. I went down to the rec center, and I joined one of those groups for old people. I been whipping their tails in BINGO. It's not bad."

A smile crept its way to my face. "I said that?" I pointed to myself.

"Oh, shut up, girl." Ms. Gloria rolled her eyes and swatted me away.

Her plant babies were strewn out on the living room floor. There were only five total, and by the looks of them, they needed a lot of love. "What happened? I come here every week to water and sing to them. Have you been checking on them?" Sitting cross legged on the floor in front of Ms. Gloria, I examined some of the yellow leaves and the dry soil. I felt the plant leaves and closed my eyes. *This one needs water . . .* I felt another one . . . *This one needs more sunlight.*

Ms. Gloria said, "I ain't been doing much of nothing, girl. I told you that. The way these puny legs been acting up and my sugar been all up and down, I just don't have the time for it anymore." Ms. Gloria pointed to her swollen cankles. "Besides, you know you always took care of them for me. You ain't been coming that much since you been seeing that boy."

"What boy?" I said with a hint of coyness. I avoided her eyes and forced back a smile.

"Oh, don't play with me, girl, you know what boy." She kicked her foot, and it tapped me in my side.

With a little giggle and lots of sass I said, "Ms. Gloria, I'm not seeing anyone, who are you seeing?"

Her eyes shot open, and mouth contorted. "Seeing? Girl, have you seen these legs? I'm seeing the doctor!"

Ms. Gloria and I fell out laughing. Her fat legs bobbed up and down in the chair as she cackled. Wiping funny tears from my eyes, I turned to Ms. Gloria and cleared my throat.

"They're leaving. For good."

She looked at me with warm eyes. "I know. His mom told me in Town House. I'm so sorry, April."

Tired of crying was an understatement, but still, the tears flowed like it was the first time I heard the news. Each time I thought about it, I couldn't believe it was really happening.

"Now tell me about this Chase."

"How did you know?" I grabbed one of Ms. Gloria's legs and held on tight.

"I heard what Keri said. I been itching to get you alone to ask about him, but it was never the right time."

I quietly sobbed. "Chase . . ." The words were caught in my throat. I swallowed and fought back the urge to change the subject. This was a summer that changed everyone, but for me it started months ago with Chase. When you're faced with choices, who do you show up as? Maybe in the face of fear and uncertainty, a newer, wiser you is born. Everyone is just trying to be better than they were yesterday, but did that mean your yester-years didn't count and you had to make the most of every moment now?

Some days you stand in the sunshine. Some days you create your own sunshine. If I wanted to get over it, I had to get through it.

Taking a deep breath, I told Ms. Gloria my Chase story. I told her the entire, gory, ugly, hairy details. Embarrassment washed across my body, and I rubbed away fine, barely there hairs on my forearms.

Ms. Gloria cocked her head and listened to every word. She popped three Tums as she shook her head and grunted when I said wolf-pussy.

When I was finished, a lightness found its way to me that said the storm was almost over. There wasn't a rainbow in sight, but the clouds were clearing. My hardest moment could also be my bridge to peace. They could both be true at the same time.

Gazing up at Ms. Gloria, I waited for her reaction.

"Come here." Her pointer finger motioned to me.

I scooted closer to Ms. Gloria and my ears piqued. It was so quiet except for her ratty, old, air conditioner.

"Let me tell you one thing, Little Caren. All I hear is what I see. Ain't nothing hairy, ugly, or funny about you. That's not the girl I know and hell, even if it was, that boy ain't got no right talking about you like that. I got half a mind to give Ivy some money and tell her to finish beating his ass. He earned that one, fair and square. You know what you need to do? Get yourself some therapy."

"Therapy? I'm not that crazy, Ms. Gloria."

"Oh, girl, hush. You don't need to be crazy to get therapy. I did it myself when my husband passed away and it worked. I fell in love with that lady therapist. I tried to give her some rice and beans when we finished because I was so appreciative."

"Rice and beans?" I giggled. "Where do I go for therapy? How do I find one?"

"This is where you get on that Spaceport and find yourself one. The Spaceport got everything!" Ms. Gloria rubbed my back as I rested my chin against her knees.

"Seriously, though. April, you can't keep holding onto this. It's too heavy for anyone to keep. This ain't yours to keep anyway. You are none of those things. And when you start to think you are, you have to say to yourself, "it ain't true!" Just like some people say, I'm a mean old cat lady. I say to myself, Gloria, it ain't true. You ain't even got no cats!"

Ms. Gloria and I cracked up until my cheeks hurt.

"Now what's going on with Shane?"

"It's just not fair, Ms. Gloria. I just . . . we just . . . There's just so much more for us to explore about each other," I grumbled. Through Shane, I became a different person. I liked to think that he became a different person through me too. It was like I was ice and when he came along, I was just existing in some gray area. He helped me unthaw and brought color back to my life.

"This is the cruel side of life, my girl." Ms. Gloria rubbed my back as I rested my head on her leg. "Sometimes when we find love, real, deep love. It's for just a fleeting moment. And we wonder, why can't I have that? Why can't I keep it? The truth is no one keeps it. They grow it. You already know that, my girl. I got to see a different side of you that I haven't seen in a long time. He brought you back to *you*. And even though he is leaving, it's now your responsibility to create your own path and be the person Shane helped bring out. He didn't change you. You changed you. His love just showed you what was already in you—waiting to be freed."

Ms. Gloria lifted my chin, and I looked up at her with tears in my eyes. "You know, I'm seventy something years old. My husband died almost thirty years ago. He was like your Shane. Always challenging me and pushing me to be better. And when he passed away, I thought, *who is going to love me like that? Who is going to be there for me?* I remember one time, we were having some of his work buddies over for dinner. I was rushing around, setting the table, cooking, and sweating. His colleague's husband leaned over to my Milton, nudged him and said, *'so in your house, who eats first? The man or the kids?'* He said it so playfully that I didn't think nothing of it and just kept moseying around in the kitchen. My Milton leaned back and said, *'Doesn't matter. No one eats until my wife sits down.'* And I just melted. That's the type of man he was."

She looked off out the window and clasped her hands together. "Now that you've seen what love is. You will find it again. Look at me. I loved my Milton something fierce. But I know I will love again. And when I do, I will be a better woman because of it. Because of my Milton. When I get these here legs fixed right, and my sugar under control, I'm going to find me somebody and imma be the best woman to them because I know what an easy love looks like. Feels like. April, you will love again and when you do, you will have *this* to compare it to. You will know what's it's like to be loved, easy. Love ain't gotta be hard, my girl. When it's right. It's easy." She grabbed both of my hands and put them to my chest. "I pray that you find an easy love. But before you do that. You give *yourself* an easy love. Let it be spoken. Let it be written. Let it be done."

Ms. Gloria's cell phone rang, interrupting her words. Keri was downstairs waiting to be buzzed up to come and do her hair. That was also the newest thing, all tenants and visitors had to be buzzed in and out. When Ms. Gloria let her up, Keri walked into the room and surveyed the scene. Plants everywhere and me with red eyes.

"Did I walk in on something?" She frowned and started setting up her hair dryer on Ms. Gloria's kitchen table.

"No, baby. I was just telling April all about love." Ms. Gloria patted my head and chuckled. "Now help me get up from this here chair so I can go sit in that chair and let Ms. Keri do my hair so I can find me a man."

I took Ms. Gloria by the arm and led her to the chair where Keri was setting up her hair station. When she plopped down, she said, "Keri. You're a pretty girl too. What do you know about love?"

I cringed, waiting for Keri's remarks.

Keri shot Ms. Gloria a glance out of the corner of her eye and moved slower while setting up her stuff. "I don't know. Whenever I thought I was in love, it ended up being some crummy guy. You never know when they're serious anyway."

My mouth flew open in surprise. Had Keri had a shitty experience with a boy too? Was it not just me?

Ms. Gloria spoke before I could get my thoughts together. She smiled and nodded at me.

"April, here did. She got a boy real serious about her. Real bad. Tell her, April. Tell her how you know when they're serious." She closed her eyes, wrapped a towel around her neck, and prepared to get her hair washed.

I took a deep breath and leaned on the wall behind me. Keri wasn't my enemy. She was a girl questioning the world just like I was. When I knew love, I saw Keri differently. I saw the world differently. I cleared my throat. "It's easy. That's how you know it's real. The love isn't hard, it's just easy."

When I walked back into our apartment a few minutes later, Milani was crying.

"Here, hold her, I have to use the bathroom." Mom laid Milani in my arms. She shuffled to the bathroom and closed the door behind her.

I looked down at Milani with her smiling face and smooth brown baby skin. She smelled heavenly. I rocked her back and forth. "I know you can understand me somewhere in there," I whispered to Milani and nuzzled her little face. "I want to tell you the story of when you were born." She stared into my eyes like she knew I was talking directly to her. "Our family was cold and just existing We thrived in the shade and kept things low-key. We moved around in the world because we had to—but we really weren't growing. Then you came along, and you brought sunshine to our darkness. Water when we were thirsty, and love. All we needed to grow was love, and that love was in part, you. Thank you of saving our family and helping put us back together, just by being born. We needed you and we didn't even know it." I cradled her and rubbed her back. Milani cooed and farted in my arms until my wrist vibrated.

"Eeeww." I turned my nose. "Moommmm! Come get her!"

thirty-six

. . .

Mom and Shanice were dressed in matching chef outfits complete with top hats and nametags. They wore white tights and long white flowing t-shirts that drowned past their knees. They had them spray-painted on the front and it said *A Taste of Love*. That was what they decided to name their catering business.

The food lined the rooftop, and all around the perimeter I smelled some of their best work. Shanice brought in her Jamaican side and set up jerk, stewed, and curry chicken with plantains and rice. Mom made all the sides: seafood salad, potato salad, fresh cucumber and tomato salad, rice, and fried chicken wings.

The spread smelled heavenly.

I held the storm door as people moseyed in and out. Mr. Fred used some of his reward money and finally got the elevator fixed.

"Hi. Hello." I nodded my head to everyone walking in as the elevator dinged behind them. I was wearing a blue jean skirt and white crop top. It was my first time ever wearing a crop top. I always thought I was too round for outfits like these and hated the way my arm meat jiggled, but when Ivy and I picked out our outfits for the day, she was determined to put me in something that showed some skin. I was one full week in without shaving, and I couldn't wait to tell Shane as I watched him and his family make their way down the hallways to the rooftop. The party was being thrown in their honor, and I wanted everything to be perfect.

When I glanced myself over in the mirror, I dabbed some perfume just behind my ears and on my wrists, just like Mom taught me. I felt good. I looked good.

"You go on and see your guests, I'll hold this door." Dad shooed me away.

"My guests?" I crinkled my face.

"Kyle! You always running your mouth! Just hold that door and hush!" Mom shouted.

She was zipping back and forth carrying all kinds of trays. Sweat was forming at her brow, but she glowed like she was in her element, doing what came naturally— serving her people.

"What's he talking about, Mom?" I plopped down into one of the lounge chairs.

"Girl, I don't know. You know that man ain't right in the head. Come help me finish setting this table."

I checked my phone, wondering when Shane and his family would make their appearance. The party was being thrown in their honor, and I hoped they wouldn't be late.

When I paddled to the table where two cakes were set up, I glanced down at them. One cake read, *Good Luck Walker Family*, the other cake read: *Congratulations, April*.

"What the . . ." I spun around. Mom, Dad, Ms. Gloria, Mr. Fred, Shanice, Jorge, Journey Love, Shane, his parents, Marcel, and dozens of other tenants were grinning ear to ear. "What's all this?" I searched their faces.

"Did you think we would let the opportunity go by without celebrating your big win? Not a chance, beautiful girl. We wanted to celebrate earlier but there was so many reporters and cops crawling the building, it just didn't feel like the right time." Mom grinned.

"Even though the Walkers were not here for long, we will remember them, and they'll always be honorary members of the brownstone. Always family." Mom took Mrs. Walker's hands and held them. They looked into each other's eyes and shared a moment, Black mama to Black mama. Dad shook Mr. Walker's hand and rubbed Marcel's head.

"And of course. We want to celebrate you." Shane stepped forward.

"You knew?" I shrieked and jumped at Shane.

Ms. Gloria cracked up laughing from her wheelchair beside the table, watching me and Shane interact.

He cleared his throat. "Uh . . . I . . I did know." He closed his eyes for a second and let himself find the words. "But you're always in my business so it's hard to keep a secret from you." Shane was wearing a button up blue shirt, khaki shorts, and a pair of crisp Air Jordans. His face held a light sheen and told a tale of his nervousness.

He was beautiful and I loved everything about him.

"We are so happy for you, and your big accomplishment. I didn't want to leave . . . we . . . we didn't want to leave without showing you how proud we are. So, this party is for us, but it's also a celebration for you," Shane explained. He held a sly smirk knowing he got one over on me.

"We have something for you." Mrs. Walker stepped forward and held out a large gift bag.

"Mrs. Walker, you shouldn't have." I looked at everyone smiling back at me.

My people.

When I rummaged through the bag, I pulled out a plants lover's dream: neem oil, fertilizer, shovels, gloves, and a custom planter's pot that said, *April Showers Bring May Flowers.* I turned around and saw so many eyes looking back at me. I used to hate people looking at me. I thought they were judging my hair, body, skin. But today I saw people who each played such a part in showing me, *me.* I teared up.

"Thank you. Thank you all for this. I don't know what to say. I feel good," I croaked out.

I checked out Ivy, standing off in a corner with her arm slung over a girl's waist I recognized from school. She waved, and when I walked over to her, she whispered in the girl's ear. The girl stood and waved as I made my way toward them.

"Becca, I'd like you to officially meet my best friend, April. You guys should've met sooner, but this coming out of the closet thing took a lot longer than expected." Ivy gave a nervous laugh.

Becca rubbed Ivy's hand, turned to me, and smiled. "Hi, nice to meet you. Ianesha has told me so much about you. I'm glad we get to finally meet and I can stop pretending I don't know who you are in school." She chuckled.

Ianesha.

Ivy's eyes danced as she watched me and Becca interact for the first time. I saw Becca many times in school, but Ivy was quiet as a mouse and was never big on introductions. When she told me she finally talked to her mom, I couldn't be prouder. Her mom wasn't all the way accepting, but she didn't kick her out of the house and disown her. They were a work in progress, and that was enough for Ivy. She was living in the daylight without the pretense of who people thought she should be.

Ivy was in love.

As I watched her and Becca gently touch each other and discuss the upcoming school year, I knew she would be okay. She would be more than okay. The closet wasn't big enough for the type of love Ianesha wanted to grow, and she finally saw that.

"My girl beat out all those other teenagers, and they had them some good stuff too. Plants and flowers I ain't never seen before. Real exotic shit. She gets it honest; I help when I can." I heard my dad say from another corner of the roof. He was sitting down at a table full of neighbors and chomping on a chicken bone, retelling my big win.

"Kyle, you ain't never put your fingers in a flick of dirt, don't be lying." Mom handed Dad a beer and laughed.

I took in all the sights and sounds around me. My home. We had been through a lot this past summer with so many changes, new beginnings, and endings.

I peered over the ledge down below, and for the first time in days, there was no police tape, reporters, and no one watching our every move. Life was getting back to normal—but yet everything was different.

Shane came up behind me and put his arms around my waist. I closed my eyes and let my head fall back into the crook of his neck. "What are you thinking about?" he asked.

"This. Everything. Me. You. I'm just so grateful. For it all." I choked back tears.

"No crying, love. This is a happy day." Shane brushed tears from my face and flung them away.

"I am happy. I am." I nodded. I turned and faced him. "You don't know what this means to me."

"You don't know what you mean to *me*." He stared into my eyes.

"Eeewww, kissy faces. You don't know what you mean to me," Corey, Marcel, and Deja mocked. They shot out from a corner of the rooftop, ran past us, and giggled. I didn't know where they came from, but then again, I never did. Some things never changed.

"Stop all that running around!" Shanice scolded. The kids ran around her, and she almost fell carrying two containers full of food. As I watched Marcel play with Corey, I noticed he had his hands in his pockets. He was laughing and joking, but he was reserved and not with his usual intensity. He scoped out the scene in front of him, and he watched everyone talking, laughing, eating, and dancing. When he saw me looking, he nodded his head and gave a small smile.

The summer had matured him too—so it seemed. He went from being a little mousy pest and Shane's little brother, to enemy of the state and then savior, only after his thievery came with the balance of riches.

Hours passed, and people laughed, ate, drank, played cards, and had a good time. The sun began to set, and with that, out came ice cream, rooftop fireworks, and more smiles.

Ms. Gloria was right. When you allowed it to be—love was easy. It was like ice cream on a hot summer night surrounded by the people you love.

thirty-seven

. . .

This was my first time really checking her out. I didn't get a good look, but now seeing her for the second time, felt like the first time. Mom, Dad, Gage, and I waited for her to show us around.

"I'm so glad to see you again. When I got your message online, I just smiled to myself. Starting your therapy journey is commendable and exciting. I think you will find something here that interests you. Something that speaks to you all." Trista smiled at Mom and Dad. Her hair was still as bright and red as ever, just like the day I met her outside when I had an anxiety attack on my way to the motel.

After it was all said and done, Phoenix Counseling Center was a short fifteen-minute walk from our brownstone. If I kept going past the bodega and made two rights and kept walking straight, I would've found it on my own.

Instead, I found it when I was ready, with the help of Spaceport.

I kept her card tucked in my jewelry box next to the piggy bank that Gage gave me. I looked at it for a few days before I sent an email through their website. Today, they were giving us a tour.

"We have traditional counseling including individual, family, and group. We also have art therapy, equine therapy, and plant club. We have business coaching for small business owners, and we have a men's group starting up pretty soon." Trista waved her arms and showed us the space. Each room had a different theme. They had a "rage room" that was filled with red and black colors. The walls were foam and someone could go in and "rage" if they wanted to be in a safe environment. I passed by a yoga room, and finally, landed in front of a white and lavender room. When I checked the wall, this one was called the Calm Down room. The ceiling had four large skylights and bright sunshine was shining through. Plants lined the room and a large, birds of paradise stood tall and leggy off to the side, beckoning for me to touch it.

"Your mom says you are a plant wiz. We could use someone to keep these babies healthy." Trista folded her arms and leaned against the wall as I peered around the room. The energy in here was good. Real good. The plants were happy, I could feel it.

"I would love to," I breathed. When I told Mom I wanted to try therapy, she assumed it was because of Shane leaving.

It was. It was also Chase.

Hopefully with the help of therapy, eventually I would tell her that.

When I returned to the foyer, Dad and Gage were talking to a heavy-set black man. He wore a t-shirt that said, *Black Men Go To Therapy."*

"Mr. Kyle and Mr. Gage, I'm glad to meet you. I'll see you next week for our first session. I think you guys will like it." He dapped up Dad and Gage and embraced them, Black man to Black man. He wasn't stuffy or uptight like I imagined a therapist to be.

He was like them.

Mom came out of the front office with a folder and a stack of papers.

"What's all this, Caren?" Dad took the folder and helped her carry her things.

Mom's cheeks reddened. "I signed up for business coaching."

Dad's eyes lit up. "Yes sir! They don't want none of East Harlem's newest business owner! *A Taste of Love* is here to stay!" He lifted her off her feet into a bear hug and dropped the papers.

"Kyle, Kyle! Put me down!" Mom fussed with Dad. She straightened her dress and frowned, but I saw her mouth creep into a smile as she blushed.

Gage and I looked at our parents, and then back at each other. Our teenage love birds who didn't know how to be parents but grew to be them. They knew it started and ended with love. I cheesed until my cheeks hurt.

So *this* is what was beyond the bodega.

Healing.

When we got home and I plopped down on my bed, I noticed a text message from a number that I would never forget. My breath caught in my throat.

Chase.

> Hey, school is coming up. I know things ended bad between us. I just wanted to make sure we were good though. No hard feelings. I'm sorry, April.

I paused and held my phone to my heart as it beat out of my chest. I went to his name contact in my phone. I scrolled down until I found what I was looking for. The BLOCK button was ready and prime for the picking.

"You don't know me at all," I said out loud, and with one tap— blocked him.

thirty-eight

. . .

Rain poured down from the dark gray clouds. The stoop was slightly wet, but I sat protected under the small awning. A few tenants on the fifth floor were moving out, along with Shane's family. People took their earnings from the reward money and were off in search of a better life, better opportunities, maybe better love.

Mr. Dawson walked by me and sludged up the steps. I waved, but he mumbled a gargled,

"Hey, girl" and slammed the door behind him. He took his earnings and still drank it away, but this time with more expensive liquor. At least that's what he told people. I prayed that whatever he chased in his drink he would find within himself.

I sat on the same stoop. In the same place. With the same overcast rainy sky, and watched Shane's family load up their car, just as they had unloaded it a few months ago. That seemed so long ago when I thought about it today.

As quickly as he entered my life, he was gone. As quickly as I had loved, I had lost.

Shane slammed the trunk closed, and Marcel hopped in the car, playing on his tablet. Shane and his mom walked toward me. His mom carried her peace lily. Her face was solemn but determined. Her family had been accused and victimized in a matter of months. She was a Black mama in search of a better life and for that, I didn't blame her. Mr. Walker had the ability to move his family wherever the NBA needed a recruiter, and now with their reward money, they had options. Isn't that what people really want anyways? Options?

"April. I would be honored if you would take care of this peace lily for me. You know, I've never really been good with these things. You brought her back to life so I thought you should have her." She smiled and pushed it toward me.

"Thanks, Mrs. Walker." I took the plant from her hands and hugged it to my chest. "I'll take good care of her." I blinked back tears. I hoped they couldn't see my tears through the rain.

"You take care of yourself, April. And thank you. For what you've done for my boy. He needed you. I'm sorry things ended this way, but if you're ever in Florida, please look us up." She nodded, and her eyes glistened as she glanced between me and Shane. I saw them shine through the rain.

"Shane. Just a few minutes, son." She nodded to him standing behind her and walked back to the car.

"So, this is it." I gave a weak smile.

"Yeah, I guess so." His mouth was tight. "I'm going to call you as soon as we get there. And we'll talk every day."

"And I'll tell you how my first day went. And I'll text you every morning, to make sure you're up."

"Everything else stays the same. Me and you. We are the same. God, I love you so much." He grabbed my face and pulled me closer and kissed my face. I heard Marcel groan from the car.

"I love you too, Shane." I cried and latched onto his broad back. I held on as tight as I could. I didn't want to let go and I didn't want him to either. Not for a minute, second, or hour.

"Shane, son. It's time." Mr. Walker walked up and patted Shane on the back.

"Okay, Dad. One second." Shane wiped his face. He used his sleeve to wipe mine too.

"I have something for you." He held up a finger and jogged back to the car. He came back with a large poster tucked under his arm. When he handed it to me, I carefully unfolded it and I was sure my knees would buckle and give out right there. Tears sprang to my eyes again. It was one of the pictures Shane and I took at the flower festival on my birthday. We were standing in a field of blue flowers, gazing at each other. We took a bunch of pictures that day posing, but this picture was a random one where we grabbed each other's face and grinned as someone photographed us.

"Shane. It's beautiful." I sniffled. "I'll keep it forever."

"You are beautiful. Don't you forget that. I don't care what anyone says. I'll beat their ass. Don't let anyone make you think things about yourself that aren't true. You stand ten toes down at all times. You are the baddest, funniest, strongest, plant loving, girl this side of Harlem. And baby, I love you. Don't you forget that."

"I won't." I nodded through my tears. "And you keep boxing. Keep fighting. Keep taking your time with your thoughts, with your words. Don't let anyone take your voice. You got this, my love. You always did." I brushed my fingertips across the scar above his right eye where all his life he had to fight. Pulling his head toward me, I lightly brushed my lips against it.

He closed his eyes, and a tear dropped down his cheek. "I got you." He grabbed my hand and kissed it.

"And I got you."

Shane's dad beeped the horn, and he hugged me once more before letting my hand go. With tears streaming down my face, I watched him and his family ride away. Even though they had already pulled away and he couldn't see me, I mouthed *I love you* to Shane.

When I looked up at the brownstone, my home; I saw Ms. Gloria, Shanice and my mom staring through their individual apartment windows down at me. Even Jorge and Journey, packing for their own journeys for love, spied us from their second-floor window. Even through the rain blocking my sight lines, I could tell from here each of them was crying. When they saw me looking, they moved from their windows, back into the shadows of their own lives.

I ran upstairs to my apartment, burst inside, and shuffled to the bathroom. Today I wore the same yellow dress that Shane loved, and that I loved too. It made me feel womanly. Feminine. I pulled it up and inspected my legs. I saw some hair budding, but I didn't freak out. I grabbed my razors and my Nair in the cabinet, and I threw it away.

I didn't need it anymore. I would be seen and *heard* from now on.

I shuffled back to my room and thumbed the first-place certificate from the show. I smiled to myself. School was in two days, and I was going back a new woman holding my head high. Not because of how my body looked. Because I was the rose that grew from concrete. I was not ashamed. I was not embarrassed. I was April— and she was enough.

I was a rare plant. I needed soil to settle my roots and a strong planter to call home. These things grounded me for new growth to push through. I flourished with good energy, and gentle love and care.

And Shane . . . Shane and I would forever be unfinished business.

This summer I got to experience love, and that was something so sweet. I also found me, and that was something that I would make sure not to lose again.

The End

epilogue

. . .

Eight months later....

"Ouch!" I rubbed my head and winced. Milani's bottle went whizzing by Mom's bare arm and plunked me right in the head.

"That girl got a right hook on her, she got that from me!" Dad grinned.

Milani giggled and cooed at him, like she knew Pop-Pop was happy. Her Mickey Mouse hat was too big for her head and fell off to the side even though we got the smallest size they had.

"Kyle, hush! Are we in the right place? I can't tell by this map, it's so confusing." Mom peered at the Disney World map and turned her head sideways. "They want you to come and compete at these event things but it's a maze to even find where you're going!"

"We're not in the right place. We're looking for Pavilion C, we're in Pavilion J." Gage carefully took the map from Mom's hand and pointed.

My phone buzzed in my pocket. Dozens of *you got this* and *we're proud of you,* text messages rained in from family and friends. The actual competition wasn't until tomorrow, but after The NY Home and Garden Show came back to the brownstone and did a special segment about my plants, people were cheering for me from all over.

Colleges were even reaching out, asking me to visit their horticulture programs.

It was almost one year from the day I won the NY Home and Garden Show: Teen's Edition. The top three winners from each state in the country all flew to Disney World and were competing in the national competition.

And I was amongst them repping New York, Harlem-bred, loud and proud.

Shipping all my plants and materials to Florida was similar to learning rocket science. Ground shipping? Priority? Next day? Flat rate? Weight? Postage? I quit three times and had a full, crying breakdown in the post office. Getting everything I needed halfway across the country and making sure they showed up in decent condition was too much to think about and I didn't want to deal with it. I drafted an email to the competition committee explaining that I, April Mays, was shitty at rocket science and therefore I would not be competing any longer.

But *Shane*.

When I told him I was quitting, it was like he heard nothing I said and asked me what he could help with. Have you ever been so confused, that when someone asked you what you need or how they could help, you couldn't even put it into words? You didn't know what you needed? Shane got on the phone with Ivy and Mom, and together, they came up with a plan to help me get everything shipped and sorted to Shane's house for safe keeping until I got there.

Even thousands of miles away, he laid down roots in my heart and they were so entwined and entangled. With each late-night phone call, Facetime, letters mailed, we became more knotted.

I carefully picked out my school clothes, paying extra attention to what pieces and colors made me feel beautiful. Yellow was still a clear winner, and when I walked into school, my head was held high. And it all happened—one summer.

What people didn't understand about me was I was a different girl. I knew love, I grew love. When it seeped into your pores and infected every part of your body, it changed you in ways that were seen and felt. I felt like a new woman, and they *saw* it. A few boys asked me out on dates. I smiled and felt giddy inside because it felt nice to be wanted. But I didn't *need* to go out with anyone, nor did I want to. The new me was new to me too. And the more I got to know her, all roads led back to Shane.

Fixing my hair from where Milani bust me in the head and dabbing gloss onto my lips, I looked myself over in a reflective mirror inside Magic Kingdom. Harlem was still thawing out and coming alive in May, but Florida was a balmy seventy-five degrees. I was a lover of simple things, but I was not a simple girl. During my last therapy session with Trista, she gushed and said, *"just one plane ticket can change your entire mood."* I turned my face up to the sky and let the sun rays bathe my bronzed, smooth skin. She was right.

Everything I loved dearly—plants and Shane included, were in Pavilion C.

Waiting for me.

After arguing over the map and a few short steps later, my heart skipped a beat. We stood yards away from Pavilion C.

He wore all white.

A crisp, white short sleeved tee-shirt, white shorts, and Jordans. His back was to me as he cut open some of my shipped plants and he was trotting around the picnic tables, setting them out. A gold necklace glistened around his neck, that I could see from here and a small 'A' pendant sat in the middle of his chest.

"Don't be shy now, girl. We done came all this way. Got us racing around the country for this boy," Dad's voice boomed.

"Kyle be quiet! It wasn't just the boy! She about to win this whole damn thing." Mom swatted at Dad's arm.

"Well, well, look who's cussing now." Dad's eyes widened and he gave a smirk.

Milani giggled at her grandparents' banter.

Dad's loud voice caught Shane's attention, and when he spun around, the scar above his right eye greeted me, as it had always did. It was slightly darker; the Florida sun had given his melanin a chocolate bath. His face broke into a wide, sloppy grin.

We jogged to each other, bumping into people around us. My heart was racing, and my mouth was dry. Would he still love me? Did he still care? I knew the answers to that already, but what would our in-person energy say?

Shane pushed past someone dressed as Mickey Mouse, and almost flung a fake Peter Pan to the side. In seconds, he grabbed my waist and pulled me toward him, kissing my face, cheeks, and forehead.

"Hey you," he breathed.

"Hey yourself." I grinned and ran a finger across the scar above his eye.

He closed his eyes. "I missed that. I missed you."

"So how's life?" My arms snaked around his waist and rested on the familiar crook in his back. I held back a giggle, like we didn't already talk every day, two to three times per day.

"Oh, you know, just growing this green thumb of mine." He lifted his right hand in my face and smirked.

"What's all this?" I pinched Shane's broad back. He felt muscular and toned.

Shane gave a smug look and flexed his arm muscles. "I've been hitting the boxing ring kind of hard. You know, just in case I have to go back to Harlem and kick some ass."

Shane and I giggled and held each other tight.

"Uhh, Shane. Nice to see you again, son. Can you unhand my

daughter?" Dad crossed his arms and shot an annoyed face between me and Mom.

On cue, Milani giggled from her stroller.

Shane and I peered around and came back down to earth. A small crowd of his parents and Marcel, as well as my family, formed a circle around us. Strangers who recognized the throes of young love stopped and stared as we loved on each other.

"Hi Mr. and Mrs. Walker." I waved to his parents under the pavilion as they waved back and grinned.

Mom stepped forward. "Hi Shane, we're so happy to see you again. You look good. Let me go speak to your parents. Me and Kyle are going to get one of those big turkey legs and then we'll be back to help set up for tomorrow. I gotta check out the food competition, anyway. April, do you want anything?" She shot out questions and comments.

"I'm okay, Mom, thanks," I whispered, never taking my eyes away from Shane's. I was hungry for nothing but him, and the way he gazed back at me and licked his lips told me he was famished too.

When Mom and Dad walked away with Gage and Milani, Shane turned to me. "You look great, girl. You know how I feel about you in yellow."

He smacked my butt and I giggled.

"You ain't been shaving have you?" He ran his fingers across my legs.

If my heart swelled any more, surely it would burst right out of my chest. The more I found me, the less I needed shavers and hair removal creams. They weren't extinct from my life, but they were on the endangered list. "Nope..." I gave a smug grin. "Not the way it was before."

And it was the truth.

"Good. I want it so thick we can try and braid it later!" Shane gave me half-serious eyes.

We fell into each other and laughed. God, he still smelled like him.

"There's a diner spot behind the pavilions. I checked the menu. They have Yoo-hoo's and ice cream." Shane raised an eyebrow.

I stepped forward, closing the space between us until I could feel his heart beating against my chest. "I've been ready for you and a Yoo-hoo for months now."

"You and Yoo-hoo? Oh, she's a rapper now too." He cleared his throat and acted like he was spitting bars.

We cracked up laughing.

Shane slipped his fingers into mine, cupped my face, and whispered into my ear, "I love you, April Mays. Ain't shit change."

I eyed Mr. and Mrs. Walker over Shane's shoulder, smiling and talking with my parents. My plants were right next to them, and despite the undertaking it was shipping them to Florida, they looked happy and healthy, waiting for me to put my love all over them.

Plants and family.

Disney World really was the happiest place on earth. "I love you too, Shane Walker." And I did. I really did.

Sometimes you had to go on adventures to find where you truly belonged.

When I slipped my hand into his and walked into Pavilion C, I knew where I belonged, and it was right beside him. A few feet away lay my plant babies. Soon, my fingers would dance around them like lace. A gentle whisper, a soft embrace, they would know I was here, and I traveled all this way for them.

For love.

In a sea of green, I found my grace, my solace, my sacred space. It was a love story that knew no end.

discussion questions

1. What are your thoughts about the brownstone building? Some tenants seemed to love where they lived, and others felt trapped.
2. Who was your favorite character and why? Who was your least favorite?
3. How do you feel about April's shaving? Did you figure out early on that it was excessive?
4. Were you shocked to find out why she was shaving?
5. Shane's speech impediment seemed to come alive when he was nervous. What happens to your body when you get nervous, and how do you calm yourself?

author's note:

Wow! My fifth book. It sounds surreal saying that. To know how far my writing has changed, but also knowing it's just the beginning. I continue to be in awe of what words has done for my life. This book is an ode to my personal love for plants. Being a plant momma myself, I had a vision of a teenage black girl who found herself through plants blooming around her. Fun fact, the entire storyline about plants came first—Shane was added later. April had a lot of low days, but in the end she understood that she existed in a world where rain and sun shine lived together.

When I wrote April Showers, I believe that's the place I was in my life. Understanding that every thought, feeling, and emotion had an opposite emotion, and all were useful. April struggled with her self-esteem, but she was always hopeful.

That is what I wish for you, finishing this book now. May you always, always, regardless of the rain in your life—remain hopeful. Your choices are:

One Day or Day One.

You can always change your circumstances.

Me? I wrote my way out of mine.

Signed,

Janay Harden
September 9, 2023
6:15pm

also by janay harden

Hey, Brown Girl

Forty-Two Minutes (The Indigo Lewis Series Book 1)

Someone More Like Myself (The Indigo Lewis Series Book 2)

Locked In (The Indigo Lewis Series Book 3)

how you can help

. . .

I'd love to hear your thoughts about April Showers! Please consider leaving a review of this book on Amazon or Goodreads.